ROOM SERVICE

Visit us at www.boldstrokesbooks.com

Praise for Fiona Riley

Miss Match

"In this sweet, sensual debut, Riley brings together likable characters, setting them against a colorful supporting cast and exploring their relationship through charming interactions and red-hot erotic scenes… Rich in characterization and emotional appeal, this one is sure to please."—*Publishers Weekly*

"*Miss Match* by Fiona Riley is an adorable romance with a lot of amazing chemistry, steamy sex scenes, and fun dialogue. I can't believe it's the author's first book, even though she assured me on Twitter that it is."—*The Lesbian Review*

"This was a beautiful love story, chock full of love and emotion, and I felt I had a big grin on my face the whole time I was reading it. I adored both main characters as they were strong, independent women with good hearts and were just waiting for the right person to come along and make them whole. I felt I smiled for days after reading this wonderful book."—*Inked Rainbow Reads*

Unlikely Match

"*Unlikely Match* is super easy to read with its great pacing, character work, and dialogue that's fun and engaging…Whether you've read *Miss Match* or not, *Unlikely Match* is worth picking up. It was the perfect romance to balance out a tough week at work and I'm looking forward to seeing what Fiona Riley has in store for us next."—*The Lesbian Review*

Strike a Match

"Riley balances romance, wit, and story complexity in this contemporary charmer…Readers of all stripes will enjoy this lyrically phrased, deftly plotted work about opposites attracting."—*Publishers Weekly*

"Everything about the writing worked for me. The book is just as smart, funny, and sexy as its two leads. The plotting works well, the pacing is perfect, the conflict believable, and the resolution even better. It also has an epilogue that's entirely satisfying and left me with the happiest of sighs…*Strike a Match* is Fiona Riley's best book yet. Whether you're a fan of the other books in the series or you've never read anything by her before, I recommend checking this one out. It's the perfect remedy to a bad day and a great way to relax on a weekend!"—*The Lesbian Review*

By the Author

Miss Match

Unlikely Match

Strike a Match

Room Service

ROOM SERVICE

by
Fiona Riley

2018

ROOM SERVICE

© 2018 By Fiona Riley. All Rights Reserved.

ISBN 13: 978-1-63555-120-4

This Trade Paperback Original Is Published By
Bold Strokes Books, Inc.
P.O. Box 249
Valley Falls, NY 12185

First Edition: June 2018

Credits
Editor: Ruth Sternglantz
Production Design: Stacia Seaman
Cover Design by Melody Pond

Acknowledgments

The idea for this book came to me while I was staying at a hotel during an impromptu winter getaway. What originated as a quick escape from life's responsibilities turned into a really fun snowed-in weekend where I met all sorts of interesting people who inspired some very interesting characters. When a blizzard strands lovey-dovey couples and single, jaded business people at a hotel during the weekend of Valentine's Day, the hotel bar is the best place to get a front row seat for Extreme People Watching. Truly. Throw in a couple blood orange martinis and half-priced Valentine's Day themed appetizers and you're sure to have a good time. Or at least hear a few good stories. Luckily, I found both to be true.

I wrote this book shortly after my first novel, *Miss Match*, but shelved it for a few years as life got in the way. But the essence of this story has stayed with me the whole time: This book is about letting go of the past and embracing the scariness of the future. This book was my future; it had to be. I needed it to be. And through great fortune, here it is.

I want to thank Kathy Creedon for coming up with the title. You're a genius. I think you're pretty awesome in general, but you're totally a title genius. Totally. The genius-est. And big thanks to 'Nathan Burgoine for supporting this idea while splashing around in the pool with me. You are such a positive force in all that you do, and I am grateful to have you in my life.

To my editor, Ruth Sternglantz, thank you for helping me find the right way to tell this story. I started it long before I met you, but the final product is a perfect mix of you and me and my inability to write grammatically correct sentences. I should be disciplined, stern-ly. See what I did there? Xo.

Team BSB: Thank you for fostering such a supportive and loving writer/editor/reader community. It's nice to know that I can shoot off a text at just about any time of day or night and reach some amazing human that I've met through my time with Bold Strokes Books.

And to my wife: Thank you for encouraging me to leave work behind and escape every once in a while. There is no one I'd rather escape with than you. Thanks for all of your support.

For Jenn.

You are the funniest person I know. And the sweetest. And most caring. And also the most passionate. You are so many things to me and there are not enough words to tell you just how much you mean to me. Ever. But I'll keep trying, because you deserve someone that will fight for you and love you as much as you love me. I am so grateful for you. Thank you for being you.

CHAPTER ONE

New York City

Tuesday was usually Olivia Dawson's favorite day of the week, but not today. No, today was clearly an evil Tuesday masquerading as a regular Tuesday. Everything was going wrong today. Like, if she didn't have *bad* luck, she'd have no luck at all. This was not the start her usual, friendlier Tuesday greeted her with. This Tuesday hated her. And she hated it right back.

At some point during the night, her apartment must have lost power because her bedside clock was blinking 3:04 a.m. and not doing its job: waking her up at the predetermined time. Thankfully, her sister Christine had texted her a million times and jarred her out of her slumber. Not that it had helped much—she was still late. But today was not a day she could be late. She had a meeting with her boss, Corrine Baylor, followed by a videoconference with the new corporate bigwig who was going to introduce an upcoming project to the team. This was the biggest opportunity of her career, on the most important day to make a good first impression, and she was late.

As she frantically attempted to get ready, she managed to trip over her sneakers and broke her favorite high heel. Her lucky Jimmy Choos. The ones she couldn't afford in grad school but had forgone anything that wasn't a noodle dish just so she could buy them for graduation. The same lucky heels that she wore on her first day at Greater Image Design Inc. eight years ago and the ones she wore on the day she was promoted to chief designer and team leader when her mentor Albie retired. These shoes made her feel confident and smart and successful. How could she possibly get through today without her lucky shoes?

She was still mourning the loss of her favorite footwear and sulking as she ate the abandoned, overripe banana in the company's kitchenette area when her teammate, Farrah Sanders, walked in.

"Good morning, Olivia. You look—" If the expression on Farrah's face was any indication, Olivia knew what was coming next.

"Like a hot mess. I know." She sighed and stirred the lukewarm, slightly burnt coffee she found at the bottom of the coffeepot.

"I was going to say that you look nice." Farrah was being polite, and she appreciated that.

"I doubt that but thank you."

Farrah pointed to the banana as Olivia tried to swallow the bite in her mouth. "You hate bananas, Liv."

"This is the kind of day I'm having, Farrah. Drinking sad, stale coffee probably leftover from the cleaning crew at night and suffering through a banana so I don't faint in our meeting. Just leave me here to die."

"It's not even ten yet, Liv. How could your day possibly be that bad?"

Olivia's shoulders drooped as she recounted the morning's events. "I overslept. I couldn't find my keys because they were playing hide-and-seek in the couch cushions. By the time I finally got to my car, I was greeted with a flat tire, and only once I nearly lost an arm trying to get through the closing doors of the bus did I realize my wallet was in my gym bag from last night. All I had in my purse was some loose change and an unused tampon and a business card from that cute girl at the mall kiosk that sells the face cream—"

"I love that stand." Farrah nodded, her expression sympathetic.

"Right? They have the best stuff." Olivia sighed. "And to top it all off, I broke my favorite shoes."

Farrah's mouth fell open and her eyes dropped to Olivia's feet. "Not the shiny, candy-apple red ones. Say it ain't so."

"It's the end of an era." Even as she said the words, she wasn't ready to accept it. She'd been mulling over repair options when Farrah walked in.

"Jeez. I think you need this more than me." Farrah opened the fridge and tossed a yogurt to her. She extended her hand and motioned toward the offending fruit. "Give me that, you look pathetic."

Olivia handed over the remainder of the banana and accepted the spoon Farrah offered her in return. Farrah's well-practiced, motherly expression gave her momentary calm.

"Maybe this isn't the best time to tell you, but uh, Hannah already called the office looking for you." Farrah looked pained. "Twice."

And there went the calm. Olivia cringed at the name. "Really?" She shot a hopeful glance at Farrah, who only frowned more deeply and nodded. "Crap." Suddenly she was feeling worse, no longer hungry and especially not inclined to return to her desk.

"I told her you were in a meeting and would call her back, but, she sounded, um…"

"Pissed?" Olivia supplied knowingly.

"Yeah." Farrah patted her on the shoulder and shrugged.

"Okay. It's fine. I can handle this." Olivia finished her yogurt and gave herself a lame pep talk before excusing herself to her desk. She had a few minutes to spare before her meeting with her boss and she had to pull herself together. Fast.

Any confidence she'd mustered during the short jaunt from the lunchroom vanished when she saw the behemoth New Horizons Industry binder on her desk. When she'd first started out at Greater Image Design so many years ago, the company had specialized in redesigning small spaces, like sprucing up outdated home offices or breathing new life into community reading areas. The projects were fun, but relatively small in scale, which was perfect for Olivia when she was learning the ropes of the business. Gradually, as the needs of the community and their clients changed with advancements in technology, the business projects and artistic opportunities flourished, and Olivia flourished right along with them. Long gone were the humdrum basement home office redesign days of the past. The future had brought sexy tech startups with young entrepreneurs at the helm that wanted to bring nature into the creative spaces they hoped would foster the development of the next great app or bioengineered cure-all. Everything was fast-paced and streamlined now. People wanted to feel like they could work and be in nature at the same time. Olivia's special brand of green space themed design was what had catapulted Greater Image Design into the stratosphere. It's also what helped them snag the New Horizons gig that was looming in that binder.

Olivia loved the challenge of redesigning an existing space. She loved the complexity of making something new from something old and outdated. Design was in her blood. And constantly on her mind. She had a tendency to be a little manic that way, her mind racing and seeing things from a different perspective than most others. That untethered creativity had served her well in this business, and by associating with the fast-growing New Horizons brand, she was sure to reach new professional heights. The deep pockets New Horizons offered with their far-reaching connections was a dream come true for Olivia. Or a nightmare. That depended on how you looked at it.

These last few weeks had been exhausting. Olivia and her team had been so slammed with work lately that she'd been counting on having the morning to review the background. So much for the best laid plans. She flipped open the cover and nearly knocked over her now ice-cold coffee. Try as she might, she couldn't shake the feeling that a dark cloud was settling over her shoulders.

"Olivia? Are you ready?" The singsongy voice of her boss sounded from over her shoulder. Corrine was her usual chipper self today. Joy.

"Yup." That was all she could muster. It would have to do.

She grabbed her drafting binder and followed Corrine to her office. It was a short walk through the design center, on the south side of the building. Olivia envied the bright corner office with the nice view of the park below. Her own desk was in an open floor plan space with drafting tables and design scraps. It was a great environment to foster creativity, as her team was spaced out evenly around her, but she still loved the quiet of Corrine's office. She could use its solitude when she had a hard deadline and Randal wouldn't stop humming nervously at the drafting table next to her. She knew if she asked, Corrine would be more than happy to lend it to her from time to time. Corrine was like that. She'd come to them a few years ago and oversaw Olivia's transition into Albie's position as chief designer. She'd been both a good boss and a great ally throughout the whole process. So as much as her zest for life sometimes drove Olivia a little crazy, she really did appreciate her. Truly.

"So, as you know, this conference call is super important. We are virtually meeting the corporate liaison of New Horizons Industry and she will be our direct contact for this project, effective immediately. I think it goes without saying that it's important we make a good first impression." She nodded to herself as she spoke, her short blond hair bobbing with her head movements. "I feel good about today. It's going to be a great meeting."

Olivia gave her a small smile and tried to absorb all the good vibes Corrine was throwing at her. But she was failing miserably. "Sure, you got it, Corrine, I'm on it."

Corrine beamed and bounced on her heels as she scooped up the files from her desk, ending their meeting and heading toward the conference room. That was shorter than expected, and Olivia was grateful.

She paused in the now quiet office and let her eyes trail over the neat, picture filled desk of her colleague. Corrine and her husband had been married for about ten years with two perfect cherub children and a golden retriever named Biscuit. They looked like such a happy, loving family. Olivia let her mind wander as she looked at a collage one of the kids had made and wondered if she'd ever have something like that one day: a wife, 2.3 kids, and a dog. But not a purebred, no, it would have to be a rescue. Something with baggage. Something like her. She sighed.

Chicago

Savannah Quinn leaned back in her chair and stretched her neck and shoulders. She had gotten up earlier than usual today to squeeze in a spin class before her conference call and she still felt a little tight. She wanted to make sure she was alert and ready for this morning. She figured there was no better way to do that than sweat it out with the cute spin teacher who always winked at her.

She shifted in her chair and looked over the open file for the hundredth time. This partnership with Greater Image Design was a big deal for her. In her new role as district head of sales and the appointed corporate liaison, the Greater Image team was now her primary focus and her success was directly correlated with theirs. She'd been doing quite a bit of research on their employees to prepare for today. She pulled up their individual and team project portfolios and reviewed their productivity via evaluations from management and peers. This wasn't protocol for her parent company, New Horizons Industry. It was something *she* had insisted on doing. She didn't get to where she was today by following the protocol of those around her. She'd always been a groundbreaker. She was bold and fierce. That's the only way she'd survived her mess of a childhood and the relationship waste that littered her past. This was a fresh start for her. Savannah believed that hard work started with her and trickled out to those around her. She was always up to something, by nature; multitasking was like breathing for her. But that dedication to work had led to other things falling by the wayside. Just as well, Savannah thought. She'd let herself lose focus in the past. Never again.

Her position at New Horizons kept her busy. Busy meant that she didn't have time to get too distracted, and that was fine by her.

New Horizons had become a force in the corporate landscape seemingly overnight. The company had branches in all major cities and specialized in constructing office buildings for businesses of every shape and size. But they'd started to get a bad rap for building ugly, gray monstrosities without any high-tech innovations. Businesses were changing, and New Horizons needed to adapt with them. Sure, their previous approach had brought in jobs, but they weren't attracting the kind of businesses that generated enough money to keep their fast-growing company afloat. They needed glitzy technology firms with deep pockets and seemingly endless investors. They wanted young blood, but they were applying old design standards. At least, that's what the market research was telling them. The recent numbers showed that they were losing opportunities due to their outdated design approach. Savannah was brought in to fix their image problem by finding a way to update their business. She'd been researching ways to do just that when she'd stumbled on Greater Image Design. Or more specifically, Olivia Dawson's impressive portfolio.

This partnering opportunity was new ground for New Horizons. And for Savannah. She'd taken this job after a messy breakup left her feeling uninspired and lost. Her little brother Cooper was attending school here, so it had made perfect sense to make Chicago her new home. Well, if you could call it *home*. She'd been working in her new position for over a year and she still hadn't fully unpacked. But having Cooper nearby made her happy. He was her only family. She wanted to be close to him in both relationship and distance. He kept her grounded in a way she hadn't felt in years.

She made a mental note to call him later today as she reached into her bag and pulled out her laptop. She arranged the desk in preparation for the conference call and thought of her little brother. Cooper was finishing up his senior year in college and would be moving on to bigger and better things soon. That scared Savannah a little. She'd gotten so accustomed to their weekly Sunday dinners with his girlfriend Amber and coming home from another business trip to find the two of them folding laundry on her couch. Her condo's proximity to his campus was intentionally convenient and even more convenient that her laundry was free when he needed it. Which was often. She never complained, though. She liked knowing that the condo was being used. She traveled more than 70 percent of the time on this job, so at least she knew someone was bringing in the mail. Sooner than she liked, Cooper would graduate and her home life would change, but on the work front, things were moving along nicely. Her new promotion to this position was a professional success that made her feel alive for the first time in a long time. Partnering with the smaller boutique firm in New York City was a big deal for her professionally and, hopefully, personally as well. She needed a new project to help her refocus on what was important in her life. Cooper was growing up and would be moving on. She figured it was time to take her little brother's lead for once.

She loaded her laptop and sent the image to the large flat screen television mounted in her office. She preferred her work in front of her, on a large scale, to best assess the situation. She moved the mouse, watching the cursor on the television screen as she pulled up the videoconference app and split the screen with employee bios. Savannah put on her headset and sipped her coffee before dialing Corrine. She glanced once more at the clock to make sure the time difference from her office in Chicago was correct and settled into her seat to start the call. She yawned, still sore from this morning's workout, and glanced longingly out the window. Today was going to be a long day.

CHAPTER TWO

B y the time Olivia got to the conference room, everyone was already sitting, facing a projection screen on the far wall. Her entire team was present, as well as some people from accounting and legal. Corrine was hovering over the speakerphone with a look of excitement on her face.

That excitement quickly faded when it was apparent that their new liaison with New Horizons, Savannah Quinn, could see them but they couldn't see her. "Uh, we appear to be having some IT issues on our end, Savannah. Hold on, sorry." Corrine looked flustered.

"Tuesday strikes again," Olivia muttered. The gray-faced silhouette in the corner of the screen where Savannah's face should have been unnerved Olivia a little. It was creepy.

"I thought you liked Tuesdays?" Her best friend and chief engineer, Reagan Fischer, stretched in the seat next to her. Besides her sister Christine and her niece, Reagan was her closest friend in the world. "Scratch that, I know you like Tuesdays. You *love* them. You are in a relationship with Tuesdays that is probably unhealthy, and you should see someone about that."

"Like you are any sort of relationship expert." Olivia accepted the half piece of gum Reagan offered with a huff.

"You tried me on for size—I think we did okay." Reagan stuck out her tongue at her and teased her. "You know, until we didn't."

Olivia laughed. That was true. Kind of. They'd briefly dated in college until they both realized they were better off being friends. Reagan was a free-spirited playgirl back then, and not much had changed in the nine years since they'd first met. "My point exactly."

Reagan looked scandalized. "Are you trying to insinuate that I'm bad at relationships?"

"Not at all. No insinuation necessary." Olivia smiled. Reagan was a lot of fun. She was tall and lean, with lush dark hair and deep brown eyes with full lashes. She'd stayed true to her college self and developed a pretty well-established reputation for being a lady-killer. Olivia was willing to bet that she had single-handedly converted half of the straight population of Manhattan one woman at a time. But a monogamist? Not quite. "You're great at *relationships*, in the plural. You just suck at monogamy."

"Who wants to be limited to one"—Reagan winked—"when you can have many?"

Olivia felt the stress of the day recede a little. She was glad she'd convinced Reagan to join the design firm when she was promoted. Reagan melded perfectly with the rest of the group and added a great mind to the artistic team in the design space. She was creative and practical at work, hard-working and diligent, but she required a little wrangling at times. Olivia and Reagan were similar enough to get along, but different enough to balance each other out. They worked well together and on days like today, Olivia was grateful to have Reagan by her side.

"So…when did you and Tuesday break up?" Reagan drew Olivia's attention back to their original conversation.

"Today. Our love affair has ended." Olivia sighed. "I *used* to love Tuesdays, but this Tuesday can suck it."

"Mature." Reagan nodded and spun the pen on the conference table in front of them.

"I try."

Corrine frowned in defeat. "Sorry, Savannah. We can't seem to get IT here in time and I know you have another meeting scheduled. We'll just have to be a little blind on our end."

"No worries. We'll have plenty of time to get acquainted over the next few months."

Savannah's voice had a gentle huskiness to it. Well, that was a pleasant change from the nasal twang of the previous contact from New Horizons, Olivia thought.

As the meeting progressed, Olivia found herself more and more drawn to the voice on the other end of the call. Savannah was direct and concise. She was organized but not patronizing, which Olivia liked. She enunciated her words perfectly and appeared to be watching the group closely on her end, even commenting on Randal's hideously wrinkled shirt with a gentle jab that got a chuckle from the conference room and

Randal himself. A sense of humor, too? This Savannah woman was getting better and better.

"Great. This is all very exciting." Corrine clapped and buzzed in her chair, her excitement palpable. "You'll be working with Olivia directly for the upcoming project, Savannah. I'm here to help, of course, but Olivia's your woman for the job."

Olivia waved to the gray face on the screen because she felt like she had to. But it was awkward. So awkward.

"So, about the project..." Corrine's expression turned more serious.

The project in question, the big secret, was not that big at all. In fact, considering some of the projects they had completed in the past, this was on the small side. It was a pilot design trial that had the potential to become a full-blown national contract if New Horizons was pleased with the outcome. The plan was to build an indoor green space that was technologically advanced in every way: climate controlled, living walls, water features, natural lighting, with smooth stones and earth tones. Business professionals who frequented the space could custom design their surroundings by tweaking the cyberinput and displays on some of the walls and ceilings. Although the basic structure would remain fixed, certain aspects of the room could be customized and mobilized. Chairs would rotate out, stones would change color, glass would tint or reflect images of ocean scenes, marketplaces in Dubai, sunsets by the Golden Gate Bridge, or the open night skies of the deep country. The design called for a lot of tech work and engineering, but the key to their success would be to develop a general process that could be applied to spaces of different shapes and sizes.

"Bottom line," Savannah said, "the hope is to create a space that can integrate whatever environments the user might be motivated by. We want to give every user a custom experience. Once we establish the concept, we'll need to send out teams to initiate the work. Your office will come up with the blueprint, and then we will ask that your chief of design, that's you, Olivia, as well as a few team members make the trip to the pilot installation sites to oversee the beginning of the project." Savannah's voice paused, then continued, "We're contracted to work with your team for three installations to ensure that we work well together and that our combined vision for the final product is met. At the end of the trial completion, we'll reevaluate the results and negotiate further involvement on a grander scale."

Savannah finished by adding, "We'll work closely with you on your home turf to make sure that everything is ironed out before the trips, so they can be short and you'll be separated from your families as little as possible. We appreciate your input on this matter. I know that travel isn't usually part of your jobs, but we want the primary brains on the project present at the start of all new installations. Continuity breeds success."

Olivia nodded as she took notes on the topic. She agreed that being present was ideal for the correct application of the design, but she had to admit, the idea of traveling didn't thrill her. She supposed it really depended on where they were going and for how long. She hoped for a tropical locale, but, considering how her luck had been lately, she doubted that would happen.

Corrine ended the call and assigned each person in the room a task to begin the process. Olivia dispatched her own team to work in pairs, organizing some ideas for the general concept Savannah requested. They were encouraged to take the suggestions and add variations along the way. They'd be installing the rooms in three sites over the next six months. One month to plan the general concept, and then travel to the sites would begin.

As they walked back to the design space, Reagan bumped elbows with her, a mischievous smile on her face. "So, Liv, you're going to be working with that Quinn lady pretty close the next few months...She had an awesome phone sex voice, so that's cool."

Olivia rolled her eyes and shoved Reagan playfully. "You are such a hornball." She couldn't help but laugh along, though. She had found herself drifting a bit at the beginning of the conference call thanks to the speaker's melodious tones. She wondered what Savannah looked like.

"You know, maybe that's exactly what you need to spice things up around here. If she is as attractive as her voice indicates, you could be in for trouble." Reagan dodged Olivia's annoyed swat in her direction.

"Ugh. You're impossible. I have enough drama in my life now as is. Last thing I need is you fantasizing some faux office romance with the sexy, faceless voice of a client liaison."

"Ha! So you do like her voice."

"Reagan, shut up. Go back to work, will you?" Olivia didn't think she could actually get mad at Reagan even if she tried. The truth was Reagan forced Olivia to live her life to the fullest, and in turn, Olivia tried to help Reagan understand that feelings and emotions were not bad things; they just made relationships more fulfilling. Reagan was a work in progress, though—she still favored a one-night stand to a second date, nine times out of ten. Olivia always assumed she would spend a lifetime helping Reagan figure that out. And that didn't bother her one bit.

As she settled into her desk, her eyes picked up the bright pink Post-its Farrah had left her. She had to call Hannah back, no use avoiding the inevitable. She might as well get it over with.

"I called you twice, you know." Hannah huffed into the phone.

"So I've heard. I was busy with a conference call. What's up?" Olivia squeezed her eyes shut and waited for the onslaught that was coming.

"You never stopped by last week, like you promised you would, and you've been ignoring my calls ever since," Hannah grumbled, her voice rising a bit.

"Hannah, look, we've been through this." Olivia sighed and rubbed her forehead. "I didn't stop by last week because we broke up, and I'm not obligated to attend your book club meetings anymore."

Hannah let out an annoyed snort. She replied, "Olivia, we both know that you were just being dramatic."

Olivia let her head fall back against her chair in frustration. Hannah was a stage five clinger, and she should never have gotten involved with her in the first place. Reagan was right, not that she would ever admit it. They had dated for three months and it was insane. Olivia had ended things almost three weeks ago—not that Hannah accepted that little fact, but still. "Hannah, look, I like you. I think you are a great girl and I had a lot of fun, but I've moved on. We're better off as friends. If I made you think anything more than that, I'm sorry. I just don't feel the same way about you as you feel about me."

The line was silent for a moment. Hannah let out a tired sigh. "Fine. Take as much time as you need to think things out. I'll talk to you later."

"What?" Olivia pulled the phone away to look at it before speaking again. "I don't need to think about it. I'm done, kaput, no más, finished. We're not dating. Please feel free to stop calling my work." She hated having to get bitchy, but this was ridiculous.

Hannah gasped in her typical dramatic fashion before replying icily, "Fine, whatever, Liv, see you around." *Click.*

Olivia groaned and hung up the phone.

Reagan hit her with an eraser and snickered before adding, "Stage. Five. Clinger. Told you. Ten bucks says she popped your tire just so you would call her for a ride to work so she could rekindle the flame." She added air quotes as Olivia hurled the eraser at her head and scowled.

"I hate when you're right." Olivia didn't bother trying to suppress the smile on her face as she opened up her web browser. She loved that her best friend was her coworker. She valued her relationship with Reagan, even if she was right about Hannah all along.

Her smile deepened when she saw a new email from Savannah Quinn. She figured this was the start of what she assumed would be a regular correspondence with her. She couldn't help but wonder back to what Reagan teased about before. Was she pretty? Was she young? Old? Married? Straight? Her voice was magical. She almost frowned at the email. She much preferred talking to this woman on the phone instead. That was a good sign, right?

CHAPTER THREE

Savannah took notes on the people introducing themselves to her on the screen. She was pleased that they couldn't see her while she was doing it; it gave her the opportunity to closely watch them as she spoke. Corrine Baylor was a peppy little woman with a cute pixie haircut who liked to use a lot of hand motions when she spoke. She was organized and friendly and chipper—damn, that woman was like a hummingbird of excitement.

Savannah breezed over the legal and accounting departments, making short notes next to their bios so she would remember them later. Her real focus was on the design team. They were the people she would be working with closely over the next few months.

She was surprised when some of the team didn't match up with her physical expectations, not that she had any really, but knowing someone on paper and then seeing them in real life gave a different perspective entirely. It all started with Randal Hogan. In front of her was a schleppy fortysomething architect with a wrinkled appearance, but his dossier showed extraordinary design ideas from his past projects that were a complete contrast to his disheveled appearance. His designs favored clean lines and modern applications of metal and glass. You'd never know he was an architectural genius by the ketchup stain above his shirt pocket.

In contrast, Devon Nguyen was exactly what she expected: a young, up-and-coming interior designer, fresh out of school with a well-trimmed fauxhawk and stylish dark-framed glasses. He didn't say much, but from the doodles she could see from her vantage point he was a great artist.

Devon was seated next to Farrah Sanders, a fellow interior designer with a specialty of incorporating flora and fauna into arid, dull spaces. She periodically nudged the younger designer to pay attention. She had a nice mothering quality to her, it seemed—her file stated that she had twin teenage girls. Savannah imagined that was an asset in time management and problem solving.

Reagan Fischer was their engineer, and she looked anything but the part of the nerd with the slide rule. She and Randal seemed like the physical opposites of their jobs. Reagan was confident and almost disinterested. Her manner was oddly attractive.

Daniel Jacobs was their master carpenter and contractor, and his expression was intense. His use of discarded machine parts paired with driftwood made for a unique custom furniture design side business that he frequently incorporated into their designs. Another diamond in the rough, it seemed.

The person Savannah was most interested in, however, was their fearless leader, Olivia Dawson. The write-up on this woman was extensive. Everything about her on paper described her as approachable but confident, creative, and assertive. She was a well-loved leader and an excellent mediator, it appeared. She'd been with Greater Image for eight years and had been promoted to chief designer after her mentor, someone named Albie Davis, retired. Something about Olivia appeared to bring out the best in this motley crew. She was rumored to be a master puzzle manipulator, someone that could solve even the most difficult design obstacle. And she was the primary reason Savannah's company had sought out Greater Image over the other dozen or so firms that had pitched their involvement. Savannah's bosses wanted to know what made Olivia tick and how she managed her team to such well-oiled perfection. She'd made huge strides in a few short years and was really making a name for herself in the industry. People were noticing. Savannah was intrigued.

When she identified herself for the first time on the video call, Savannah was struck by her natural beauty. She had long dark hair that fell in loose curls from a sloppy but cute bun. She chewed on the end of her glasses while she jotted down notes. It was sort of adorable how her brow scrunched with thought before she answered Savannah's questions.

She reviewed the timeline and drafted the first of what she assumed would be *many* emails to Olivia.

From: Quinn, Savannah
To: Dawson, Olivia
Subject: Project Locations and Dates
Hi Ms. Dawson,

It was a pleasure having the opportunity to meet you and your team today. I wanted to follow up with you regarding the site locations and projected deadlines. I will be coming out to your office in about a week to start going over your preliminary concept designs. (See the attachment for specs of the first location.) We will figure out the travel timeline at the conclusion of that week, depending on your group's progress. Our first location is Denver, CO. We have a second site in Phoenix, AZ, that is slightly larger. Our final site is in Chicago, IL, which is not far from the corporate office, so there will likely be the most scrutiny on this location. Let's make sure it's perfect. Sound good? Have a great day. I will be in touch.

Savannah

She was careful with her word choice. She wanted to be professional, yet approachable. They would be logging a lot of long hours together and the last thing she wanted was to start off on the wrong foot.

An email notification popped up as her administrative assistant, Annabelle, read through her schedule for the day. That was quick. She scanned the text as Annabelle reminded her of the afternoon meeting with her boss, Kenneth Dodd. She nodded distractedly and reread the email, smiling at Olivia's mention of the video call.

From: Dawson, Olivia
To: Quinn, Savannah
Subject: Re: Project Locations and Dates
Hey Savannah!

Sounds great. I will get the team started working on the project immediately. I'm available for a phone meeting anytime after eleven a.m. on Friday. I look forward to hearing from you! If you want to make it a video call, let me know—I'd rather have IT be prepared so I don't have to talk to a gray face the whole time. Thanks. :)

Olivia

Olivia's response was the perfect mix of business and playfulness. The smiley face at the end wasn't lost on her. Savannah typed back a quick response and closed the window to focus on Annabelle's ramblings. The partnership with Greater Image Design was exactly the type of professional boost Savannah had been waiting for, and it was time to get started.

CHAPTER FOUR

Olivia and her team had been working hard the last week. Randal, Reagan, and Daniel had been brainstorming over the general room specs Savannah had sent over in her initial email. Devon and Farrah were working on the computer-aided-design program to figure out the best placement in the room for the living wall to foster their green space approach. Olivia's time had been split between mobilizing the team into action and reviewing the less than thrilling details of the newly formed partnership with New Horizons. She loved the freedom and creativity her position allowed her, but she disliked the administrative responsibilities. Luckily, Corrine and the legal team worked out the nitty-gritty stuff, but Olivia was still on the hook for knowing some of the ins and outs of New Horizons. She'd done a little review. Sort of. Kinda.

"How's all that paperwork crap?" Reagan set down a coffee in front of Olivia.

Olivia smiled and sipped the cup. "Oh, you know, thrilling."

"Yeah, I don't envy you at all." Reagan nodded and glanced back at Randal and Daniel. "The guys wanted to head out for drinks after work. You in?"

Olivia let out a quiet sigh. She wanted more than anything to be able to join her colleagues. After this long-ass week, a drink sounded like heaven. But Savannah was arriving from Chicago today and was swinging by the office to set up a workstation.

"I don't think I can. Savannah gets in later tonight. We're meeting here first and then I think Corrine wanted to do a welcome dinner or something."

"Oooh, Savannah," Reagan teased, fluttering her eyelashes.

"Oooh, Savannah, what?" a husky voice asked from behind Reagan.

Reagan froze. Her mouth stuck in the shape of a small *o* as she turned to face the new voice. Olivia would have laughed if she wasn't so captivated by the tall auburn-haired woman who stepped into her line of sight. She was gorgeous. Her bright, fashionable heels were a perfect contrast to the dark pencil skirt, expensive-looking blue silk blouse, and dark blazer she wore. The designer bag on her shoulder and matching luggage by her side confirmed Olivia's initial impression: this woman had style. And if the raised eyebrow over those steely gray-blue eyes was any indication, she had attitude to match.

"Reagan, right?" The redhead extended her hand with a small smile. "I'm Savannah Quinn. I believe you were saying something?"

Reagan paused before she shook Savannah's hand and, to Olivia's horror, unabashedly checked her out. Like, full-on scoped her. That familiar, confident smile settled on Reagan's face and Olivia cringed, knowing full well what was coming next.

Reagan leaned back against the drafting table and assumed her usual arms-crossed position that Olivia had seen her do a million times when she was trying to impress a woman and act disinterested. "Oh, yeah, sorry. I was inviting Liv here out for a drink after work. You're welcome to join us. I'm buying."

She lowered her gaze and Olivia thought she might be staring at Savannah's chest. Which resulted in her looking in that general direction as well. Crap. Reagan was hitting on their client's liaison and now they were both looking at her chest. Abort. Abort.

Olivia cleared her throat and did everything in her power to ignore Reagan's entire existence in this world. She smiled at Savannah and leaned forward to shake her hand. "Hey, I'm Olivia. It's nice to finally meet you."

Savannah smiled back and returned her greeting as she adjusted the bag on her shoulder. She glanced back at Reagan, who was poorly concealing her leering, and Olivia watched in disbelief as Savannah leaned forward and stage-whispered, "My eyes are up here, Reagan. Let's try and remember that, okay?"

A blush formed on Reagan's cheeks as she swallowed quickly and jerked her eyes up to Savannah's, nodding as she stepped back. "Okay, well, think about it and get back to us. Uh, see ya, Liv."

Olivia tried and failed to contain a laugh. She'd never seen Reagan blush like that, well, not since that time she accidently walked in on her loudly singing Cyndi Lauper in the shower with a pink shower cap on during college. But they were not ever to speak of such occurrence, so she filed it back in the blackmail file of her brain. No, this was different. Not many women so easily resisted Reagan's charms when she turned them on. She could tell she was going to like this Savannah woman very much.

"Here, let me introduce you to the team and show you around. Corrine is here somewhere." She frowned as she looked around the open floor plan for her. She could have sworn she was just here.

"Great. Thanks."

After the quick tour of the space and some brief introductions to the team, Olivia walked her guest into the right rear conference room. This was her favorite room in the office, even more than Corrine's quiet sanctuary down the hall. It was located along the far wall of the building and contained a long conference table with a projector and phone system in the middle of the table. It was relatively small compared to the other conference areas in the office. It only had seating for eight people. But one wall of the room was made up entirely of windows overlooking the lush pocket park below. This was why she loved this room.

"This place is great." Savannah looked around the room, her eyes lingered on the view.

"Yeah, it's my favorite place to sneak away and think." Olivia faced the window, her fingers tracing the leather seam on the seat in front of her while she thought out loud. "That's a little view of Coleman Park. It's a nice inspiration for the upswing of green applications in design. It helps remind you of the endless possibilities outside these four walls." She paused, realizing she was babbling. "Sorry, it's been a long day."

"No need to apologize, that was beautiful." Savannah surveyed the room once more. "So, this is home base?"

"Yup, this is your new office. Feel free to make yourself at home. Anything you need, just ask and I will send one of the minions to get it," she joked and nodded back toward the design center.

Before Savannah could reply a soft rap rang out against the glass. Corrine opened the door with an apologetic frown. She walked in and introduced herself to Savannah with an enthusiastic handshake before turning to Olivia and saying quietly, "Hey, Liv, can I chat with you?"

"Uh, yeah, sure." Olivia glanced back to Savannah. "Excuse us a minute?"

Savannah nodded before placing her bag on the table and pulling out files.

"What's up, Corrine? You okay?" Olivia cast a concerned look at her boss, who was tapping her foot anxiously in the hallway outside the conference room.

"Yeah. Aidan broke his ankle at soccer practice and David is picking up Allie at her friend's house to meet me at the hospital. Can you take Savannah out to dinner? Make sure she gets to her hotel and gets settled? Please?" Corrine pleaded and reached out to grab Olivia's hands.

"Of course, sure, no problem. Be with your kids. Let me know if you need anything else."

"Thanks so much, Liv. I owe you."

"No worries, I got this." Olivia smiled and added, "Go."

Corrine reached into her purse and pulled out a packet. "In here is all the introductory background paperwork I did for her—make sure she gets it. She's staying at that hotel off Fifth Avenue that we usually use. We have reservations for seven at Machiavelli's. I called to adjust it from three people to two. It's all set." She let out a weary sigh. "Okay, I'm off, I'll call you tomorrow."

Olivia reentered the conference room to find Savannah standing by the window and lazily scrolling through her phone. She took a moment to appreciate the way Savannah absentmindedly scratched her ankle, and watched with rapt attention as Savannah's hand traced up her calf, massaging it briefly, before she moved higher and smoothed down the front of her skirt. The light from her phone shone back on her face, illuminating her features. It gave Olivia a chance to observe her more closely, her high cheekbones and perfect jawline complemented by her pale skin and flawlessly applied makeup. She shifted and her auburn hair fell in loose waves around her face, almost veiling her profile from Olivia's unobserved admiration. Didn't she just get off a plane and take a more likely than not sticky and cramped New York cab ride to Olivia's office? Shouldn't she look a little travel worn or something? Olivia thought about what Reagan had said before and her stomach knotted. Savannah was every bit as hot as her phone sex voice promised. It was clear—Olivia's only hope for surviving the next few months of living out of hotels and working with this woman hinged entirely on what happened next. Maybe if she was lucky, Savannah would be an absolute bore at this work dinner. That would make her less appealing, right?

She cleared her throat to draw attention to her presence. "Sorry about that, Corrine had a family emergency, so I'm going to be your tour guide for the evening." Olivia stepped toward the table currently occupied by five neat piles of folders, a laptop, and stainless-steel coffee mug.

"Oh? Is everything all right?" A concerned frown settled on Savannah's face as she slipped her phone into her blazer pocket.

"Oh, yeah, her son has a soccer injury. She's got to go be Super Mom."

Savannah nodded and paused, adding with a raised eyebrow, "Do you have a family also? I don't want to keep you from them."

The blush that Olivia felt creep into her neck felt unwarranted. She tried to ignore it and shook her head. "Me? No. I have a cranky landlady and a love affair with fine wine. That and this job keep me pretty busy."

Savannah laughed. She joined Olivia at the desk and pulled out a chair before gesturing for Olivia to join her. "Well, I love fine wine and I have a healthy work ethic. We should get along swimmingly."

That was exactly what Olivia was dreading.

❖

They spent a few hours going over the progress of Olivia's team on the project before calling it a night. After dropping Savannah's gear at the hotel, they headed to dinner. Olivia checked the time and made a mental note to come up with some excuse to leave in an hour or so if the night was dragging on.

To her dismay, Machiavelli's was fun. Olivia found herself chatting easily with Savannah. They discussed everything ranging from art to current events to comparing their favorite celebrity gossip rags. Savannah was funny and engaging. This dinner felt more like a meeting with an old friend than a business meeting. Well, that or a really fun first date. Olivia couldn't decide which one, and that worried her a bit.

"All right, so, lay it on me. Tell me all about this team of yours." Savannah leaned back in the booth, cradling her wine delicately in long, pale fingers. She casually circled the rim of the glass with her forefinger and Olivia tried not to obsess over how sexual the move looked to her.

"Oh, we're at that point in the night, eh? Is this a gentle interrogation because you think I've let my guard down?" Olivia glanced at her own near-empty glass.

"Of course it is." Savannah's smile widened as she leaned forward and topped off Olivia's glass before placing the bottle back on the table. "Spill."

"Okay. I accept your challenge. But you have to split dessert with me, because there is no way we are leaving here without tasting the tiramisu. Deal?"

"That's it? Easy. Done." She extended her glass toward Olivia to clink in agreement.

"Okay, well, Randal and Daniel get along well. Randal is a super genius, but he has trouble with—"

"Dressing professionally?" Savannah offered.

Olivia liked her playfulness. "I was going to say using an iron, but yeah, basically." She chuckled before moving on. "Daniel is intense but agreeable, in small doses. He's a mad genius. Devon and Farrah complement each other by bringing experience and youth to design. They also argue like mother and son occasionally, but they figure it out." She smiled as she remembered a particularly ugly fight that started between them over the use of social media slang as graphic art on the walls of a bedroom in the home of a wealthy businessman. Devon was pushing for shock value and relevance to express the mogul's son's passion for YouTube blogging. Farrah was appalled when she learned what some of the abbreviations stood for, particularly the placement of a really cool graffitied *#UNF* over his bed. She argued that no mother wanted to know that the *Universal Noise of Fucking* might be associated with her kid's bed, ever. There might or might not have been a resultant near slap fight and threats of grounding by Farrah to a bemused Devon. Olivia had to separate them for five days on different projects until they agreed to mediation, *American Gladiators* style, at a dojo downtown. That had been at Reagan's suggestion. "And you met Reagan—she's great. She has a wonderful mind and is a real creative force. She tends to really push the envelope on structural design. Randal and Daniel keep her pretty well grounded, while managing to not stifle her too much."

"And she's into women," Savannah supplied nonchalantly as she forked the recently arrived tiramisu.

Olivia paused remembering the occurrence earlier in the office. She raised her eyebrow curiously. "What makes you think that?" She wanted to know if it bothered Savannah that her colleague was into women. She'd have to brace herself for that knowledge if they would be working closely together these next few months.

Savannah finished her bite before looking intently at Olivia. "I'm observant." She paused. "And she was talking to my tits, so that kind of gave it away."

A reflexive laugh tumbled from Olivia's lips as she shook her head and stabbed a piece of the shared dessert. "Yeah, she's, umm...subtle." She added hurriedly, "But she works well with boundaries and I will make sure she makes eye contact when she speaks with you. I'm sorry for that." She wasn't sure why she felt the need to apologize. Reagan was a big girl, and she made her own decisions in life, good or bad. "Is that a problem for you? That she likes women?"

An unidentifiable expression crossed Savannah's face. "No, not at all." She smiled and brought another piece of tiramisu to her lips, holding it there before asking, "What about you?"

Olivia's attention was on the fork, hovering closely to Savannah's lips, so she almost missed the question. Was Savannah asking if she was into women, too? "What?"

"What's your role in the team? In your own words, I mean." Savannah slipped the dessert past her lips as she waited for Olivia's reply. Olivia reminded herself not to stare.

"I'm the ringmaster to the three-ring circus." Olivia scooped up the last bit of dessert and popped it into her mouth. She wasn't sure if it was the wine, the fatigue of the week clouding her mind, or the present company, but something about this dinner felt oddly more intimate than a business meeting. "I keep the wheels turning, the gears well lubricated, and the clock ticking along happily. Corrine gives me veto power and free creative rein to tweak all submissions as I see fit. It gives me the chance to foster everyone's greatest strengths while allowing me to maintain my own creative design ideas. It's sort of the best of both worlds: management and art." She shrugged as she sipped her wine and leaned back into the booth.

Savannah appraised her from across the table and nodded. "That sounds lovely. And it sounds like you like your job."

"I do. It's fun and rewarding and I've got a great team."

"Well then, I'm looking forward to spending more time with you and them. This should be a good experience for everyone involved."

The look Savannah gave Olivia made her think that maybe Savannah was talking about more than just work. Or the wine was making her horny. Either way, tonight had turned out better than she had planned.

CHAPTER FIVE

It was amazing how many moving parts this new project involved. Savannah considered herself an organized, structured person, but this was trying even for her. Her days were long and she frequently found herself working once she was back at her hotel room for the night. There seemed to be an endless number of loose ends to tie up in preparation for the groundbreaking at the Denver site. But the week flew by and before she knew it, her time in NYC was nearly over. The realization made her frown. That meant her daily routine was going to come to an end and she wasn't sure how that made her feel.

Over the past week, she and Olivia had fallen into a steady routine of sipping morning coffee while discussing the daily agenda. They reconvened around lunchtime to discuss the project and the team's ideas, and met back up to finish the workday, conferring with Corrine and one of the Denver site managers via video call.

Savannah found herself looking forward to her time with Olivia. She liked the easy conversation and whimsical energy Olivia brought to the table. The hours between their meetings were filled with boring administrative issues and dull calls to corporate or ironing out site details for Denver. Savannah caught herself more than once watching the clock for when Olivia might pop back in. And today was no different. Except of course that it was. It was almost her last day here. And for some reason, that thought left her feeling a little unsettled.

She was finishing up a call with her boss Kenneth when she heard a soft rap on the glass of the conference room she had taken over as a temporary office. Olivia smiled at her from the other side of the glass and waved. She motioned for her to come in, glad to see her back so soon after their morning coffee chat.

"Back so soon? A girl could get spoiled." Savannah heard the words leave her mouth and wondered what wild incantation she must be under for her to actually speak the words she was thinking. Clearly her filter had been damaged during last night's fitful sleep.

"You looked tired this morning. I figured you could use a little pick-me-up. Besides, lunch is *so* far away." Olivia scrunched her nose and handed her a granola bar. "It's dark chocolate and peanut butter, but it's high in protein. So that makes it the perfect midmorning snack. It's got, like, all the food groups in it."

"As long as it's got chocolate, I'm sold." Savannah accepted the bar and sighed. "I have to admit, I'm going to miss this."

"The granola bar? You haven't even tried it yet. You could hate it." Olivia pointed to the bar and shrugged.

"That seems highly unlikely." Savannah opened the bar and took a bite. "Yeah. No. Wow. This is good. Like, super good."

Olivia cheered and dropped a file folder onto the table as she plopped into the chair next to her, lounging and offering her a broad carefree smile. "I keep a stash in my desk for when brainstorming sessions result in an absence of three square meals a day. I get hangry if I don't eat."

"Hangry?" That was a new one for Savannah.

"Hungry, angry. I'm like the Hulk when I miss my midmorning snack. The granola bar is for the safety of others, not for myself." Olivia nodded solemnly.

"Well then." She raised her bar and held her hand over her heart. "This is for the people."

"You're a true patriot," Olivia deadpanned.

Yeah, she was definitely going to miss this.

As if reading her mind, Olivia asked, "So, if not the granola bar, then what are you going to miss?"

"Hmm?" Savannah stalled. She hadn't meant to be so candid before but she didn't see a way out of it now. She decided to be honest. "This. I'm going to miss my coffee partner." She pointed to the now empty wrapper between them. "And my newly appointed snack savior."

"Where am I going?" Olivia looked confused. Savannah was reminded how cute she thought Olivia looked when her brow furrowed. Olivia had all sorts of cute mannerisms. And hot ones, too, she'd noticed. But she was trying not to think of those at the moment.

"Well, eventually, you're going to Denver. But I meant me. I'm leaving tomorrow and I'm going to miss our little routine. It's been fun."

Olivia's mouth dropped open and she sat up in her chair. "Oh. I'd sort of forgotten you were on loan to us from New Horizons."

"I know what you mean," Savannah replied, letting her gaze settle momentarily on the slight pout Olivia had on her face. Olivia looked… sad. That was what she'd been feeling before that she couldn't place— it was sadness. Savannah didn't want to leave. It appeared that Olivia didn't want her to leave either.

Corrine knocked and opened the door simultaneously. "Hi. Am I interrupting something?"

Savannah decided it was better not to point out the fact that Corrine hadn't really given the knock a chance to announce itself. "Uh, no. What's up?"

"Good." Corrine came in like a whirlwind and within seconds she was standing between them at the table, talking a mile a minute. "Okay, so, we'll be sending Randal, Daniel, and Reagan out to Denver first. Then Olivia and the rest of the crew will head out a few days later to get everything started. All in all, we have about two weeks to iron out the details. Is there anything else we need to meet on before you leave tomorrow? I want to make sure this first installation goes well."

Savannah appreciated Corrine's enthusiasm. She'd been an asset, even if she was a little like a wayward spinning top at times.

"All that's left are the final outlines and specs." Olivia picked up the folder she'd brought in with her. "They just need a quick review from you lovely ladies and then they're ready for New Horizons."

"Great. Thanks." Savannah took the file from Olivia and thumbed through it.

"Good. This is all very good," Corrine said. Her head bobbed so quickly Savannah worried it would bobble right off her shoulders. Olivia rolled her eyes. Evidently, they were on the same wavelength.

Corrine clapped suddenly, jarring them both. "We should do dinner as a group before you leave."

More time with Olivia? Okay. "Sure, that sounds great."

"Excellent." Corrine spun on her heel, facing Olivia so abruptly that Olivia leaned back in her seat. "Let the team know. Let's celebrate our hard work."

"Okay, will do." Olivia's words fell on deaf ears since Corrine had breezed out of the room before waiting for Olivia's answer. "I love that woman, but sometimes she's a bit—"

"Much?" Savannah put the folder down and pushed it away. She wasn't interested in working right now.

"Exactly." Olivia sighed. "I'm glad you noticed. I was really starting to like you and I wasn't sure if we could still be friends if you didn't agree."

"No need to worry. I'm completely on the same page with you." Savannah uncrossed her legs to stretch and could've sworn Olivia's eyes flickered downward. Olivia all but confirmed it when she looked up and blushed. Savannah held her gaze, curious as to what Olivia might be thinking. She'd been instantly attracted to Olivia since that work dinner her first night here and the feeling didn't fade when Olivia gave her a tour of some of her favorite NYC haunts before this week began. But they had been so busy with work since then, she'd all but pushed that attraction out of her mind. Not that that was really possible. But she'd tried. And here they were on their last workday together and Olivia was watching her uncross her legs. Like she'd caught Olivia noticing her chest when Reagan introduced herself to Savannah last week. Savannah didn't miss that either. But she'd thought that maybe it was nothing. It was probably nothing. Except maybe it was something.

Olivia opened her mouth like she wanted to say something when another hurried knock interrupted them. Just like before, the person on the other side of the door didn't wait for a response before barging it.

"Jesus. What is it with that door today?" Olivia grumbled as Devon's face appeared in the doorway.

"Hey, Liv? Can I get tomorrow off? My sister popped into town sorta unexpectedly, and I—"

"Yeah, Devon, fine. Just fill out the form and leave it on my desk." Olivia hurried him out of the doorway with a wave. She turned back to face her when Savannah's phone rang.

They seemed destined to be interrupted. Savannah looked at the caller ID and frowned. It was Kenneth. "I have to take this."

"I'll leave you to it." Olivia rose from her seat and headed for the door.

Savannah stopped her. "One last debriefing tonight before drinks later?"

Olivia turned and smiled. "I wouldn't miss it."

Savannah couldn't wait for this day to be over.

"All right, all right. Focus, people. This is the last time we get to socialize before we become nomads." Reagan held up a glass to toast.

"Let's all agree to get along as best we can and to steal as many mini shampoo bottles as possible."

Savannah clinked her glass with the rest of the group and they cheered in unison. Devon was off with his sister, and Farrah had other plans, so tonight's group was only Daniel, Randal, Reagan, and Olivia. Corrine had stuck around for a few appetizers but had ducked out to check on her kids, who were home alone since her husband had to work late.

Olivia was sitting to her immediate right and seemed to be distracted by something. She was looking off into the distance in that far-off way one does when they have something on their mind. Reagan had asked her something twice and Olivia hadn't responded. Savannah wanted to know what she was thinking about.

"Liv?" Reagan repeated with a smirk.

"Hmm? What?" Olivia replied, shaking her head as if to lift the fog.

"Where'd you go?" Reagan nudged her before reaching over and finishing off the rest of Olivia's drink. "You snooze, you lose, friend. Next round is on you." Reagan excused herself from the booth, shuffling past Randal and Daniel toward the restroom before Olivia could reply.

"Rude," Olivia muttered as she looked longingly at her empty martini glass.

"You all right?" Savannah leaned close and asked her quietly. The bar was packed and the crowd boisterous. She was glad they had a little corner booth right off the main bar, which gave them a little privacy and intimacy without removing them from the social lightness of the evening. Plus, it afforded her the luxury of seeing Olivia's hazel eyes sparkle in the low lighting of the bar without it being creepy that she was so close and watching her so intently. She'd have to make a lot of eye contact to hear her over the ambient noise. She didn't mind the excuse to be close.

"Yeah, I'm just...I don't know, out of it today." Olivia shrugged. "I feel like I'm in sort of a fog."

Savannah waved to the bartender for another round. "Are you worried about the design project?"

Olivia shook her head. "No, I don't think so. I just feel like I'm forgetting to do something important."

Savannah watched her closely as she decided to test the waters a bit, feeling emboldened by the martini she'd just drained. "It's because I'm leaving tomorrow, huh? You're sad?"

Olivia blinked, her mouth slightly agape until Savannah winked to give her an out.

Olivia chuckled. "Yeah, that's it, you caught me."

That was the second time Savannah had intentionally probed Olivia. She was fishing, no point in pretending that she wasn't. She'd had an inkling that Olivia might be into women over their first dinner together when she'd intentionally asked her the ambiguous follow-up question to their Reagan discussion. She'd gotten the nonverbal response she was looking for then, and it was confirmed this morning when she caught Olivia watching her shift in the chair. Savannah wasn't worried about whether or not Olivia was into women. Mostly she was curious as to whether Olivia was into *her*. That would make this a very interesting few months. It wasn't like she was looking for anything serious, but Olivia was funny and smart and attractive. She'd be a fool to ignore their chemistry.

The bartender came over with a full tray of drinks, setting them down one by one, and when Olivia reached under the table for her purse to pick up the tab, Savannah placed her hand atop Olivia's and halted her progress. Olivia's eyes shifted up to hers and she smiled, letting her hand linger on Olivia's for longer than was necessary.

"I've got this round—you get the first one in Denver."

When Olivia didn't refuse, or move her hand away from Savannah's, she considered it a win.

Savannah had to laugh at the way the night had unfolded. Around the third round of drinks, Randal and Daniel had excused themselves for the night but not before tripping their way out of the bar. She had to admit, she'd expected them to hold their liquor better. Although it was pretty hilarious watching Randal sway into Reagan on his way out just as she was hitting on some unsuspecting straight girl at the bar, dumping the contents of her drink on said straight girl. That in and of itself was funny enough, until the straight girl's boyfriend got back from the bathroom and lunged at Randal, probably assuming that he was the perpetrator of the crime. Luckily, Daniel stepped in and smoothed things over with just enough time for Reagan to sneak away and out the door. That left just Olivia and Savannah at the table, shaking their heads and laughing.

"She's got some serious lady balls." Savannah chuckled as she watched the confused boyfriend attempt to help his date, who was actively avoiding eye contact with Olivia and Savannah, knowing that they had seen everything that went down.

"Yeah. It's always interesting with Reagan around." Olivia finished off her drink before stacking the empty glasses and pushing them aside. She glanced over to Savannah and asked, "How often do you travel? I mean, are you ever home?"

Savannah paused, sipping her drink before settling her gaze on Olivia. "I travel quite a bit. Sometimes three weeks at a time to one place or another, other times I'm home for a month or two at a time, it depends."

"Air quotes on home, huh?" Olivia didn't miss a thing.

"I'm sort of new to Chicago. I'm a recent transplant. I haven't really unpacked yet." Savannah hoped that wasn't too vague. She'd rather not discuss that part of her life just yet. Light and easy was fine by her, right now.

"Does all the traveling ever get boring? I imagine waking up in a new place all the time is difficult." Olivia looked at her empty water glass and frowned. Savannah pushed hers to Olivia and was rewarded with a bright smile.

"You get used to it. Although I would be lying if I told you there weren't days when I didn't know where I was and had to call down to the front desk to figure out what city and time zone I was in." She was aware of how pathetic that sounded, but it was true.

"How do you make it work? I mean, all that jet-setting, how do you manage a family or a relationship? I don't think I could do it..." Olivia shook her head. "I'm a terrible packer. There is no way I could just scoot around the country with one neat little bag like the one you showed up to my office with."

Savannah gave her a small smile. "You find ways to make things work. You'd be surprised what you can do when you have to." She paused. "But with that being said, the goal of this launch is to limit my time on the road. To give me a sense of home base—you know, like the one I have in your office, only more permanent." She sipped her drink again, tracing the tabletop lightly with her fingers. She'd rather not discuss the relationship part of that question. Olivia didn't seem to notice.

"Is that what you want? Eventually, I mean. To be in one place?" Olivia was facing her, leaning against the back of the booth. She looked so relaxed. And her skin looked so soft. She played with her mass of dark curls as she spoke and Savannah found herself captivated. She wondered if those curls were as soft as her skin looked. The desire to touch them was increasing by the moment.

"Yes and no. There's something nice about not being tied down, if that's what you're asking." Savannah's response was automatic, but hearing the words come out of her mouth gave her a pang of regret. She wondered if she had sounded callous. She hadn't meant to. There were pros and cons to this life. "It's complicated."

"I'm fascinated by you," Olivia said. "The fact that you are entirely mobile blows my mind." Her curls bounced as she shook her head. "I'm a pretty rooted person. I value the sense of home I get from my little apartment. I like movie nights with my friends and walks in the park along familiar routes. I like knowing that my sister and niece are only a fifty-minute flight away at any given time. I don't think I could handle being untethered and entirely free from the familiar place I've grown accustomed to."

Savannah considered this for a moment, looking around the bar as she thought. She took in the small group of businessmen after work, throwing darts in the corner and sharing a pitcher of beer. Her gaze settled on a couple on a date at the bar, his hand on her knee as she laughed and touched his arm affectionately. She wondered if she was missing something. If she was missing the anchor that everyone else here had. She had that anchored life with her ex, Gwen, before Gwen's infidelity ruined everything. There was a sense of loss around the familiar domesticity that came with a relationship, that was true. She missed it. Part of it, anyway.

She kept her gaze on the bartender as he wiped down the bar with a rag when she replied, "I think that eventually everyone wants stability and routine in their lives. So, yes, I guess I do want to end up someplace, sometime, on a more permanent level. I don't know if I've found that place just yet, or if I ever will." She was surprised by her own honesty in the moment. She blamed it on the empty martini glasses on the table in front of her.

"You will," Olivia replied. "You'll find that place. Everyone needs roots somewhere. Sometimes it just takes longer to find the right spot. But you'll find it."

"You seem very confident in that assertion." Savannah had found in the short time that she'd known her that Olivia seemed to have a way of framing things in such a manner that they seemed quite attainable. Even the most daunting of tasks. She liked this about her new colleague. She felt very comfortable addressing big things like her nomadic tendencies in a very unassuming way.

"I am," Olivia replied with an affirmative nod. "Piecing things together is my full-time job: everything has a place. Sometimes you just need to look from a different angle or with a fresh set of eyes, but all puzzles have a solution."

Savannah finished her drink and thought about the many ways that statement could be interpreted. She had a preference as to which way that might be. Time would tell if her wish came true. "Well, I guess we'll just see about that, won't we?"

CHAPTER SIX

Denver

Olivia glanced down at her phone once more as she tapped her foot, waiting for the cab to pull up. She'd landed about forty minutes ago, collected her bags, and managed to corral Devon and Farrah to meet her at the arrivals curb in time for their designated pickup, except there was no cab in sight. The flight had been bumpy and she had been sandwiched between two rather unfriendly passengers, both of whom took turns falling asleep on her shoulders. The last thing she wanted to be doing right now was wait around for some cabbie to get her. All she really wanted was a shower and a stiff drink, the order of which was negotiable.

"Thank God for technology. I hate flying," Devon grumbled and cracked his neck while playing with his phone. He had been whining off and on since they'd met at the gate in LaGuardia, and Olivia's patience with him had run out about an hour ago.

Farrah stood behind him, brushing lint off his shoulders before fixing her hair in the window of the terminal behind them. "Hey, Liv? Are we meeting everyone at the hotel or…?

"Yeah, when the cab finally gets here, we'll check in and meet briefly to discuss the schedule for the next few days." She looked at the clock on her phone again but she just got more annoyed when she saw the time. She really should stop doing that.

Just as Olivia was about to blow her stack, a large black SUV with tinted windows pulled up and out of the passenger side popped Savannah with a large smile on her face.

"Welcome to Denver."

Olivia let out a heavy sigh, her shoulders relaxing a bit at the sight of Savannah. She'd been looking forward to seeing her again. She'd had this nervous energy buzzing through her for the whole flight. She shouldn't have been surprised that she felt much calmer now that Savannah was here. She knew damn well that part of that nervousness was about seeing Savannah in person after their recent text exchange. "I thought there was a cab picking us up."

"Why? Are you disappointed?" Savannah teased her as she helped Farrah lift her suitcase into the back hatch. The driver emerged and began helping Devon with his bags on the other side of the vehicle.

"No, no, not at all. I'm sort of relieved." Olivia placed her own luggage in the back. "My only cab experiences are on the mean Manhattan streets, so I wasn't sure what to expect."

"Well, I figured you guys would be tired and I heard the weather wasn't ideal on the flight out, so I commandeered the hotel's shuttle and Ernesto here." Savannah nodded toward the driver. "Ernesto seems to know all the best restaurants in town."

As Olivia settled into the back seat of the van, she let her mind wander. Over the past few weeks, she and Savannah had communicated daily via email or phone. Sometime along the way they had swapped numbers and begun texting outside of work. At first it was just about work details, things they had forgotten to include in interoffice memos or little notes on some design features that Olivia had late-night inspiration about.

The conversations were harmless and innocent, until the last few days, when their texts had more to do with seeing each other again than about work. Olivia had started things three days ago, sort of unintentionally. Well, that wasn't entirely true. She'd had a feeling that maybe Savannah was flirting with her at the bar that last night before she'd left town, something about the way she was looking at her. There wasn't anything in particular, but something just told her that maybe her immediate attraction to Savannah was reciprocated. She'd thought about this a lot. So when it came time to pack, she figured there wasn't any harm in asking Savannah what she should wear. No harm there, right? *hey, what's the weather like there? what do I pack for clothes?*

Olivia didn't think it was too odd a question, although she was aware she could just look it up on her weather app. This was more of a…conversation starter of sorts. You know, get Savannah thinking about what she might be wearing.

There was a pause before Savannah answered. *It's warm, dry. Pack sunglasses, it's bright here*

She added some specificity for round two. *so like, skirts or pants?* Savannah's reply came fast. She had her attention. This was good. *oh definitely skirt weather, pants for cooler evenings. altho I can see if formal gowns are necessary...*

It took exactly three seconds for Olivia to type a reply. *formal gowns? R we attending something fancy?*

Savannah replied: *well, I expect a certain standard of dress when in my presence*

Well then, that was something. She could practically hear those words coming out of Savannah's mouth in that husky voice which made her feel all sorts of things. She hesitated for a moment, writing and deleting her text before settling on something playful as a response. She added the winky face for good measure. *oh i c. someone should tell Randal that. Ok, i will make sure to up my packing game ;)*

Savannah texted back: *I'm excited to see the final selections.*

Suddenly, Olivia was much more excited about this Denver trip. So much so, that the following morning, with a little too much caffeine and some downtime, she texted Savannah again. Just to see if yesterday was a fluke. *ok, so i think im all packed. what's the coffee like there? should i pack some?*

The response was immediate. *it's good. i will make sure they have 1% milk at the ready*

Olivia jumped right in for the full flirt. *oh, u remember how i like my coffee? that's sweet. :)*

There was a pause and Olivia wondered if maybe she'd crossed a line. The ellipses bubble hovered next to Savannah's name, until: *do u remember how i take mine?*

Booyah. That was definitely a flirt back. Of course she remembered how Savannah liked her coffee. She'd spent the better part of a week staring at Savannah's mouth the whole time they had their morning meetings. She could probably pick her lipstick color out of a lineup without any trouble as well.

Olivia: *skim milk, one splenda ;)*

Savannah: *u got it. :) hurry up and get here, we have work to do.*

She remembered smiling the rest of the day, feeling victorious. But she knew her victory would be short-lived. Their relationship needed to stay light and playful. The flirting couldn't go anywhere. And as she looked up to catch Savannah smiling at her in the rearview from the front seat of the SUV, she reminded herself that she would not flirt with her client's liaison, she would not stare at her lips when she talked, and she most definitely wouldn't start falling for her.

❖

The ride from the airport to the hotel was quick. Ernesto pointed out interesting sights along the way and told them little facts about the Mile High City and about fun hiking trails near the hotel. Savannah watched Olivia and Farrah in the rearview from the passenger seat of the SUV. Farrah was nodding and smiling at all the information, occasionally leaning back and saying something to Devon, who had put in an earbud and was zoning out. Olivia was reclined in the seat, her sunglasses pushed up onto her head, loose dark curls hanging freely, each curl more perfect than the last—soft looking and gorgeous. Her eyes were directed toward the mountain view as they drove along, occasionally flicking toward Farrah from time to time.

Savannah found herself staring. She averted her eyes and slipped on her shades when she caught Olivia glancing up and smiling at her in the mirror. Olivia had the most beautiful smile; she had small dimples and perfect teeth with full lips. Savannah let the near-black lenses of her sunglasses hide her appreciative gaze. She was surprised when they finally pulled up to the hotel, not realizing that she had spent the better part of the ride entranced.

Savannah waited in the lobby while Olivia and the rest of her team checked in to their respective rooms. It was late in the day and the construction workers had gone home, but when they arrived at the design space, Randal and Daniel still had on their hard hats and were poring over some graph paper with a calculator. Reagan was firing crumpled paper basketballs into the waste bin and posing with every successful completion.

"Liv! Thank God you guys are finally here." Reagan swept an arm across her forehead dramatically. "These guys have been boring me to death."

She jerked her thumb toward Randal and Daniel, rolling her eyes when they grunted in response. She sidled up to Olivia and hooked her arm. "Anyway. How was your flight, girl?"

"Bumpy. And cramped. But we made it." Olivia adjusted the bag on her shoulder as she glanced around the skeleton of the room. "How's it been here?"

Randal cleared his throat. "It's good, Liv, everything looks good. They'll put up the dividing wall over there, tomorrow. And they're taking orders for fabrics and plants tomorrow, too, so they'll be here by the end of the week."

Daniel nodded and adjusted his hard hat. "Yeah, everything looks totally manageable. The crew here is really good."

Savannah stepped forward, pulling out a rolled-up blueprint and draping it across the nearest drafting table. "This is the outline the guys and Reagan have come up with for the construction schedule. We're hoping that Devon and Farrah can look at some samples in the morning and have some firmed-up plans by the early afternoon."

Savannah watched as Olivia slipped her arm out of Reagan's and walked toward the drafting table. She placed her bag on the floor and appraised the print as Reagan and Devon began playing an aggressive one-on-one paper basketball game nearby. Savannah's gaze followed Olivia's fingers as she outlined the dividing wall and walked her fingertips along the layout for the wall of glass that would be controlled by the computer system to adjust its tint and the scene viewed on it. When Olivia paused at the dotted lines at the edge of the room and looked up at her, Savannah had to remind herself that she was there to work, not ogle.

Savannah stepped forward and pointed to the far corner of the space. "This is where the water feature will go. It will require less plumbing here and it will help separate the zones of the room."

Olivia nodded and leaned closer to the print once more to examine the details. Out of the corner of her eye, Savannah saw Reagan make a crazy jump shot toward the trash and careen into Olivia, sprawling her forward toward the table. Savannah barely got her hands on Olivia's waist in time to prevent her from face-planting on the blueprints.

Olivia looked a little stunned, her hands settling on Savannah's still wrapped around her waist. She took a breath and stepped toward Reagan with her fist raised. "Seriously, Reagan? What are you, five?"

Reagan spun on her heel, waiting to see if she made the shot before checking to see if Olivia was okay. "You good, Liv? Did you see that shot?"

Savannah loosened her grip on Olivia, but kept her hand at Olivia's lower back surveying her cautiously before shooting a glare at Reagan. It seemed as though Reagan was going to be more than a handful.

She cleared her throat and pulled her hand away as Devon and Reagan resumed their game, oblivious to the annoyed mutterings of their team leader. Savannah distanced herself from Olivia in that moment. She used a conference call with a vendor as an excuse to be noncommittal when they invited her to dinner. It was better this way. Although she might have entertained a little flirtation with Olivia over the past few weeks, actually touching her sparked a different reaction in Savannah. She enjoyed the feeling of Olivia in her arms far too much even though it was brief and arguably protective in nature. She wasn't even going to delve into the momentary flames she saw when Reagan was so flippant with Olivia's safety. That was an introspection for another day. It was decided. Touching Olivia was something else entirely, and Savannah needed to keep her hands and mind in check.

CHAPTER SEVEN

Olivia probably would have launched the water bottle that was on the drafting table at Reagan had she not been momentarily stunned by the warm hands around her waist. In all the weeks that they had worked together, Savannah had only touched her twice: once at the bar to stop her from paying, and then again, right now. Savannah's hand settled at her lower back and stayed there as she admonished Reagan. It grounded her.

When Savannah pulled her hand away, Olivia looked up at her. The expression on Savannah's face was unreadable, but her eyes, her eyes were so interesting. They were blue, but they were gray, too. And they were brewing with something, like a slow rolling storm was moving through them. Olivia was disappointed when Savannah left without agreeing to join them for dinner. She was disappointed with herself for feeling disappointed, too.

They pored over the specs for a little longer before the guys decided to go to an off-site steak restaurant that Ernesto had pointed out before. The ladies decided to head back to the hotel and try out the lounge downstairs.

Reagan and Farrah were already sitting in a booth by the time Olivia got down to the restaurant in the hotel lobby. Farrah was laughing about something one of her daughters had posted on Facebook and was showing a video to Reagan. Reagan was smiling like an idiot at the screen in front of her.

"What could possibly give you that shit-eating grin, Reagan?" Olivia teased as she slipped into the seat.

"It's only the funniest video of a kitten and a puppy fighting over a cheese stick ever. In the whole world. I checked." Reagan crossed her heart to make it official.

"You have such a soft spot for animals. You better watch out, or it'll kill your reputation for being a badass." Olivia looked over the drink menu.

Farrah piped in with a hearty laugh. "If only all those poor women knew that little Reagan was a softy."

Reagan pouted, crossing her arms and narrowing her eyes. "Are we picking on Reagan tonight? Because if we are, I might go make friends at the bar with that hot ass in the black skirt." She nodded toward the silhouette of a woman at the edge of the bar, shrouded in darkness except for her impossibly tight skirt and killer red heels.

"Oh, yeah?" Olivia challenged. "And what makes you think she's going to fall for your game? I mean, we're in Denver. No home-field advantage for you, my friend."

Reagan leaned back in her seat and quirked an eyebrow at Olivia. "You wanna make a wager, Dawson? Because I bet you a Scorpion Bowl that I can get her number in two drinks or less."

Farrah scoffed. "Are you serious? Hanging out with you two is like attending a frat boy convention of idiocy."

Reagan feigned offense and shot Olivia another daring glance. "What do you say, Liv? Drinks on you if I get the digits?"

Olivia knew Reagan could be charming when she wasn't being a total jerk, but there was no way in hell that perfect ass in that unbelievable skirt was going to fall for her charms. No way in hell. "You're on. And if you don't get them, in two drinks or less, dinner is on you."

"Dinner?" Reagan leaned forward mockingly. "Ooh, you drive a hard bargain, Dawson. But since I am convinced I got this in the bag, you're on." She extended her hand to Olivia to shake, only to pull it back at the last minute and sweep it through her dark hair with a laugh. "I'll be back. Don't wait for me to order—I think I see something much better than what's on the menu."

Farrah groaned and shoved Reagan out of the seat.

They watched her with amusement as she wandered to the other side of the bar, ordered herself a drink, and gestured toward the beautiful woman in the corner, still hidden from view by a curtain of dark hair and a blind spot in the lighting. The bartender nodded, mixing a drink and walking it down the bar. He placed it in front of the mystery woman. The woman kept her head down, but Olivia could see from the moving lips of the bartender that they were talking about something. The gestures he was making as he spoke looked oddly sexual and he pointed toward Reagan, who was approaching slowly while shooting a taunting glare at Olivia. She puffed out her chest in victory as they all watched the mystery woman take the glass and spin it before sipping it slowly.

Reagan was only three steps away from the woman when she stepped into the light: the mystery woman with the great ass was none other than Savannah. Olivia choked out a laugh so violent that she started to cough and Farrah had to slap her back to keep her from dying.

Savannah sipped the glass as she walked toward their table away from Reagan, who was standing very still, her eyes wide in a comical way that made Olivia laugh even harder.

"Ladies." Savannah held up her glass in a mock toast before slipping into the booth next to Olivia, who was hysterical with laughter next to Farrah, causing the booth to shake beneath them. Savannah toyed with the rim of her glass, placing her other hand on the table over the menus and idly tapping her fingers as she waited for her seatmates to settle down.

Olivia wiped tears from her eyes, clutching her gut as she spoke. "H-hey, Savannah. Fancy meeting you here."

Farrah snorted and Olivia's laughing redoubled. It was contagious.

Reagan was still frozen in her spot near the bar, seemingly trying to figure out what she should do next. In the end, she quickly downed her drink and stepped back to the table. She slid next to Farrah with a false grin on her face. "Savannah. How nice to see you here. Staying for dinner, I hope?"

Olivia roared with laughter and covered Savannah's hand on the tabletop with her own before she gasped out, "Yeah, stay. Reagan's buying dinner."

"Oh?" Savannah asked.

"Yup. Reagan bet us that she could get the hottie in the skirt's number, in two drinks or less. Tell us, Savannah dear, you didn't happen to share your cell number with her, did you?"

Savannah tapped her chin in mock consideration. "You know, that never came up."

Farrah lost it at that point, gagging on her water and shaking her head as Reagan huffed in annoyance next to her. "That'll teach you to peacock around, Reagan," Farrah said, wiping her eyes and sighing. "That's the best laugh I've had in a while."

"So, you like my ass in this skirt, huh?" Savannah's expression was playful. "I especially liked that you asked the bartender to add some hand gestures, just in case I didn't get the memo. But really, thanks for the drink, Reagan."

Olivia couldn't stop vibrating with laughter. She slid her hand off Savannah's as she wiped at the tears in her eyes. Her sides hurt from laughing.

The waiter came over and surveyed the women curiously. "Would you like to hear the specials? We have quite a few choices on the menu tonight."

Olivia burst into another fit of giggles and Reagan grumbled before ordering another round of drinks for the table.

"Not that I'm complaining at all, but what made you decide to join us?" Olivia was elated but trying to play it cool. And if the easy smile on Savannah's face was any indication, it was totally working. Definitely.

"The conference call fell through. I stopped down to get a drink to take back to my room with the intention of doing a little more work. I hadn't planned to intrude on your dinner, until Reagan propositioned me." Savannah's laugh made Olivia's insides heat up.

"It's no intrusion at all. I'm glad you're here." Olivia covered her mouth with her hand to stop herself from doing something insane like telling Savannah she looked pretty tonight, and that she'd noticed Savannah had changed from her previous outfit of the day. Because that wouldn't be weird or creepy at all.

Savannah's smile widened. "Me, too."

Something behind the glint in Savannah's eyes when she answered Olivia told her this was going to be a very fun night.

CHAPTER EIGHT

Olivia groaned the next morning when the sun peeked through the curtains, blinding her and inciting a gentle throb in her head. Although she'd had her fair share of cocktails, she still remembered everything that happened in vivid detail. And the details reminded her that last night had been ridiculous.

After Reagan had accidentally sexually harassed Savannah, they made it a point to antagonize her the rest of the night. There were appetizers and some food and shots. Lots of shots. By the end of the night Farrah and Savannah practically carried Reagan to her room before unceremoniously dropping her on the bed with two bottles of water and some ibuprofen. Farrah offered to hang around and tuck Reagan in for the night and Olivia had been grateful. Normally, she would be more than happy to have a drunk slumber party with her bestie, but with Savannah nearby looking delicious and her inhibitions lowered from all that tequila, she was glad Farrah could fill in just this once.

Olivia was pretty buzzed by the time she and Savannah hit the elevators, and she was swaying a bit and bumping the walls as she waited. Savannah had merely laughed and helped her step into the elevator as she placed her hand along Olivia's hip to keep her from tripping over the threshold.

"Why are you so damn sober?" Olivia tried to limit the amount of slurring evident.

Savannah had shrugged. "Because Farrah and I skipped the last round of shots and substituted with water. That's why."

"No fair. Reagan was paying—you have to go full throttle in such in-instances." Olivia closed her eyes momentarily, which was a mistake, and she swayed a little more before reaching out to entwine her fingers with Savannah's to steady herself.

"Well, if that was your intention, I think you were very successful." Savannah loosely held Olivia's hand as the elevator doors opened to Olivia's floor. "Come on, let's get you to bed." Savannah stepped out of the elevator and gently tugged Olivia with her, pausing before she asked. "Which room is yours, Liv?"

Olivia giggled and tucked her chin, nervously dragging her toe on the carpet. She'd looked up to find Savannah watching her expectantly. She'd nodded toward the left corridor and pulled Savannah along with her. She probably should have been focusing on walking in a straight line, but she was too happy thinking about the fact that Savannah had just called her *Liv* and not *Olivia*. It was cute. She hadn't done that before. After a few more steps, Olivia stopped short in front of her room, pulling Savannah's hand in the process. She pointed toward the closed door. "This is me."

"You need a hand getting it open?" Savannah was holding Olivia's purse and surveyed the key card lock with mild amusement.

"I can do it. I'm not wasted, just buzzed." Olivia smiled and reached her free hand toward her purse, pulling out the key card and stepping toward the door, but not quite getting to her intended destination as she was jerked back. Her hand was still in Savannah's, who was standing behind her.

"You'll have to let go of my hand if you want access to the room, I'm afraid." Savannah scrunched her nose. "It's sort of a two-handed job, getting into a room."

Olivia frowned, Savannah was right. She *did* need two hands. To be honest she had sort of forgotten that they were even holding hands at all because it had felt totally normal. She let out a defeated sigh and released her hold on Savannah before stepping forward and unlocking the door on the first try. She turned and smiled in triumph. "Success!"

Savannah laughed and shook her head as she followed Olivia into the room and set Olivia's purse on the dresser.

"Thanks for walking me to my room. It was very gentlewomanly of you." Olivia took Savannah's hand again before she leaned in to press a kiss to Savannah's cheek. She paused there a moment, only pulling back when she realized that this was Savannah Quinn, her colleague, not her best friend or her girlfriend. And she probably shouldn't be kissing her on the cheek, at all, even a little.

"Um, sorry, I think I momentarily lost my mind there." Olivia stepped back and pressed her fingers to her lips, because her lips were sort of buzzing right now from touching Savannah's cheek. But more than that, she did it to stop herself from uttering something she couldn't take back. Something like, *Gosh, your skin is soft*, because that would be bad. Very bad.

Savannah nodded and stepped back and Olivia appreciated the distance. She didn't trust herself like this. It was good Savannah was more sober. "Good night, Olivia. I'll see you in the morning."

Olivia mumbled good night and watched as Savannah stepped out of the room and closed the door silently behind her.

Fast forward to now, and here she was, squinting at the clock, about seven hours later with a throbbing headache and the realization that she totally almost made a move on Savannah. Well, maybe she sort of did. She groaned in frustration as she sat up slowly, willing the room to stop spinning. She gulped down some water and grabbed an apple out of the complimentary fruit basket on her way to the bathroom. Just as she was stepping toward the sink, she noticed a piece of paper that had been slid under the door. She leaned forward to pick it up, being careful to brace herself on the wall, and silently prayed that bending down wouldn't make her headache worse. It did.

> *Olivia,*
> *Hope you had a good night's rest. I moved the usual morning meeting until eleven, so take your time getting to the design space. Devon and Farrah are working on the fabric decisions now. We'll finalize them at the meeting later.*
> *Savannah*

Olivia smiled at the note. She was grateful Savannah had bumped back the morning meeting. It was awfully thoughtful of her. Olivia let the warmth of that thought wash over her as she stepped into the shower. She reminded herself to thank Savannah when she saw her later and let herself imagine all the ways she'd like to do just that.

❖

Savannah had spent the morning working in her room. After last night, she'd slept pretty soundly, although not for long. She found herself wide-awake only four hours after falling asleep. She didn't feel tired, though. She felt surprisingly refreshed.

She'd started the day answering emails and making calls from her room until it was a little after nine in the morning. When she got to the design space she was surprised to see not only Randal and Daniel but Reagan, working together and directing the construction team here and there. Reagan looked a little ragged, but awake and functional. That was unexpected.

"Good morning, Reagan," Savannah greeted her. "How are you today?"

Reagan looked up at her with eyes wide and a slight blush on her cheeks before brushing her hair back and resuming her cool-as-a-cuke facade. "I'm good, how are you?"

"Good." She decided to go with it. She glanced over at the contractors. "Things progressing as they should?"

"Yep, looks right on schedule. Are we still doing the morning meeting?" Reagan reached forward and scooped up some papers from the drafting table as she turned to face Savannah again.

Savannah had pushed the meeting back to give Olivia and Reagan some time to recover. She had sort of instigated their shots last night and was feeling a little remorseful. But just a little. "No, I bumped it back to eleven so Devon and Farrah could go over the textures and come to a decision." It was partially true—she had hoped they would be productive.

"Oh, cool," Reagan replied casually and glanced at Savannah again, seemingly unsure of what to say.

"It's fine, Reagan, really. Last night was fun. No big deal." Savannah lowered her voice to keep the conversation between the two of them.

Reagan nodded and let out a sigh of relief. She paused for a moment, as if she was going to say something, before seeming to change her mind. "Okay, good. I'm going to get back to, uh, it. See you in a bit." She walked back toward the guys hovering over the drafting table by the window and got to work.

Savannah's attention was called toward Farrah and Devon, who were standing by the water feature's intended location. They were holding up swatches and paint samples. Devon had made the astute observation that they could sync the water pressure to adjust with certain backdrops—more aggressive flow for the hiking imagery, replicating a far-off waterfall, versus the slow, gentle descent of a babbling brook paired with the starry night scene they had planned. Savannah waved over the head contractor and Daniel to discuss whether this was a feasible request. Everyone seemed to think it was a stroke of genius, and a worker was dispatched to find the equipment to test it out. Farrah came up with a fabulous idea to camouflage the fixture mechanisms with a native, living moss found just outside the city that she had read about in prep for the trip. The water supply would feed the living moss, which would also contribute to the lushness of the fountain area. This slightly changed their plans for the next two days, but Savannah was pleased with the innovative thinking. This team worked so well together.

❖

By the time Olivia stepped into the design space, things were moving quickly. The dividing wall had been assembled and was being drywalled. Devon and Farrah were working with Savannah by the water feature. Savannah was talking to someone on the phone, nodding in reply and speaking to Daniel to convey whatever message she needed to. Olivia cradled the coffee in her hands while she let herself appreciate Savannah's outfit today. She was in a black dress with a bright teal belt and matching pumps. The dress was formfitting, but professional, and very, very flattering. Savannah, it seemed, had a fantastic wardrobe. She had the phone tucked to her ear as her fingers worked furiously over the screen of the tablet in front of her. Olivia could see her pulling up windows as she talked.

"She does have a great ass—I wasn't wrong about that," Reagan whispered. "And I know you've noticed that, too."

There was no point in denying it. She was obviously appreciating Savannah's assets from here. And Reagan would recognize what that looked like better than anyone. She looked over at Reagan. "Yeah, well, at least I didn't try to get in her skirt with a sad pickup line and some obscene hand gestures." She nudged her shoulder into Reagan.

"Ugh, don't remind me." Reagan groaned and squeezed the bridge of her nose. "She was pretty cool about it, though. It could have been a big thing."

Olivia nodded. It *could* have been a big thing. But that didn't really seem like Savannah's style, not that she had any real idea about her or her style per se. But she wanted to, and that worried her a bit.

"She's mysterious, which is hot," Reagan continued.

"Agreed." She really was.

"And she's got this sexy put-together vibe thing going on," Reagan added.

Olivia sighed. Shit. She totally did. "Completely."

"And that voice—"

"Don't even get me started." The more time Olivia spent with Savannah, the more she wanted to listen to her say all the things. Forever. "She's the total package."

"I wonder what she's like in bed…"

Olivia whipped her head in Reagan's direction just in time to catch Reagan giving her a sly smirk.

"Gotcha."

Olivia felt a flush settle on her cheeks. Reagan had been baiting her. That sneaky bastard.

"I knew you liked her." Reagan's nose wrinkled as she smiled.

Olivia pouted. "Is it that obvious?"

"Probably only to me. And anyone who heard you gush about her joining us for dinner last night."

Olivia winced. "Yeah…that was not my smoothest moment."

"It's cool. Having a little crush might be good for you. You know, it might loosen you up a bit. You could use a little fun since you dropped Hurricane Hannah." Reagan took the coffee out of Olivia's hands and drank it.

Olivia was going to point out that she needed that coffee to live but decided the distraction it provided was worth it. Olivia didn't mention kissing Savannah last night, nor did she mention that she'd gotten the impression that Savannah had been flirting with her all along, too. She decided to let Reagan think it was a one-sided crush, because maybe it was. But she sincerely hoped it wasn't.

As if sensing she was the topic of conversation, Savannah looked up at the two of them and waved. She ended her phone call and stepped toward them, ducking under some electrical wires and over some spools of construction supplies before reaching them. "Ladies."

"Hey." Olivia shifted her weight and stepped a little away from Reagan so as not to set off any more alarm bells with her bestie.

She saw Reagan regard her curiously before looking back up at Savannah. "It looks like we're all set on our end. We're meeting before lunch, right?"

Savannah made eye contact with Olivia while she answered

Reagan. "Yes, why don't you round up the group and we'll get started a few minutes early so they can duck out for a longer lunch."

Reagan nodded and walked toward Randal, where she clapped him on the back and laughed when he almost dropped his graphing calculator in surprise.

Olivia stood there, waiting, thinking about what she should say. She had figured that addressing things directly was the best way to go. She *had* kissed Savannah on the cheek after all. But part of her wanted to pretend it didn't happen, probably the same part that wanted to pretend she wasn't immensely attracted to her. That same part was currently screaming at her to stop staring at the woman's lips but was obviously being ignored. She had Reagan to thank for pointing out all of Savannah's best qualities. Jerk.

"Lost in thought?" A knowing expression spread across dark pink lips as Savannah tilted her head down slightly to catch Olivia's gaze.

Olivia had the distinct feeling that Savannah was flirting with her. Savannah's eyes flickered down to Olivia's lips for a moment before returning her gaze. Olivia decided to go for it. "Mm. I was just wondering what color lipstick you use—it's such a unique shade."

Savannah quirked an eyebrow, licking her lips before she replied, "Is that so?"

Her voice was velvety soft with a little more huskiness than usual as she added, "It's a combination of two colors. I blend them with my finger and apply a gloss to seal in the color." She brought her index finger to her lips, hovering over them in a mock reproduction of her blending method. Olivia was enchanted. Savannah dropped her hand, breaking the trance and asked in the same quiet tone, "How did you sleep?"

Now she knew Savannah was flirting with her. Olivia took a half step closer and reached out to brush a bit of plaster dust off Savannah's shoulder. "Good. Like the dead. The way one does after being taunted into tequila shots."

Savannah's eyes followed Olivia's hand from her shoulder back down to her side. "Hey, I merely suggested that Reagan might have a higher tolerance for alcohol than you. At no point was that a personal challenge for you to pound 'em down."

"Everything sounds like a challenge after a pitcher of margaritas," Olivia teased before taking a more serious tone. "Thank you for making sure I got to my room in one piece. I appreciate it."

There was a hint of a smile on Savannah's lips as she replied, "Of course, no problem." She paused and added, "It was my pleasure."

Olivia bit her bottom lip and looked past Savannah at her team that was assembling by the drafting table—they were ready for the meeting. She decided this would be her only chance to say what she needed to without someone around listening. She reached out once more and lightly ran her fingertips along the hand holding the tablet in front of Savannah's chest. She spoke softly. "And thanks for pushing back the meeting."

Savannah's eyes followed her fingers. She fluttered her fingers under Olivia's tentative touch and gently rubbed her index finger against Olivia's for a moment. She looked up at Olivia once more and stepped back, just like she had last night. Her smile looked subdued, almost hesitant, when she replied, "Anytime."

Olivia got it. They made eye contact briefly, and it occurred to Olivia that there was a silent agreement passing between them: they couldn't do this. Olivia got the sense that they both knew it. She nodded and sighed. She was already too interested in Savannah. If she didn't cool things off now, she was doomed. This was just the way things had to be. She couldn't let an attraction to her colleague get in the way of the biggest professional opportunity of her career. This project had to work. It just had to. And it wasn't going to if she spent all day dreaming about her coworker. She needed to grow up and tackle this like an adult. A celibate adult who was not kissing Savannah on the cheek to say good night and daydreaming about what might have happened if she'd asked her to stay. Olivia tried not to think about how long it'd been since she'd let off a little steam. She really could use the release right about now.

She stuffed that feeling down and shook her head as she walked toward her team. There wasn't time for that kind of thinking. It was time to get back to work.

CHAPTER NINE

Savannah couldn't remember a busier week. The rest of the time in Denver had flown by. In order for them to get everything done before Olivia and her team had to leave, they all had to put in long days. Randal and Daniel left on Thursday but Reagan stayed behind to make sure the lighting installation was up to spec. She would be departing with Olivia and the rest of the team tomorrow in the early afternoon. Savannah was ready to be back on her own to prepare for their next project site but, admittedly, had mixed feelings about Olivia leaving.

The space was just about ready and all the materials were in place and picked out. The final coats of paint were being applied and the electrical inspector was scheduled to sign off on the computerized wall panel and water feature later today. All that was left was detail work and testing the space, all of which could be done without Olivia and her team. Savannah would leave a few days later once the project was complete.

Friday was a sort of free day for them. The local crew would be busy all day, but Olivia and her team didn't need to be at the project site except for a quick debriefing at the end of the day. Savannah had encouraged them to take off on their own, and they went out to do some sightseeing with Ernesto. They weren't slated to be back until the late afternoon, which was fine by Savannah. If she was being honest, she needed a little time to herself. The growing tension between her and Olivia hadn't dissipated with time—it had gotten exponentially worse.

Their workdays went on forever, and it was impossible for her to avoid interacting with Olivia. After their nondiscussion about the kiss at the end of the night of drinking, Savannah had tried to steer clear of contact. But it seemed like the gods were against her. First, there was the afternoon meeting where Olivia's leg brushed against

Savannah's, eliciting an involuntary shudder from her. And as soon as the touch happened, Olivia pulled away. Olivia had glanced over at her anxiously, and they made just enough eye contact that Savannah had missed a question from Daniel and had to ask him to repeat himself.

She changed her seat at the conference table for the next meeting. She sat off to the side so as to resist the urge to watch Olivia chew on the end of her glasses in that cute way she did when she was thinking. That worked out well for about fifteen minutes until Randal tripped over his untied shoes and dumped the contents of his drink in Savannah's lap. Luckily the drink was cold, but unluckily, Olivia came to help her pat her skirt dry. Which just led to awkward contact and strained smiles between the two of them.

So having Olivia off the premises today was exactly what Savannah needed.

Savannah excused herself from the design space and informed the general contractor that she was going to hit up the pool for a midday workout before their afternoon meetings. She let him know he could come find her if absolutely necessary, but she made it pretty clear that she was hoping to be left alone. He seemed to understand, and she was grateful he didn't try to make small talk. All she wanted to do was work out a little of this buzzing energy and try to calm the overwhelmed feeling that was settling over her. It wasn't that the project was too much; truthfully it had come together rather nicely. No, she had this sort of looming sense that something wasn't quite right. She chalked it up to lots of late nights bent over drafting tables with an attractive female colleague for long periods of time and no real expenditure of pent-up energy, sexual or otherwise.

The pool was quiet, except for a few older ladies laughing and gossiping in the shallow end. The lanes were open for laps and that was all Savannah really cared about. She wasn't here for leisure. She was here to help herself focus and get some clarity. And that clarity, she had learned, only came to her with a little hard work.

As she slipped off the terry cloth robe at the edge of the indoor pool she thought about how things had changed in the past few weeks. She'd been so immersed in this project that the little progress she had made on settling into her Chicago apartment had all but ceased. Her apartment was still barely unpacked. She'd spent so much time traveling that there didn't seem to be time to add knickknacks and personalization to the clean off-white walls of her one-bedroom condo. Gwen had been the one who added things like picture frames and candleholders to the background. Savannah had gotten rid of everything they had shared as a couple when she moved out of their place. She had no need for things that would collect dust.

She lowered herself into the water and cleared her lungs, taking in deep breaths as her body adjusted to the temperature. Her life hadn't always been this way, the way of the traveling wind without roots. She'd had a plan once, a steady, comforting life plan that involved settling down and starting a family with Gwen. But that was a distant memory now.

She let the sad memory wash over her as she sucked in a sharp breath and turned underwater in the pool, finishing her ninth lap. Her strokes were long and confident. Her years of swimming in high school and college took over and guided her through the motions in a rehearsed, automatic way. Around her fourteenth lap she felt a gentle fatigue settle in her chest, and her arms began to burn as she turned into the final leg. She had pushed herself harder than she'd anticipated, but it felt good to feel her body strain and struggle to maintain its grace in the water. When she emerged from her final lap, she pulled in a few deep breaths before she noticed someone clapping nearby. She pulled off her swim cap and looked up to find Olivia perched on a lounger nearby. She was smiling and holding a towel in her lap.

"I had no idea you were a swimmer," Olivia said with a look of glee.

Savannah took a few steadying breaths, trying to slow her heart rate as she looked up at her unexpected audience. Olivia's hair was down, hanging in loose natural curls past her shoulders. She was in dark jeans and a fitted T-shirt with her sunglasses resting in her hair. She had a sun-kissed glow to her, likely from the hike she'd told Savannah she was going on today. Olivia leaned forward slightly to extend the towel toward Savannah, making the V-neck of her shirt pucker and expose the tops of her breasts to Savannah's view.

Savannah's heart rate picked right back up again.

She let out a slow exhale as she pulled herself from the pool and accepted the towel with a gracious smile. "I swam in school. It helps me stay fit and clear my head." She kept her eyes on Olivia and watched as Olivia tried to subtly check her out. She dragged the towel across her abdomen and up her arms for good measure. "How'd you find me?" Savannah would have been lying if she said she wasn't happy to see Olivia. Or that she was happy to see Olivia checking her out, either.

Olivia leaned back on the lounger, resting on her elbows. She appeared to be struggling to make eye contact. "Uh, I stopped by the design space and they told me you were taking the morning off. The contractor mentioned you were hitting the gym. So I ventured down to see if you needed a spotter." Olivia's expression was playful.

"Is that so?" Savannah mulled that over before she rested her foot on the lounger next to Olivia. She bent forward, slowly toweling off her legs. She was pleased to catch Olivia's gaze following the path of her hands. "How was your day trip?"

"Huh? Good. It was…good." Olivia seemed distracted.

Savannah felt a bead of water drip from her hair and begin its descent between her breasts. She brought the towel up to her chest and Olivia's head jerked up with it.

"You know," Savannah teased in a deep velvety tone, "someone with a little less confidence might think you were a stalker. Since you showed up here with a towel and all."

Olivia laughed and turned so she was facing Savannah more fully. "Someone a little less confident?"

Savannah knew they had wandered into flirting territory again and indulged a little. She stood back up and lowered the towel, going out of her way to gently drag her nails across her flat stomach just to see if she could get a rise out of Olivia. So far, she had her audience captivated.

"Yeah. I happen to be a very graceful swimmer, so drawing a crowd isn't a new thing for me." She paused her hand over her navel, slowly circling around it and dragging down a bit until she hit the top of her briefs before she added in a low purr, "Although I'm not always so closely monitored while I dry off. That's sort of new for me."

Olivia licked her lips and raised an eyebrow in Savannah's direction, almost as if taunting her. She stood and turned before she bent to pick up a nearby water bottle she must have brought with her. Savannah's gaze dropped downward and she let herself admire the way Olivia's ass looked in those jeans.

Olivia paused there and looked over her shoulder at Savannah. "Really? And do you always towel off so seductively? Or is that just for my benefit?"

"Hmm." Savannah let her eyes linger a little longer. There was no sense in the unnecessary pretense when such a pleasant view was so close. "Touché."

Olivia offered the water bottle to Savannah. She took it and brought it to her mouth before she rolled it along her bottom lip. After taking a sip, she stated quietly, "I like your jeans."

"I noticed." Olivia took the water bottle back and sipped it. Savannah felt wet all over again when Olivia made no attempt to conceal the way her eyes traced over Savannah's body. "I like your bathing suit."

"Thank you." Savannah reached out and pushed a rogue curl behind Olivia's ear. Olivia's eyes fluttered closed in response and Savannah wanted to kiss her in that moment. She had a feeling Olivia's lips would feel like heaven. She thought about those lips often.

The sound of water splashing and children laughing shattered Savannah's reverie. She pulled back her hand and ran it through her damp hair as Olivia's eyes blinked back open. "This is probably not a good idea."

Olivia pouted, and Savannah wondered what she tasted like. "Yeah, probably."

They stood there, standing close, not talking, but watching each other for a few moments before Savannah let out a heavy sigh and frowned. "I should probably go shower before our meeting."

"Yeah, that's probably a good idea." Olivia's shoulders drooped. Savannah felt the same way.

Savannah wrapped the towel around her trunk and stepped back just enough to clear the fog that had settled over her mind. That same fog was also sending little sparks down into her abdomen. "See you at the meeting?"

Olivia nodded and Savannah turned to leave before she lost her willpower to resist her colleague. As much as she wanted to see where this would go with Olivia, she knew that the success of the project depended on her remaining unbiased throughout its entirety. These three installations were merely an audition for the bigger contract that New Horizons was dangling in front of Olivia and her team. From what Savannah had observed, Olivia and her team were more than qualified for the job. In fact, they were excelling at it. She'd found herself more and more impressed with every obstacle they overcame. This was a slam dunk for them. And yet, she also knew that her reports and opinions were going to be weighed in her superiors' decision process at the end. She had to make sure she could separate her professional feelings from her personal ones. But the more time she spent with Olivia, the less confident she felt in her ability to do that.

CHAPTER TEN

Olivia was pleased that the staff meeting was brief. They reviewed the final details and scheduled a videoconference for the unveiling next week, so her team could see the final product. There were a few kinks to work out with the computer, and one of the reflecting walls was on the fritz, but they had been assured that all would be worked out by the Denver crew over the weekend in preparation for Monday's reveal. Savannah let them know that she would stick around to make sure everything was perfect before jetting back to Chicago for another project that was in the works. The group decided on one last dinner together before they separated. Her team chose an off-site sushi restaurant that had hibachi for Devon and Farrah, who preferred cooked cuisine.

They sat in a U around the hibachi grill watching as the chef made onion volcanoes and flung shrimp around between his spatulas in artistic displays of agility, then into his hat, before hitting the grill again.

Olivia loved the group's dynamic. To her left, Devon and Reagan were sake bombing and high-fiving as they picked at the teriyaki plates in front of them. There might or might not have been dramatic diving catches for bits of lobster or shrimp that the chef tossed to them from the grill. Farrah and Savannah were discussing some celebrity scandal over glasses of plum wine to Olivia's right. They got along so well outside of work, which was reflected in their professional collaboration.

Olivia let her eyes settle on the blue and white flame that flickered in front of her, allowing it to pull her into a trance. She had spent the better part of the afternoon not concentrating on anything. After she had tracked down Savannah at the pool, her head was swimming with all kinds of thoughts. There had been such blatant flirting, and clearly they wanted the same thing. So why couldn't it happen? An office romance here or there was far from taboo these days. Would it really be such a bad thing?

A nagging sensation in the back of her mind made her think it might be. This contract was a total game changer for her. The possibilities at the end of these three trial installations were endless. She could write her own ticket if this all worked out. She'd be foolish to risk screwing this all up by getting involved with Savannah. Especially since her track record with women wasn't nearly as great as she would have liked. For as much shit as she gave Reagan for her constantly changing relationship status, the truth was that Olivia hadn't managed to keep a serious girlfriend in...forever. More likely than not, this thing with Savannah would blow up in her face and derail this entire project. It wasn't worth the risk.

But try as she might, she could not for the life of her ignore Savannah. She had to actively stop herself from watching Savannah eat, her eyes continually drawn back to her lips. It was distracting and enticing all at the same time. She watched as Savannah paused her conversation and reached into her pocket. She frowned, mumbled something about corporate, and left the table to take the call.

Olivia nodded in agreement to the question Farrah directed toward her, maybe in an attempt to pull her into her conversation, something about the *Dancing with the Stars* roster. But her gaze followed Savannah's ass until she was out of the room. Seeing Savannah in next to nothing, dripping wet, did absolutely nothing to quell the aching lust that had been brewing over the past few days. Olivia zoned out whenever Savannah spoke. That voice, it was just so smooth and raspy. She glanced down at her plate, picking up a shrimp with her chopsticks while Devon talked to the other women about going out to party that night.

Olivia was only half listening. She was chewing slowly and thinking about all the things that perfect voice could whisper in her ear. She remembered the low, throaty chuckle Savannah purred out earlier at the pool, and she shifted in her seat, uncomfortable in her pants. They had made eye contact earlier, over dinner, and she saw Savannah's eyes flicker to her lips again, like before. She liked the way it felt to be admired by Savannah. There was something so carnal about the way her eyes widened and a little smile danced across her lips when she looked at Olivia. It made Olivia want to jump her, immediately, and maul her face. Which would be completely unacceptable.

"What do you say, Liv?" Reagan asked, nudging her elbow.

"What's that?" Olivia replied, looking up at Reagan.

"Devon wants to hit up a place called Flashes and grab some drinks and dance a bit after dinner. It's supposed to be a pretty decent gay bar around here. You in?"

"I'll pass. You kids are too young for me." Farrah laughed and sipped her wine. She shook her head at Devon when he started to tease her about being his hag for the night. Their friendship was so cute.

Olivia mulled it over. She didn't want to go to a club and dance with some stranger. She wanted to spend some more time with Savannah. Not that that was even an option.

"Liv, c'mon. It's our last night here. Let's meet some locals." Reagan flashed a mischievous grin. "Plus, it's been like forever since you got laid."

"You're such an ass." Reagan was right, though—she could use a distraction. Maybe she could even convince Savannah to tag along. That would be the best of both worlds. "All right, I'm in."

"Yes!" Reagan and Devon slapped hands and danced in their seats while Farrah shook her head and warned them to behave.

Olivia slipped away from the table to use the restroom. She scanned the lobby for Savannah. She frowned when she didn't see her and wandered into the bathroom to wash her hands and freshen up her makeup. If they were going out, she might as well make an effort. She pushed open the door and walked right into Savannah, who appeared to be exiting while checking her phone.

"Oh, I'm sorry." Olivia stepped back.

"You sure you didn't walk into me on purpose?"

Olivia laughed. "I can think of better ways to brush up against you than when entering a bathroom."

"Is that so?" Savannah quirked her eyebrow and held open the door as she gestured for Olivia to enter.

"Mm-hmm, like, for instance..." Olivia paused and considered whether her invitation would be well received. She decided to go for it. "Devon and Reagan want to hit up a bar not far from here to get some drinks and maybe dance."

Savannah let the bathroom door close and leaned against the sink, listening intently.

Olivia felt a little nervous while Savannah surveyed her with such curiosity. It was intimidating. "Would you like to join us?"

Savannah cocked her head to the side and appeared to consider Olivia's request.

Sensing Savannah's hesitance, Olivia decided to stack the deck in her favor. She stepped closer and leaned her right hip on the sink so that she was facing Savannah. She traced the fingers of her right hand along the marble of the sink in a slow zigzagging pattern. Savannah's eyes were drawn to the movement.

"I would really love it if you came along." She walked her fingers until they were just millimeters from Savannah's hip before she stopped and reversed directions.

Savannah kept her gaze on Olivia's fingers and let out a quiet sigh. "I think that might be a bad idea."

Olivia frowned as she looked up into the conflicted expression on Savannah's face. She waited for Savannah to elaborate.

"Don't you think this is hard enough as it is? Without any encouraging circumstances like liquor and dancing and standing so close." Savannah's voice dropped to a near whisper as she uttered the last word. Olivia could feel the intensity of her gaze on her face. Savannah's eyes paused at her lips before she trailed her gaze down over Olivia's body. It was the first time she had explicitly checked out all of Olivia. Especially in this close proximity. It excited her. The tension between them was electric and felt unbearable. It was like a force field of humming pressure, invisibly separating them, and Olivia wanted Savannah to cross it.

Olivia let out a frustrated sigh. Savannah's words were in serious conflict with her body's signals. She watched as Savannah struggled to keep herself still. Her hands fidgeted angrily by her sides, like she wanted to touch her. It was once again clear they both wanted the same thing. Olivia wanted to feel Savannah, but she couldn't force her either. She frowned again and broke eye contact. She turned her attention to the mirror in front of her and slowly started to put her walls up. She needed to stop looking at Savannah and her gorgeous face or else she would do things she couldn't undo.

"You're disappointed." Savannah stated the obvious and Olivia resisted the urge to cringe. She didn't like feeling so powerless. Or so easily read.

Savannah took in a breath. "I want to—" She turned and stepped behind Olivia. She was close enough that Olivia could feel the heat resonating off her body. She was close, but not quite touching.

Olivia looked up at their reflection to find Savannah watching her. Her eyes were dark and her expression was serious.

Savannah continued, "I want to stand close to you. I want to feel you." Savannah hovered her hands over Olivia's shoulders—not touching, just hovering. It was maddening.

Olivia's skin felt like it was burning under Savannah's non-touch. She could feel the heat of Savannah's hands through her shirt and along her arms before those hands paused above Olivia's hands, which she pressed against the cool marble to help ground her. Savannah's eyes were getting darker, dangerously darker, and Savannah's pink lips turned into a small, teasing smile.

Savannah brought one hand up and brushed the hair off Olivia's shoulder, exposing her neck. She leaned infinitesimally closer and breathed across Olivia's skin in a low, throaty purr. "Do you have any idea how hard it is, to be this close to you and not touch you the way I want to?"

Olivia shuddered and closed her eyes as she felt Savannah's hot breath on her neck. She was taunting her, making her clit throb. She shook her head as she willed her body to be still, but she felt like her knees were going to buckle. She felt wet.

"Do you know how badly I want to..." Savannah trailed off with a sigh.

Olivia opened her eyes to see Savannah's lips almost touching the shell of her ear. Savannah smiled as Olivia's breath hitched in response. She was having trouble breathing and being still. But she didn't dare move too quickly. She wanted to see how this would play out.

The fingers of Savannah's right hand danced over Olivia as she spoke. "It would be too hard"—she entwined Olivia's fingers with hers and pressed Olivia's palm against the cool marble to accentuate the word *hard* before she licked her lips—"to be that close to you and not touch." Savannah stepped forward and pressed her front to Olivia's back, pushing Olivia's hips into the sink. "And that just wouldn't be fair, would it?"

Olivia whimpered and closed her eyes. She bit down on her bottom lip as she felt Savannah's breasts press against her back. Her fingers curled reflexively and Savannah held her hand in place against the marble. The husky murmurs in Olivia's ear had her head spinning. She was so turned on that she didn't know what to do or say.

Savannah sighed in her ear and her left hand fell to Olivia's hip. She squeezed gently before she pulled her fingers out of Olivia's and stepped back. "Have a good time with your team tonight. Thank you for inviting me."

Olivia let out a shuddering breath and met Savannah's gaze in the mirror. Olivia could see her chest moving up and down rapidly in her reflection. She felt out of breath. Savannah flashed her a knowing smile as she stepped away and reached for the door.

The door pulled open and Reagan slipped in. She greeted Savannah quickly as Savannah left the room.

"Hey, Liv? You okay? You look weird." Reagan shot her a concerned look before she disappeared into the stall and closed the door.

"Um, yeah, fine. Just a little tired, I think." Olivia was a terrible liar. She was glad Reagan was behind the stall door and couldn't see the glowing blush of arousal that was all over her neck and chest. She thanked the heavens that Reagan came in when she did and not a minute earlier. Although she was so hot and bothered by the interaction that maybe it would have been better if it was interrupted. She thought about this for a moment and shook her head. No, it was definitely worth every agonizingly teasing moment of privacy with Savannah. And even though she felt horribly sexually frustrated right now, she wouldn't change a minute. That voice, in her ear, breathing on her neck, taunting—

"Liv? What is wrong with you?" Reagan interrupted her thoughts as she stood next to her at the sink and washed her hands.

"Nothing. I gotta pee." Olivia tossed her a lame excuse and hid behind the stall door until Reagan left.

CHAPTER ELEVEN

After the bathroom exchange, Olivia was positively buzzing. When she got back to the table, everyone had already finished their meals and was chatting about the club. Reagan invited Savannah to join them. Savannah politely declined and offered to cab it back to the hotel with Farrah, giving no indication this was her second invitation. She claimed to have to make some work calls.

Olivia slid into her seat and avoided looking directly at Savannah, because it just made her body hot and her heart rate pick up. The one time they did make eye contact, when the check was paid, she could have sworn she saw that mischievous glint in those gray-blue eyes again, the same one Savannah had had at the pool, in the bathroom, and recently, in her dreams. She gulped and reached for her water.

When they arrived at the club, it proved itself to be just the distraction Olivia needed—dimly lit, with a full bar. That was pretty much all Olivia cared about. They lined up shots along the bar and nodded their heads to the thumping house music as they talked intermittently while checking out the other patrons.

Devon found a cute gay boy in a plaid shirt to slink off with and Reagan quickly cozied up to a blonde with big hair and minimal clothing. Olivia settled into a seat at the bar and sipped her cocktail as she toyed with the straw. If she was being honest with herself, she would admit that she didn't want to be at the bar. She'd rather be chasing Savannah through the hotel or spending some much needed alone time working out her sexual frustrations. There was a lesbian couple next to her, obnoxiously making out with each other, and the spectacle was nauseating because she was envious. She quickly downed her drink and stepped toward the dance floor to release some of her tension.

The beat picked up and the overhead lights flashed brightly colored shapes on the floor. People writhed around her in singles and pairs for a few songs as she got lost in the music. A pretty brunette sidled up to her and danced a bit before she stepped in closer and placed her hands on Olivia's hips. Olivia smiled at the woman and matched her movements. She shook her hair in front of her face and focused on the beat of the music. The woman stepped up behind her and loosely encircling her waist. She started dancing closer. Olivia closed her eyes and tried to focus on the touch. She tried to enjoy it, but all she could think of was Savannah behind her in the bathroom teasing the shit out of her. She let herself imagine that it was the sultry redhead for a song or two, before she caught Reagan at the bar gesturing to her. She finished the dance and thanked her impromptu dance partner before slipping through the crowd.

"Hey!" Reagan called out. "Who's she?"

Olivia shrugged. She hadn't even attempted to get the woman's name. Her mind was elsewhere.

Reagan rolled her eyes and handed Olivia some fruity concoction. "Devon and I are thinking about heading back to the hotel. Are you ready?"

Devon was kissing Mr. Plaid Shirt in tight pants next to them and was completely oblivious of their existence. Reagan's blond friend wandered over with a martini and a crooked grin.

"Hey, I'm Candy." She smiled and shook Olivia's hand before sipping her drink and leaning into Reagan's chest.

"Of course you are." Olivia shook her head. "Yeah, I'm ready. Let's go." She finished her drink and handed the empty glass to Reagan before calling out to Devon and pointing to the door.

The cab ride back to the hotel was *interesting*. Both Reagan and Devon were bringing back guests, so Olivia sat in the front with the cabbie, who had a funny accent and liked to talk about fishing, a lot.

By the time they returned to the hotel it was well after midnight. The lobby was deserted, so of course their arrival sounded like a herd of elephants running through a glass factory. Devon and Plaid Shirt were stumbling hot messes. Reagan at least appeared to be sober enough to press the correct elevator button, but the way Candy was sucking on her neck made Olivia decide to take the next elevator car instead. The last thing she wanted was to be the fifth wheel in an elevator porno.

The doors closed and Olivia shut her eyes and took in a deep, steadying breath as she waited. She didn't really want to go to sleep right now, but she also didn't feel like watching bad television in the hotel bed either. She exhaled, and the silence of the lobby was interrupted by the soft melody of a piano. Olivia opened her eyes and glanced around looking for the origin of the sound. The lobby was empty except for an older gentleman sitting behind the check-in counter. He was reading the paper and seemed oblivious to the tune.

Olivia walked away from the elevators and across the lobby toward the sound. It sounded like it was coming from the hotel bar. The bar—a U-shaped metal surface with eight equally modern looking bar stools— was a few steps down from the lobby. A few flat screen televisions were positioned on the walls behind and to the right of the bar but the entire left side was made of glass with a view overlooking the mountains. The entrance to the hotel's restaurant was across a communal meeting area furnished with comfy sofas and lounge chairs.

She stepped up to the bar and asked for a glass of water after she decided that she had no desire to drink. The bartender looked exhausted. One lonely businessman sat at the bar, nursing a beer. His face looked worn and his tie was pulled loose. He looked like he had traveled across the world and back. His wrinkled suit matched his heavy eyes. Olivia suddenly felt tired, too. Maybe it was the company she was currently keeping.

She shook her head to ward off the sudden fatigue and stepped away from the bar and toward the couches facing the view. The soft melody was still playing somewhere near the entrance to the restaurant that had long since closed for the evening. She walked along the wall of windows and looked out at the mountain view as she followed the inviting sound. At the other end of the lounge sat a baby grand piano and a single floor lamp that appeared to have been dragged from a sitting area nearby. The lamp was tucked off to the side and barely illuminated the keys and the person playing the beautiful music.

Olivia stood there silently and enjoyed the music as her eyes adjusted to the darker corner of the lounge area. It was then that she realized she knew the musician. Sitting perfectly straight with her eyes closed and playing without sheet music was Savannah. Olivia watched Savannah's fingers move fluidly across the keys. They sped up and slowed down as the song began to come to a close. When the music stopped, Savannah opened her eyes and reached for the glass of wine that rested atop the piano. Realizing that she was sort of staring, like a creeper, Olivia cleared her throat to announce her presence.

Savannah turned her head quickly in surprise, nearly dropping her wineglass in the process. She smiled when she recognized her admirer. "That's twice today you've crept up on me. You sure you're not a stalker?"

"I promise you, I'm not. I just seem to find myself stumbling upon you."

Savannah sipped her wine and set it back atop the piano before starting up a new song. "Now, now, that's not entirely true, is it?" she teased. "You sought me out at the pool. I vaguely remember you holding a towel."

"Yeah, that's true, I guess."

"I meant to ask you before—what made you come find me?" Savannah held her gaze, as her fingers moved along the keys and hit each note without looking at her hands. Olivia was impressed. She was quite good.

Olivia paused and thought about the question. She didn't have a legitimate reason. She'd come back from the day trip and wanted to see her. She'd found herself standing by the entrance to the pool, scooping up a fresh towel and wandering in. She'd just missed spending time with Savannah. And it hadn't occurred to her until this moment. She hesitated, mulling over whether to fib or be honest, finally deciding on honesty.

"I guess I just missed you. I don't know." She shrugged as if it was a normal feeling, but knew that it wasn't.

Savannah's grin widened. She seemed pleased by this information.

"Have you played long?" Olivia asked, eager to change the topic to something less serious.

"Since I was young. I took lessons as a child and hated it." She looked down at her hands as they continued to gently hit note after note. "I grew to appreciate the training as I got older."

"It's beautiful." Olivia's gaze settled on Savannah's perfect profile; her red hair was swept up into a loose bun. She was wearing a soft looking but snug black top over expensive jeans that she had paired smartly with black leather boots. She looked casual yet chic, with simple diamond studs in her ears and a single floating diamond necklace.

Savannah waved her over to the bench and slid down to give her some space. "Come here, I'll teach you."

Olivia hesitated before she joined her. She sat next to Savannah and placed her water by Savannah's wine. She rolled her shoulders more to release the sudden nervous energy she had rather than because she felt stiff.

"So, this is just a simple background piece I learned a million years ago." Savannah spoke quietly. "It's fairly easy—the notes are very repetitive. I'll play the low end, and you play the high end. Okay?"

Olivia nodded. She was listening but she was also enjoying how close they were to each other again. She also made note of how fantastic Savannah's perfume smelled this close. Savannah continued to play with her right hand while she placed Olivia's fingers on three keys with her left.

"Okay, when I give you the cue, I want you to press this one, then this one, then this one." She gestured with a nod to each key as she brought her left hand back to the keyboard. "You ready?"

Olivia took a breath and they began to play. Savannah cued her with a nod or a quiet word until the end of the song, at which point Savannah sped up her playing and reached her left hand between Olivia's to strike one last note to finish the song. She held the note before releasing the pedals slowly and pulling back her hand.

Olivia caught Savannah's hand as she tried to pull it back. Olivia entwined their fingers and pulled their hands into the space between them on the bench. "Thank you. That was fun."

Savannah looked down at their joined hands. The outside of her hand pressed lightly against Olivia's thigh. "Anytime."

That sexy, low purr was back again.

Olivia was convinced that she would do just about anything Savannah asked in that tone. It was addicting. She was pretty sure she could listen to Savannah read the phone book and still get turned on.

Savannah reached for her wine and sipped it as her thumb rubbed along Olivia's skin. "How was the club?"

"Fine, it was fine." Her eyes flickered to Savannah's lips on the wineglass. She was envious of the goblet. "Devon met some cute cowboy." Savannah nodded and hummed. She offered the glass to Olivia, which she took and sipped at before she continued. "Reagan met some barely dressed blonde. Needless to say, it was an interesting cab ride back here." She placed the glass on the piano and shifted in her seat so she was straddling the bench and facing Savannah. She was careful to maintain their hand position.

"And you?" Savannah asked as she mirrored Olivia's new position.

"And I, what?"

"Did you meet anyone interesting?" The question came across as nonchalant, but Savannah's gaze was focused on their clasped hands, not Olivia's eyes. It was as if she wasn't sure she wanted the answer. Olivia thought that if their roles had been reversed, she would have been jealous. Could Savannah be jealous? The thought amused her.

She squeezed Savannah's hand lightly and pulled it onto her leg as she slid forward a bit. She pressed Savannah's palm flat against her thigh and laid her hand on top of it to hold it there. "No, my thoughts were elsewhere."

Savannah looked up at her, an almost hungry look in her eyes. Olivia met her intense gaze until Savannah broke the stare and reached for her wine. She dragged her thumb along the seam on the inside of Olivia's knee as she hid her mouth behind her wineglass.

Olivia felt herself starting to get warm. It was hot in there, in the darkened corner of lounge, in the middle of the night, with Savannah's hand on her thigh and her finger teasing along the seam of her jeans. She felt positively sweltering.

"Well, I'm sorry you were distracted." Savannah wore a sinful smile as she placed her glass atop the piano again and squeezed Olivia's thigh.

"No, you're not," Olivia challenged and slid forward that last inch until their knees were touching. "You're not sorry."

Savannah licked her lips and bit her bottom lip as she whispered, "You're right. I'm not."

That was all Olivia could take. The closeness. Savannah's hand on her knee. Those eyes. That tongue wetting her lips. Her perfect fucking teeth pressing down on that bottom lip. That sultry voice. That was it. She leaned forward and tilted her head to hover close enough to Savannah's mouth to feel her breath against her lips.

"Me neither," she whispered before closing the distance and pressing her lips against Savannah's.

CHAPTER TWELVE

Savannah froze and her eyes fluttered closed as she felt Olivia's plump lips press against hers. At first, she just stayed there a moment until her body caught on to what was happening and responded fully. She pressed into the kiss and let out a soft hum. She felt Olivia squeeze the hand Savannah held to her thigh while her other hand trailed up to cup Savannah's cheek. Any hesitation Savannah had about deepening the kiss fell by the wayside when Olivia teased her tongue against Savannah's bottom lip. All the teasing and the taunting caught up with her and before she realized what she was doing, she was pulling Olivia into her body, up onto her lap.

Olivia's surprised gasp only fueled Savannah's desire. But when Olivia leaned forward and sucked hard on Savannah's tongue and lips, Savannah worried that things were escalating too quickly.

"Savannah. *Please.*" Olivia moaned against her mouth and she forgot everything else. She tugged her closer and positioned Olivia's legs on hers so their centers were almost touching. The kissing itself was fucking mind-blowing, forget the fact that Olivia molded against her like this was a well-choreographed dance they both knew. Olivia whimpered and rolled her hips against Savannah's, and all Savannah could do was scratch up her back to keep her close. The feeling was incredible. She had no idea how badly she had wanted Olivia pressed flush against her like this.

"Jesus," Savannah murmured and broke the kiss to explore the soft skin of Olivia's neck. She'd wanted more than anything to suck on that skin earlier in the bathroom. And since they'd already crossed the kissing boundary, she figured she might as well experience the rest of the forbidden territory.

Savannah latched on to Olivia's pulse point and Olivia shuddered in response, pulling Savannah's mouth back against hers. Olivia's plump, pouty lips overwhelmed her. The gentle rolling of Olivia's hips picked up and Savannah let herself experience all the things she'd daydreamed about doing to Olivia if she ever got the chance. She slid her hand into Olivia's thick curls and tugged gently, pulling her head back to expose more of her neck. Olivia rewarded her actions with a deep moan, and one hand dropped from Savannah's jaw to her waist. Olivia clawed at the waistband of her jeans and Savannah pulled her closer still, desperate to increase their contact.

Olivia rolled her hips harder this time and Savannah ached at the friction. Olivia's heaving chest against hers was hypnotizing enough without the insistent roll of her hips. Savannah licked along Olivia's jaw and breathed in deeply her scent, a mix of alcohol and perfume and sweat. She couldn't get enough of it. She reclaimed Olivia's lips with a more forceful kiss encouraged by Olivia's hands at the back of her neck. Olivia scratched at her hairline and Savannah's insides tightened. She pulled Olivia's bottom lip between her teeth and sucked it into her mouth as her palm moved from Olivia's back to her ribs. She massaged along the flesh of her rib cage before teasing her thumb along the outside of Olivia's breast.

"*Fuck*." Olivia hissed and Savannah moved her hand forward a little more, just barely cupping Olivia's breast through her shirt. Olivia shivered and Savannah felt the grinding start to catch up with her.

"You have the best lips." Savannah tried to slow down the kiss. She could practically feel the heat of Olivia's center pressing against hers with each and every roll of Olivia's hips. Savannah was more than turned on. She was on fire. But if they continued this little game of kiss and grind, she would come right here on this piano bench, fully clothed, like some overly hormonal teenager on a first date with a hot girl. And Olivia was most definitely a hot girl. Savannah had to stop this before it went too far.

Before she had a chance to slow things down, Olivia shifted on her lap and shuddered. Savannah paused their kissing to glance down. In this position, Olivia's crotch was directly against her belt buckle. She rolled her hips forward against Olivia's to test a theory, and Olivia shuddered again and this time a throaty moan accompanied the reaction.

Savannah rolled against her again, because hearing that moan was positively heavenly.

"Savannah." Olivia's tone was a warning and she considered her options. She wanted more than anything to see Olivia come undone from her touch. She wanted to taste her and experience every tremor of pleasure she could with Olivia. But not like this.

She leaned forward and licked the shell of Olivia's ear as she whispered, "As much as I want to make you come, this isn't how I imagined it happening."

Olivia turned her head and captured Savannah's lips. Her hands took Savannah's and guided them to her cheeks. Savannah cradled her face, and the desperation slowly melted out of the kiss and their lips moved against each other's almost sweetly as they gasped in unsteady breaths. Olivia was cradled in Savannah's arms, partially sitting on her lap, as her hands combed softly through Savannah's hair, and Savannah felt safe and at home in her embrace. When she tucked her face into the side of Savannah's neck and kissed the skin softly before nuzzling it, Savannah wondered what she'd done to find such a magical creature. Whatever it was, she'd do it a thousand times more if this was the outcome.

Savannah let out a contented sigh as she let the smell of Olivia's shampoo and perfume soak in. She wrapped her arms more tightly around her and dipped her head to kiss Olivia once more.

"So, about that thing you said before"—Olivia was so close she could feel her breath across her lips—"tell me about that."

"Which thing? The thing about you having the best lips?" Savannah couldn't remember if she'd said all the things she was thinking. Part of her hoped she hadn't. Her mind was a complicated place when it came to Olivia.

"No. That's a fact." Olivia kissed the edge of her mouth. "I meant the part where you told me you imagined this." She gestured between them before she reached forward and traced her fingers along Savannah's collarbone. This time it was Savannah's turn to shudder. "I want to hear more about that."

Savannah took Olivia's hand in hers to try to gain some composure. She helped Olivia slide off her lap and put a little space between them on the bench. She felt shy all of a sudden. She took in a deep breath and reached for her forgotten wineglass. As she sipped its contents, she weighed the pros and cons of being honest in this situation. She handed the glass to Olivia, who brought it to her lips to drink as Savannah replied, "I would be lying to you if I said I didn't. It's crossed my mind a few times."

Olivia's lips lingered on the wineglass and Savannah worried she'd shared too much. Olivia merely smiled behind the glass. "Yeah, I know what you mean."

Well, now. "Oh, do you?" Savannah took the glass from Olivia and placed it aside. She caressed Olivia's cheek with her thumb as she asked, "Anything in particular you'd like to share?"

Olivia pressed her index finger to her lip in thought, then replied, "Um, there may be a daydream about the drafting table that seems to continually occur…"

Savannah quirked an eyebrow at her. That was it. She would never look at a drafting table the same way again. And considering they would be around a lot of drafting tables the next few months, that would make things very difficult. Savannah frowned as that thought went from a very naughty place to one of a painful realization: they were going to have to continue to work together, for months.

Savannah's hand left Olivia's cheek and a look of concern crossed Olivia's face. "What's wrong?"

She exhaled as she stood from the bench and shifted uncomfortably in her now wet underwear. She pulled Olivia up to her and wrapped her in a tight embrace as she pressed a soft, lingering kiss to her lips. She held it for a few moments as she willed her brain to forge this into her memory. She wanted to remember the feeling of Olivia's full lips on her own. The feeling of her body close. The smell of her perfume. All of it.

She sighed as she ended the kiss. "I frowned because this really can't happen, Liv. We are going to be working together for months, and I can't focus around you as it is. I mean, forget about me being able to sit at a drafting table with you," she teased before rolling her eyes in frustration. "I'm sorry, but this just…it just can't."

"Okay. I'm going to stop you there. This *can* happen." Olivia gestured between them again. "In fact, it *is* happening. We can't exactly deny the chemistry, Savannah. It's palpable. What's the harm in giving it a chance?" Olivia seemed convinced. Savannah wasn't so sure.

"And what if it doesn't work out—" Olivia's lips were on hers again and she forgot how to form words.

"And what if it does?" Olivia had a point. "Look, I realize we both have a lot at stake here. You're a client I hope to build a long-term relationship with. You have to deliver an unbiased evaluation of our work. But as long as we can be up front about how things are going and try to be realistic, we can handle this like adults."

Savannah still wasn't entirely convinced, but the feeling of

Olivia's lips on hers was too good to resist. "Let's make a deal. Why don't we see how things go? No expectations. Just two people—"

"Who happen to be insanely attracted to each other," Olivia supplied.

"Right. Just two people who are insanely attracted to each other, working together, and seeing how things go." Savannah wasn't even sure she was making sense in this moment. Olivia had that effect on her.

"Perfect." Olivia paused. "Why do I get the feeling that the kissing has ended for this evening?"

"Because it has." Savannah wanted some time to think about this a little more. She couldn't think with Olivia's breathy little pants in her ear.

Olivia pouted and Savannah felt her libido start to dial back up. "Liv. You've got to put that pout away if you want us to remain *friendly*." Savannah rubbed her thumb over Olivia's protruding bottom lip. "Because that pout is really hard to ignore."

Olivia nipped at her thumb. "I have enough friends, Savannah."

She'd walked right into that one. "Fair enough."

Olivia smiled and pressed a soft kiss to the edge of her mouth. "Just think about it. Think about it and know that I think you are smoking hot and want to have lots more of these piano lessons."

Savannah chuckled as Olivia stepped back and began slowly walking away backward. "Have a good night, Liv. See you in the morning for your flight."

And just like that she was alone again with her thoughts at the piano, feeling no more in control than she had the moment Olivia had entered her life. And for the first time in a long time, she didn't mind not being in control.

❖

Savannah accompanied them to the airport the following morning, not out of obligation, but more out of a desire to see Olivia once more before they parted ways. She wanted to make sure things were okay between them. Well, as okay as nearly dry-humping your colleague to climax in the dark corner of a hotel lounge could be okay.

Devon and Reagan had both shrugged off their guests from the night before as they stumbled into the car, with hair disheveled and sunglasses firmly planted over their eyes. Farrah just laughed at them, making comments about them reaping what they sowed. Olivia laughed that infectious, bubbly laugh and shook her head. Savannah didn't miss the way her eyes drifted to Savannah's in the rearview. That small smile on her lips told Savannah that things would be fine, but she still felt a little unsure.

Last night had been…hard. It had been hard keeping her hands to herself. It was hard not violating the piano with Olivia sprawled out on top of it. And it was hard walking away. It had been hard. No way around it. She'd had to force herself to go back to her room alone. Even then, she was restless. Her hand had wandered to the waistband of her pajama pants in an attempt to quell the throbbing Olivia left her with. But she decided against it. She needed to release some of this tension, but she didn't know how she felt about releasing it to thoughts of a woman just a few doors down who was probably in the same frame of mind. That felt a little too real for Savannah to stomach. How easy it would be, to knock on her door and decompress together. Needless to say, she slept like absolute shit. Vivid dreams of hazel eyes and full lips and moaning in her ear kept her up most of the night. She wondered if Olivia felt the same way. She hoped she did.

When they finally arrived at the airport, Savannah started to regret her decision to tag along. She wasn't exactly sure how the whole good-bye thing was going to go.

She hugged the team and thanked each of them for their hard work. She told them she looked forward to their next project, which was just a few weeks away. It wasn't like her to hug people, but she wanted to uphold the farce so she could embrace Olivia once more without it seeming odd.

Olivia smiled at her. She stepped into Savannah's open arms and whispered, "Last night was both lovely and awful—I didn't sleep a wink."

Savannah smiled and pulled Olivia closer. "Something on your mind?"

Olivia leaned back and stepped out of the embrace but remained close. "Yeah. You. And those gorgeous piano fingers."

She was going to make this excruciating, wasn't she? Savannah decided she liked Olivia more in this moment than ever before. "You have no idea the amount of beautiful music these fingers can make."

Olivia glanced over at her team, who appeared to be joking with Ernesto, before looking back at Savannah with her eyebrow raised.

Betraying her intention to keep things friendly, Savannah leaned close once more to add, "Maybe I'll show you sometime."

"I'd like that." Olivia's expression was earnest.

"Ready to go, Liv?" Reagan asked behind dark shades as she gingerly rubbed her no-doubt throbbing head.

"Yeah, let's go. See you later, Savannah. Thanks for seeing us off." Olivia gave her a wave and linked arms with Reagan as she headed into the airport.

Savannah watched them disappear around the corner and hoped she hadn't made a big mistake.

CHAPTER THIRTEEN

The following weeks went by surprisingly quickly for Olivia. Savannah videoconferenced the launch of the Denver room to the Greater Image team while they began working on the Phoenix project that following Monday. It had come out great. Olivia could not have been prouder, and Corrine was so giddy she practically grew wings and flew around the office. The celebration was short-lived, though, because the next site was right around the corner.

The Phoenix project was considerably larger in size and complexity. The basic outline they had used for Denver would suffice as a guideline only. This site was vastly different from the last: Instead of a newer build like the last trial, New Horizons had acquired a building in the historic district of Phoenix and had tasked Olivia's team with bringing their unique design ideas to a beloved, but much older architectural space, while insisting they keep nearly century-old charm intact. There were more oddly shaped walls, structures, restrictions, and details than the first project, requiring a lot of math and science work this time around. Devon's and Farrah's input was limited until they knew the final room layout. They bounced around a few signature pieces that New Horizons wanted to include, but a lot of their work would be done on-site. Reagan, Randal, and Daniel, on the other hand, were up to their elbows in prep work, and Olivia was juggling a little bit of everything to keep the team afloat.

Olivia sat in on half a dozen videoconferences with those three and Savannah to try to make things as seamless as possible. The head of the Phoenix crew was on the calls as well, but there appeared to be a scheduling issue regarding the launch date. The historical district in which the building was located was celebrating some significant anniversary around the time of the unveiling, and New Horizons wanted to speed the launch up a week so that VIPs could see the space during the citywide celebration in hopes of facilitating increased interest in expansion possibilities for the rest of the calendar year.

This put a significant strain on Olivia's team. They were asking for a project completion in four weeks that would normally take five or six. But the exposure would be incredible, and Olivia knew that if she and her team could deliver a more complicated end product in a shorter time frame, Greater Image Design would come out looking, well, great. As an added incentive, not that they needed one, New Horizons was offering a short vacation upon project completion to Olivia's team at one of the Phoenix-area resorts they partnered with. It was an all-inclusive stay for everyone involved, on New Horizons' dime. So that wasn't half bad. As long as every person involved understood that the project needed to be completed in the shortened schedule with perfect outcomes. No pressure or anything.

She'd gone over it with her team and everyone seemed to be on board, excited even, so she knew they would put in the extra effort.

Outside of the schedule shake-up, the days following Olivia and Savannah's little make-out session were initially quiet. Professional emails were cc'd to the group and consisted mainly of setting up meetings and deadlines. Gradually, she and Savannah had started to extend their videoconferences by a few minutes, just the two of them making idle small talk when the team left the room. Olivia still stood by her feeling that it was foolish to ignore their mutual attraction but realized it was probably equally foolish to encourage it. Still, they had managed to keep things light, even if she felt like their eyes spoke volumes more than their lips.

It wasn't until a few days into the final week before heading to Phoenix, when Savannah texted Olivia a work question after-hours, that the playful banter turned into a heated flirtation. Since then, it had been a pretty regular occurrence for them to flirt via text.

Their text flirting had been mostly harmless. A winky face here and there. A few brief references to piano benches or questions about how the morning coffee was. There were a few good-night messages, nothing major. The texts danced along that line of appearing slightly more than friendly to someone who might pick up their phones but could easily be excused away if need be. But today's texts would have been particularly difficult to disguise.

Earlier today, Olivia was discussing what materials her team would need in the design space. Everything was fine until she asked for a few drafting tables. Then things escalated rather quickly, probably because Savannah took it there, commenting, *those are distracting*, at which point Olivia replied something along the lines of, *only if used inappropriately*, followed up shortly with, *I like to work with a firm surface under me, you know, when I get my hands dirty.* Savannah's tongue-wagging reply emoji gave Olivia all kinds of visuals for the rest of the afternoon. And not that Olivia would ever admit this to anyone, but she was rereading some of those texts when her sister called and interrupted her.

"It's been impossible getting ahold of you lately," Christine complained. To be fair, that was true.

"I know. I know. I've totally sucked at the sister thing lately. Work is insane." Olivia was glad to be home alone tonight. It was the first time in forever that she had nothing planned. She was savoring the quiet.

"I'm not a fan of this traveling thing. I never know when I can call or what time zone you're in. It's bananas."

Olivia could hear her little niece echoing *bananas, bananas* in the background and her heart grew a thousand times. She couldn't wait to see her. She must be so big now.

"Well, buckle up, Buttercup, because the next stop on the list is Phoenix." Olivia poured herself a glass of wine and breathed in its aroma. It was heaven.

"Phoenix is hot stuff. Pack your antiperspirant—we both know how you sweat," Christine teased.

"I'm going to ignore that." Olivia plopped down on the couch and crossed her legs. "How's Mackenzie?"

"She's good. She made a bunch of new friends in her afterschool music class and has since declared she will be a professional tromboner. I tried to tell her that's not the correct title for that, nor is that a life goal, but she's four so it fell on deaf ears."

"I love that kid so much." Olivia's face hurt from smiling.

"She's a character—I'll give you that." Christine laughed. "We miss you, Liv." Now she sounded sad. "I was joking about the traveling thing before, but in all seriousness, I need some sister time and Mackenzie has been asking about auntie cuddles."

Guilt washed over Olivia like a tidal wave. Christine and her husband were getting a divorce, and although so far it was amicable, it couldn't be easy on her sister. "Soon, Chris. Soon. I promise. Once Phoenix is behind me, I'll have a little more wiggle room."

"Until Chicago," her sister pointed out.

"Right. Until Chicago. But then it's all clear and the project is done. And hopefully New Horizons is thrilled and this is the professional growth I've been dreaming about." Olivia didn't like to say it out loud too much, but she was really proud of this opportunity. And she wanted to be successful.

"I know. I'm just jealous because you get to spend so much time with this Savannah chick. She sounds hot." Mackenzie parroted that in the background and Christine told her it was time for bed. "I gotta put the little boogie to bed because it's past her bedtime. Talk soon?"

"Yes. Love you, Mack! And you too, Chris." Olivia was glad she had a chance to catch up with her sister, even if it was brief.

"Bye, Auntie." That kid was the cutest.

Olivia closed her eyes and was letting the weariness of the day fade from her shoulders when her phone rang in her hand.

"Forget something?"

"I don't think so. Should I have?"

She'd answered it without looking because she figured it was Chris calling her back for some reason. Imagine her surprise when Savannah was on the other end of the line.

At first, Olivia thought she might have dozed off and was dreaming. It wouldn't be the first time that thoughts of Savannah danced across her subconscious. Olivia opened her eyes and looked at the cell phone screen. Yup, it was definitely Savannah and not a dream.

"Savannah. Hi."

"Hey." She could hear Savannah's smile in her voice.

"Calling, huh? No more texting?" Olivia teased but she preferred this. Any time she could listen to Savannah's voice was her favorite time.

"Um, I'm driving. I have a meeting over cocktails and I needed some information about the Phoenix specs, but I know it's after nine thirty your time, so I figured you might not check your work email this late. Is this a bad time? Am I disturbing you?"

Olivia appreciated how thoughtful Savannah was being. "You never disturb me. What's up?"

"That's nice to hear." Olivia could hear a faint clicking noise in the background. It sounded like the turn signal of a car. Savannah asked, "Did your team come to a final decision on the water feature? I know it was a big hit in Denver—it's like the focal point of the room there. I wasn't quite sure what they thought about replicating it on a much grander scale in Phoenix. Have you guys discussed it?"

"Yeah, we're going to pitch a few ideas to the Phoenix crew and see what they think. I like the way it offers that calming effect in the space, you know? I think we should stick with it." Olivia had discussed this at length with the team and they were all in agreement.

"Okay, good. Great." Savannah paused. "How was your day?"

Olivia noted the change to that phone sex tone she loved so much. It brought her thoughts back to the texts from earlier. "Good. Distracting, but good."

"Oh? Why was it distracting?" Savannah's tone was playful.

"Oh, you know, some woman keeps texting me mildly suggestive things. All day long. That kind of distracting."

Savannah laughed. "Is that so?"

"Mm-hmm. It's torturous."

"She sounds like a nuisance. Want me to say something to her?"

"No, I can handle her." Olivia wondered if that was true.

"And how do you plan to do that?"

Olivia got the feeling that this conversation was about to take a different turn. It was dangerous talking to Savannah on the phone. At least by text she had a chance to pause and think before hitting send. Talking on the phone made it almost too easy to instigate something more.

Olivia glanced around her apartment and decided to take this call into her bedroom, to get a little more comfortable. "Well, for starters, I would ask her nicely to stop, and see where that gets me."

"And if asking nicely doesn't work? What then?"

"Well, then I would have to let her know there is a time and place for such banter. And that there are consequences if she doesn't heed my warnings." Olivia closed her bedroom door and set her wineglass on the bedside table.

"Consequences? Those sound interesting. Tell me about them. What kind of consequences?"

Savannah was baiting her. She took it.

"No more phone calls. No more texting. And I wouldn't tell her that I'm all alone in my apartment right now." Olivia could feel the beginnings of arousal pooling in her lower stomach. She liked this game.

"Does she ask about that? Does she want to know things like… what are you wearing?"

Olivia pulled in a deep breath and took a hearty sip of wine as she pondered what might happen next. Savannah was asking her hypothetical questions that were stirring up all kinds of nonhypothetical feelings. She clicked off the overhead light and settled onto her bed before turning on her bedside lamp. "She hasn't yet, but I feel like she wants to, like it's going there. I just think I should prepare myself."

"Maybe it would help if we practiced. You know, I'll pretend to be the person distracting you, and you answer like you think you would. Would that be helpful?" Savannah's voice was dripping with naughty intention.

Olivia was hypnotized. "Yeah, that might help."

"All right. So, Liv, where are you right now?"

Olivia smiled at the use of her nickname. "In my room, on my bed."

"Is the door closed?"

"It is, but I live alone so that's not a big issue. Why?" She settled farther into the bed.

"No reason." There was a pause. "What are you wearing?"

"I don't know if that's an appropriate line of questioning." Olivia played along as she felt herself start to get turned on. She could feel the heat crawling up her neck at just the hint of where this might be going.

"I'm just curious—it's okay. Tell me, what are you wearing, Liv?" Savannah remained in character and goaded her gently.

Olivia felt herself starting to melt into the sound of Savannah's voice. She closed her eyes and focused on her breathing in an attempt to slow it a bit. "I'm wearing jeans and a button-up shirt."

"How many buttons are open at the top of your shirt?"

Olivia glanced down: the top three were undone, showing just a hint of cleavage. She liked this shirt because it made her tits look great. It was tailored in all the right places to be professional but sexy at the same time. She'd changed out of her skirt when she got home and pulled on a pair of jeans to run to the store but she hadn't bothered to change her top yet. "Three." She breathed out.

"And tell me, the jeans, are they like the ones you had on at the pool that day? You know, so I have a point of reference."

Olivia wondered if Savannah added that last bit to uphold the pretense of role-playing for the intention of setting boundaries. They had clearly veered off course in that department. She wasn't about to stop it. "Actually, they're the same pair."

When Savannah moaned, Olivia decided to forgo the game entirely. She wanted to know what Savannah was thinking, fuck pretenses. "You remember my jeans? Did you like them?"

"They were memorable. I'm a fan." Savannah hummed and Olivia flushed.

She dragged her fingertips along her collarbone and let herself remember the appreciative gaze Savannah cast her by the pool. "I have that effect on people."

"You're pretty unforgettable, especially in those jeans," Savannah drawled.

"Anything particularly memorable?" Olivia closed her eyes and traced her fingers along the collar of her shirt as she remembered Savannah's touch, her lips along her neck.

"Your lips," Savannah husked. "I love the way your lips feel on mine."

Olivia moaned.

"Do you remember the taste of my mouth on yours?"

"Fuck." Olivia's pulse quickened as she remembered their time on the piano bench. Oh, she *definitely* remembered. She thought about it often, more than she'd like to admit.

"Do you remember how it felt with my hands on your hips? When I pulled you onto me?" Savannah's voice was thick. Her words were slow and deliberate.

Olivia whimpered. She didn't think she could ever forget the way it felt. She kept her eyes closed as she let herself become absorbed into the conversation. She soaked up Savannah's breathy sex voice, one syllable at a time.

There was a pause on the line before Savannah quietly commanded in the most seductive voice Olivia had ever heard, "Olivia, I want you to unbutton your shirt."

"Jesus." Olivia felt that heat from her neck start to spread through her body. It traveled across her chest, down her abdomen, and settled right between her thighs.

"One button at a time, Liv. Do it." Savannah purred across the line and Olivia's fingers shook as she complied.

"Okay." She was surprised how affected by Savannah's soft command she was. It made her shudder with want. She could feel that familiar stickiness against the crotch of her jeans as she undid each button, slowly, one by one. She let out a heavy sigh when her shirt was completely undone. Her breath was shallow and short. "All right."

"Good girl," Savannah cooed and Olivia was positively soaked. "Unbutton your pants, Liv. Unbutton them and slide them off your hips. But do it slowly. All right?"

"Mm-hmm." Olivia abandoned any attempt at speaking in full sentences. Not after that last little exchange. She was barely keeping it together long enough to fulfill Savannah's request. Everything in her body screamed for her to just make herself come to the sound of Savannah's voice, but she knew she should wait, see where this went. It was wonderfully torturous.

After a moment or two, Savannah asked, "How's it going, Liv?"

Her fingers were deliberate as she unbuttoned her jeans and slowly lowered the zipper like Savannah asked. She pressed her hands onto her hips and hooked her thumbs under the denim as she eased her jeans down her hips, over her ass, and past her knees until she could kick them off. She trembled as she looked down at herself, near naked but feeling surprisingly warm.

"Pants free." She licked her lips and waited to hear what Savannah had to say.

"Mm, Liv, what kind of underwear are you wearing?"

Olivia looked down the smooth plane of her body, over her breasts, and down to her panties. She squeezed her thighs together to help lessen the throbbing and a soft moan accompanied the action. "A black push-up bra with lace, matching thong..."

"That sounds so hot." There was a pause. "Liv?"

"Yeah?" Olivia was breathless.

"I want you to think of me, okay?" That wasn't any problem at all. "Think of me and use your left hand to massage your breast, over your bra. Can you do that for me?"

Well, fuck.

"Okay." Olivia slid her palm up her naked stomach to loosely palm at her breast. Her nipple pebbled under her palm and she groaned as the throbbing between her legs intensified.

"Harder, Liv. Massage it harder." Savannah's encouragement was making her feel light-headed.

"Shit," Olivia gasped out as she did as she was told.

"I want you to roll your nipple between your fingers, Liv. Think of my hands and tease them."

"Oh my God." Olivia pinched and plucked at her nipple. She

kept her eyes closed and bit her bottom lip as she envisioned Savannah touching her, breathing into her ear, coaxing her on. Her unoccupied hand gripped at the blanket next to her and squeezed the fabric with frustration and pleasure as she waited. She was getting restless. "I wish you were here."

This time Savannah moaned. "Me, too, babe. Me, too." Savannah took a breath over the line. "Imagine me there, over you, breathing against your neck. I want to lick under your jaw and suck on the skin under your ear. Your skin is so soft, Liv…"

Olivia's hips canted up at Savannah's words. Her chest warmed at the word *babe*. Her heart pounded at the thought of Savannah kissing her neck and hovering over her. She let herself believe that it was Savannah's touch winding her tighter and tighter. "You feel so good."

"Olivia." Savannah's tone was serious. "I want you to run your other hand down your stomach and drag your nails along the skin. Do it slowly, then tell me what it feels like."

Olivia slid her hand from her left breast to her right. She continued massaging and teasing as her right hand released the blanket and settled under her panting chest. She danced her fingers along the skin as her blunt nails sent shock waves through her body the closer she got to her panties.

"It feels…" She struggled to string coherent words together. "It feels, ugh, unbelievable. So hot. Fuck. Please." She was getting antsy. She didn't think she had ever been this turned on by someone just talking to her. It felt so good. She needed a release and she wanted Savannah to talk her through it. Now.

Savannah muttered a quiet curse. "I want you to touch yourself. Slip your fingers under your panties. Are you wet for me?"

Olivia moaned deep and loud into the phone as her right hand paused at the band of her thong and flitted along the elastic before she slipped under. "Oh God." She cried out as she reached the hot, wet flesh. She saw stars as she glided up and down and collected the wetness on her fingers. "I'm so wet, Savannah. Fuck. I'm so, so wet."

"Liv." Savannah sounded hungry. "Rub circles on your clit, Olivia."

"I'm so sensitive. It feels so good." Olivia felt possessed. Her hands moved across her body almost greedily while Savannah dictated the speed and pressure. She continued to coach and encourage her with that liquid sex voice. Olivia clenched her eyes shut as she felt herself start that steady climb while her hand worked faster under her panties, rubbing over the wetness. Her clit throbbed as she imagined Savannah touching her and bringing her higher and higher.

"Imagine my hand, Liv. Imagine me there, over you, holding your hips still as I touch you. You feel so good. You're so wet. I love the heat. I want to feel it all. I'm kissing along your neck, Olivia. I'm licking down your chest and sucking on the skin as I make tight circles on your clit. Can you feel me, Liv? Are you close for me?"

Olivia gasped and panted out, "Savannah, I'm so close. Please, I need to…" Her hips rocked up to meet her hand as she pressed harder on her clit and she felt herself reach the point of no return. She bit her lip and scratched at her chest, imaging Savannah's hot mouth working its way down her sternum, between her breasts. "Savannah, I need to, I—"

"C'mon, baby. Come for me. I want you to. Come for me." Savannah sounded breathless now and Olivia didn't hesitate to comply.

Her breathing staggered before it stopped momentarily as she reached the precipice and crashed back down. Her heart was racing and her breaths came out unevenly as she felt her body relax into the bed. She continued her gentle ministrations as the aftershocks rolled through her body and sent tingles through her legs into her feet. She let out a satiated sigh as her hands fell limply to her sides. A soft chuckle spilled from her lips as she realized she just got herself off to Savannah's voice. She was quiet for a moment as she listened to Savannah's breathing, which seemed faster than normal. "Shit. Did that just happen?"

Savannah laughed. "Mm-hmm. That definitely just happened."

Olivia let out a contented sigh. She felt like she should be panicking in this moment, but she just felt happy. "Hey, Savannah?"

"Yeah, Liv?"

"You have the sexiest voice I have ever heard. I just thought you should know." Orgasms were like truth serum to Olivia. She had little if any control over the things that came out of her mouth during or after. It was a thing.

Savannah's panty-dropping chuckle rang out across the line before she answered and Olivia swooned a little. "Really? We just did what we did and the first thing you wanted to tell me immediately following is that you think I have a sexy voice?"

"Yes. It seemed like a very important thing to tell you in the moment." Well, it did.

"Thank you." Savannah's voice was softer now. "I'm looking forward to seeing you in a few days."

Olivia giggled. "Yeah, me, too."

A comfortable silence fell between them before Savannah let out a heavy sigh. "Hey, as much as I don't want to go, I sort of have a business meeting, oh, about ten minutes ago that I have to get to."

"Oh God, I totally forgot." Olivia was recovering safely in her bed, but what about Savannah. "Where are you right now?"

"Um, in the parking lot, in my car, sitting outside the restaurant." Savannah sounded a bit embarrassed.

"Jesus. I'm sorry. You must be…" Olivia cringed.

"Wet? Sexually frustrated? Unreasonably turned on before a business meeting? Is that what you were going to say?" Savannah teased with a laugh.

"Um, yeah." Olivia scrunched her nose as she replied. "Is all that true?"

"Oh, yeah. Totally. I'm a mess right now."

Olivia wondered if that was true. What she would give to see the look on Savannah's face when she came… "I sincerely doubt that. I'm sure you look stunning, as usual."

"You're sweet." Olivia could hear the car door open and close over the line. "I have to get to this meeting but I'll call you later if it's not too late. Is that okay?"

"I'd like that." Olivia sank deeper into the comfort of her bed as a feeling of tranquility settled over her. "Good luck at your meeting."

"Talk to you soon." They exchanged good-byes before ending the call.

Olivia lay there wondering what they'd just done. It was one thing for her to be attracted to Savannah and for them to flirt. It had been another thing to make out with her on the piano bench. But phone sex? Phone sex was something else entirely. She didn't regret it— if anything, it made her want to see Savannah that much more. She wanted to experience everything Savannah had to offer, in real time, not just over the phone. Just thinking about it made Olivia feel warm and tingly again. No reason to let that go to waste, right?

CHAPTER FOURTEEN

Phoenix

Savannah made sure to call Olivia after the client meeting like she'd promised. And every day since then. They exchanged cute, flirty texts bidding the other good morning and good night, or spoke briefly about work before asking how the other person's day was going. It felt completely normal. Well, except for the part that they didn't directly discuss *that* phone call. The one that took what had been happening between them to a different level. That call remained alluded to, but never openly discussed. And Savannah had mixed feelings about that.

All along, Olivia had been the one encouraging Savannah to put down her walls and let the chemistry they clearly shared ignite. And yet, something told Savannah to cool her heels. As much as she wanted to see where things went with Olivia, part of her was also hesitant. Even if she could put aside the complicated working relationship they shared, she could feel the ghosts of her past getting in the way.

Her last real relationship had nearly ruined her. After college, she'd been in a serious relationship with her college love, Gwen, and there was talk of marriage. They had plans for a family and a menagerie of pets. But things hadn't worked out. Gwen had struggled with depression after the loss of her mother and started an affair with someone she'd met in a bereavement group. She'd pulled back from Savannah months before Savannah had caught her in the midst of her betrayal. Everything fell apart very quickly after that. The whole thing was so jarring to Savannah, that, for a few days, she just did nothing at all, ghosting past Gwen and letting the hurt settle in. Then one day, Savannah came home to an empty closet in their shared bedroom.

Savannah was alone, without any real closure, and had a household full of painful memories and responsibilities to sort through.

She didn't date seriously for a few years after that. Her work had become her life. She'd downsized her existence to a twelve hundred square foot loft and resisted anything serious in the relationship department. She had flings, or frequent bedmates, but nothing lasting. It was easier that way. None of it ever felt like a *forever* thing to Savannah. She had thought she had a forever thing with Gwen and she'd been wrong. That relationship had ended even with Savannah trying her best to make it work. So, she changed. She changed her job, changed her city, changed her sense of permanence. When things got rocky with a woman she was interested in, she didn't even try to make it work. She just let it fall by the wayside.

But what was happening with Olivia was unlike anything she had experienced before. This wasn't like one of the flings she'd had after her relationship with Gwen dissolved. But it wasn't like the relationship she'd shared with Gwen either. This was something different.

She really *liked* Olivia.

She looked forward to hearing from her and seeing her. And that made her nervous for a few reasons. She didn't want to get too attached—they lived in two different cities and their time together had an expiration date. Plus, she didn't really know all that much about Olivia. Nor Olivia about her. They'd kept it light. Well, light*ish*. Physically they appeared to be a good match. But Savannah wasn't sure if she was ready to broach the emotional stuff yet. If ever. Whatever they had was working the way it was, why change it?

She thought back to that night on the phone. She'd been amazed that she'd reached her destination safely and didn't careen into a tree while Olivia's breathy moans filled her ear. That phone call and the incredible sounds that came out of Olivia's mouth were the only things she could think of lately. The Phoenix installation couldn't come fast enough.

"I want to make sure this goes off without a hitch, Savannah." Kenneth Dodd had a jolly, booming voice that matched his large, rotund frame. He looked like a younger version of Santa and his mannerisms echoed the comparison. Savannah had heard gossip that he had been quite a shark of a businessman when he was younger, but her only experience with him had been easy-breezy. If anything, she thought him a bit oafish and unhelpful. She'd not experienced any of the shrewdness of the legend. He was a middle-aged, balding white man with bright red cheeks and a deep laugh, who never seemed to be concerned with anything, ever. He was freakishly calm, at all times, which unnerved Savannah, who was used to a fast-paced, high-energy approach to management. Her whole life was deadlines, conference calls, emails, and meetings—all things that should consume Kenneth's time as well, but he just never seemed bothered. He was odd. That was the only way she could describe him. Odd.

"Of course, Ken. That's the plan. Did you receive my evaluation of the Denver site?"

"Right, yes. Looks like they're doing great work. Go team." .

Savannah had been swamped with prep work since she'd arrived in Phoenix. In order for them to meet the accelerated deadline, everyone had to be working around the clock in preparation for Olivia and her team to arrive. She had back-to-back meetings on the day Olivia's flight landed and would be unable to meet Olivia and her team at the airport as she had hoped to. She wanted a chance to get Olivia alone, talk about things in person, and try to get a feel for what she was thinking. But there was just too much to do in such a short time. And this phone call was one of them.

Kenneth rambled on and on about the excitement this project was generating and told her a seemingly endless story about nothing in particular until he finally ended the call. Savannah glanced at her watch. Dammit. She was going to be late. That man could talk and talk and talk. She seriously wondered if he just liked to hear his own voice. She grabbed her personal cell phone and dialed her brother.

"I thought you forgot about me." The sound of a video game machine gun was in the background.

"Sorry, Coop. It's been insane." Savannah ran her hand through her hair and exhaled. "How's Chi-town?"

"Meh. Busy. School is busy. Life is busy. The usual." Cooper sounded distracted.

"Is this a bad time?" Savannah knew the answer.

"I'm sorry, Sav. I'm kinda in the middle of something. I just wanted to let you know that Dad called." Cooper sounded shy.

Savannah and her father did not get along. They barely spoke and saw each other even less. But Cooper was still in school, so if she had a relationship with her half brother, she still sometimes overlapped with her deadbeat father. "Oh? What'd he say?"

The sound of gunfire paused. "He wanted to know about parents' weekend and visiting. I didn't tell him we had plans. I don't want him to impinge on them. You know how he can be."

She sighed. That she did. He was grandiose and obtuse. Entitled and narcissistic. Being around him was exhausting. She was grateful for his decision, but Cooper sounded anxious. "Okay. So is there a problem?"

"He wants to crash my dinner with Mom."

"Yeah, so?" Two birds, one stone. Savannah thought this sounded like a better alternative to a meal with her father alone.

"He met someone. He wants to bring her along." Ah. There it was.

Sure, he did. To rub it in Cooper's mom's face, no doubt. Savannah would bet her life savings that this woman was young and pretty. That's how her father liked them. Her father had dumped Cooper's mother a couple of years after Cooper had been born. Just like he did with all the women in his life—he left them. Cooper and his mother were close. No doubt this made him feel uncomfortable.

"Tell him no, Coop." Savannah didn't have many regrets in life, but she did feel badly about the way things had gone with all the women that followed Gwen. It wasn't anyone's fault really—she just wasn't ready. She didn't feel the connection and her heart was still reeling from the first time. But part of her was angry with herself, too. She had grown up with a father who thought people were expendable. She didn't like the way she'd easily shrugged off the women in her recent past. It felt like something he would do. That was not a comparison she ever wanted. The only good thing that man had ever done in his whole life was have her brother, Cooper.

Her brother cracked his knuckles. He did that when he was nervous.

"Coop. You're an adult. Tell him to fuck off with his Barbie doll rent-a-girlfriend. If he can't sit through dinner with you and your mom and Amber without showboating this week's arm candy, then he can't go. Simple as that."

"Yeah." The sound of gunfire resumed. "You're right."

"I know I am. Just try. If you don't want him there at all, that's fine, too." Savannah felt bad. She knew how things were with her father. She knew how Cooper must be feeling. But she'd grown out of that kind of guilt and shame. She wasn't interested in her father's negativity or need to impress people. Cooper was still learning, but Savannah had seen enough of that behavior for a lifetime. "Call me if you need anything, Coop. I'll talk you through it."

"Thanks, Savannah. When are you home again?"

"Couple of weeks."

"Great. Okay. I gotta finish killing these zombies before Advanced Chem later. Love you. Thanks for the pep talk."

"Love you, Coop."

She glanced at the calendar in front of her. Was it really a few weeks until she was back home again? When did she get so accustomed to being someplace else all the time? She thought of Olivia and about the feelings Cooper stirred up when he brought up their father. She had failed at her past relationships by not even trying. Her thoughts circled back to Olivia. Olivia made her want to be in one place for a longer period of time. Olivia made her want a lot of things. She looked at the clock again—they would be landing any minute. Maybe she could wrap up here and meet up with her at the hotel. She wanted to get her alone, to talk to her. She nodded to herself and made the decision. She could work on the rest of this later. Tonight, she needed to see Olivia. Alone.

Olivia couldn't help but frown when she saw the hotel transport van without Savannah in it. She had been secretly hoping Savannah would meet her and greet her with a tight embrace and some secretly whispered seduction. She wasn't that surprised, though. The Denver installation was very close to the hotel they were staying at; this time around the project space was much farther away. It would have been ridiculous to expect Savannah to leave the design space and get back to the hotel just to take another vehicle to personally pick them up. But she still couldn't shake the disappointment she felt.

The ride from the airport to the hotel was quick. Devon and Farrah were chatting about the flight with the driver and picking his brain for good haunts in the area. They'd be in Phoenix longer than they'd been in Denver, so there'd be more opportunities to explore and see some of Phoenix's culture. The boys and Reagan had arrived a few days before, just like last time, to get things in order since.

Once Olivia and her team checked into their hotel rooms, a hotel driver shuttled them over to the design space. The room was in the far east corner of a nearly century-old building that overlooked a man-made pond with mountains in the distance. It was gorgeous in its bare-bones setup, so rich with history and architectural charm. The space would be unbelievable once Olivia and her team had a chance to work with it.

Daniel and the head contractor met them at the door, handing them each hard hats and giving Olivia the newest blueprint plans. Randal and Reagan were seated at one of the drafting tables going over numbers and drawings. Reagan was in her usual grunge-chic outfit, her hair brushed sloppily over her shoulder in that perfected just-out-of-bed look. Randal was his usual wrinkled self, looking worn-out already, and it was barely midday. Olivia shook her head. At least they were consistent.

She glanced around the space in search of Savannah. She was on the phone, standing by the far window reading her tablet and juggling some documents at the same time. She had on a hard hat and her forehead was creased in concentration as she shook her head in response to the person on the other end of the line. She was wearing a nicely tailored navy-blue power suit with a skirt that hugged her ass in a way that should be illegal. Olivia let herself appreciate the view until Savannah noticed she had an audience. A sly smile spread across Savannah's face as she glanced over at Olivia. She winked before resuming her phone call and Olivia's heartbeat increased. Savannah was all kinds of sexy, and even in a hard hat across a crowded room she made Olivia's heart thump just a little more enthusiastically.

Try as she might to get Savannah alone, she was unsuccessful. The day was long and before she knew it the team was breaking up, and they were assigned different cars back to the hotel. Savannah had ducked out early to meet with some representatives from New Horizons in the hotel bar to go over the schedule again.

It was after seven that evening before Olivia finally settled into her hotel room. She fell back onto the queen bed and spread out like a starfish on the soft comforter. She closed her eyes and listened to the gentle hum of the air conditioner as she tried to unwind. It was very warm in Phoenix, a dry, arid heat, but her room was cooled to a comfortable seventy-four degrees. She contemplated her dinner options: room service, the hotel bar/restaurant, or off-site. She hadn't even unpacked yet, but all she could think about was how soft this bed was and how tired her body felt from all the travel of the day.

She must have dozed off because when she blinked her eyes open again it was just after half past seven. She stretched on the bed and sat up slowly before she walked to the bathroom and grabbed one of the plastic-wrapped glasses on the sink to fill with water. She ran the cold tap for a few seconds, then filled the glass and took a sip. The water was warm and she gagged at the unexpected temperature. The ice bucket on the side of the sink caught her eye and she scooped it up. She grabbed her room key card and stepped out into the hall in search of the ice machine.

The machine was around the corner from her room, down the hall, past the elevators, tucked in an alcove at the corner of another long corridor of rooms. She leaned against the wall and pressed the button on the machine until her bucket was almost completely filled.

"Hot?" A familiar velvety voice pulled Olivia from her daze.

Olivia looked up and caught Savannah sending her a curious look. "What?"

"I asked if you were hot." Savannah nodded toward the ice bucket, which was currently overflowing because Olivia was staring at Savannah's lips and not paying attention to what she was doing. Savannah reached out and gently ushered Olivia's hand away from the button to stop the ice chip mountain that was beginning to form.

Olivia flushed and looked down shyly at the mound of ice that was slowly littering its contents onto the floor.

Savannah still loosely held Olivia's fingers in her hand as she stepped closer. She ducked her head to catch Olivia's gaze. "I didn't get a chance to say hello to you earlier. How are you?"

Olivia tilted her head to the side. "I'm good. Better now." She licked her lips. "How are you?"

"I'm good," Savannah replied as her gaze fell to Olivia's lips. Olivia felt her body heat up as Savannah's eyes lingered. Savannah reached forward and pushed a stray curl behind Olivia's ear. Savannah's fingers brushed lightly against her cheek and Olivia closed her eyes at the sensation.

When she blinked them open again she found Savannah watching her. Savannah's hand dropped to her side and grabbed an ice chip from the overflowing bucket. She popped it into her mouth and she stepped forward a little more as she entwined her fingers with Olivia's. She glanced up and down the hall before she leaned in and breathed icy cold air across Olivia's ear.

"Before, when I asked if you were hot, I wasn't asking about you specifically. I already know *you* are hot. I just meant, you know, temperature-wise."

Olivia exhaled a shaky breath. The cool air on her skin made her break out in goose bumps, but Savannah's lips in such proximity to her ear made her burn up.

She whimpered softly when Savannah's free hand dropped to her hip and squeezed.

"Have dinner with me tonight." Savannah brushed ice cold lips across the skin under Olivia's ear before she pulled back, surveying her.

Olivia gulped. Savannah was still standing close. She was close enough for Olivia to smell her perfume—it was delicious. She took a minute to compose herself and squeezed Savannah's fingers in hers as she replied, "I'd love to."

Savannah stepped back a bit farther as she skated the ice chip along her bottom lip with her tongue. Olivia watched with rapt attention as she sucked it back into her mouth with a knowing smile.

"Hey!" Reagan popped around the corner with the phone cradled to her ear. "I was just calling you, Liv. Wanna grab a bite?"

Olivia felt her eyes bulge when she heard Reagan approach from behind her. She watched Savannah's face for any glimmer of emotion as she withdrew her hand from Olivia's. Savannah's smile faded as she surveyed Reagan over Olivia's shoulder. Olivia got the impression that she was less than thrilled at Reagan's arrival. She felt that way, too.

"Oh, hey, Savannah." Reagan stopped next to Olivia. "Got dinner plans?"

Olivia watched Savannah's eyes narrow with what looked like irritation. Olivia couldn't think of a worse time for Reagan to fly around the corner and invite her to dinner. She figured the irritation was mirrored in her own face when Savannah glanced back at her with a small apologetic smile before she answered.

"Hey, Reagan."

"Whoa. Got ice, Liv?" Reagan poked Olivia in the side and spilled a few more ice chips onto the floor.

"Yeah, this machine spits them out faster than I was expecting." She turned to face Reagan because she didn't want to be rude. Even if she did want Reagan to disappear into thin air.

"So, ladies…dinner?" Reagan repeated as she glanced between them.

Savannah stepped back farther and leaned against the wall. Olivia watched as she swallowed the end of her ice chip and raised her eyebrow in apparent contemplation.

Olivia figured she had two options and one was decidedly more intimate than the other. They were dancing along that line again—what was appropriate, what was not. Reagan's option was the much safer bet. It was friendly and harmless. It would look suspicious if they both declined her offer. Olivia had no problem with the direction her relationship with Savannah was going, whatever direction that might be. But she wasn't about to make an announcement to her team and especially not to Reagan. She could feel the frown on her face, and a subtle nod from Savannah confirmed they were on the same page.

"Yeah, sounds good." Savannah nodded encouragingly toward her. "Olivia, you in?"

"Sure, sounds great. Let me just drop off my, uh, ice." Olivia felt flustered. And disappointed. And annoyed.

Savannah struck up a conversation with Reagan and Olivia slipped back to her room to figure out what had just transpired.

Olivia deposited the ice bucket on the bathroom sink and sank onto the edge of the tub with a heavy sigh. Fuck. As much as she loved Reagan, she really, really didn't want to entertain Reagan or her ramblings over dinner. She really, really wanted to see what Savannah had in store for her instead. That ice thing was like the hottest thing anyone had done to her in the name of seduction. Well, minus the phone sex thing. She was so screwed.

She shook her head, letting her curls tumble around her face. Savannah made her all kinds of nervous. It was the kind of nervous that made you feel clumsy and inarticulate. Ever since that phone call, Olivia had struggled to keep her words and actions in check. It had taken all of her willpower not to jump Savannah in the design space when she was bent over the table looking at specs with Randal, or when she was laughing at some awful joke Reagan fed her, or when she was smiling down at her phone reading a text Olivia had sent her from across the room just to see how she would react. It was getting hard to behave. They both so obviously wanted the same thing, but they really needed to figure out what that meant and how that was going to happen.

Olivia stood with a frown as she surveyed herself in the mirror. She fixed her mascara, touched up her lip gloss, and resigned herself to a very different dinner than the one she would have preferred.

❖

Savannah and Reagan were in the hotel bar waiting for a table when Olivia made her way to them. Savannah noticed that she'd changed into a dinner outfit. She looked great.

"So I just told her that I needed some space. You know?" Reagan shook her head and sipped her beer.

Savannah sipped her martini and she tried to be polite while she feigned interest. But she wasn't really listening. She hadn't been able to stop thinking about Olivia since they were interrupted earlier. The stray ice chip in her martini was not helping her focus in the least.

"Oh, please don't tell me you're boring Savannah with your dating woes, Reagan," Olivia chimed in with an exaggerated eye roll. "I'll get my order to go if that's the case."

Reagan scoffed and flashed a look of mock offense. "Whatever, Liv." An evil smile crossed her face as she narrowed her eyes. "I was just going to tell her all about how you and I used to date."

Savannah's head whipped toward Reagan. She must have misheard her. "Did you say something about dating?"

"That was a million years ago, Reagan. No need to dig up ancient history." Olivia looked nervous.

"Aw, c'mon, Liv." Reagan slipped her arm around Olivia's waist in a one-armed hug. "We had some good times. Remember that foam party in West Village A—"

"Enough," Olivia bit back and shrugged off Reagan's arm. Savannah watched as her eyes threw daggers in Reagan's direction. This didn't seem like a discussion Olivia wanted to have in her presence.

Reagan looked momentarily wounded until the hostess finally appeared and ushered them to their table. Savannah said nothing. She chose instead to sip her drink and watch the tension rise between Olivia and Reagan. That was an interesting disclosure. She wasn't sure how she felt. Was she a little jealous? Maybe. No. She was more curious, she decided. Something she would inquire about later.

Farrah joined them shortly after they were seated and engrossed them in a story about her teenage daughters and the adventures of dating. Farrah seemed to notice the increased tension between her team members, and Savannah saw her nudge Reagan in the ribs while she continued to engage in a conversation with her.

Reagan apologized under her breath and Olivia dismissed the apology with a tight smile. She'd been making a lot of eye contact with the salmon in front of her.

Savannah excused herself from the table to use the restroom but waited nearby unobserved on the return trip when she overhead Farrah chastise her tablemates.

"What is wrong with you two?" Farrah looked between the two women. "Marital quarrel?"

Savannah could see Olivia shake her head and mutter something, but she couldn't hear what.

"C'mon. Lighten up. It was a joke." Reagan pouted and mirrored Olivia's defensive posture.

Farrah looked between the two of them again and shook her head in frustration. "You two are worse than my teenage girls. Spit it out. What's wrong?"

Olivia said nothing but Reagan said, "I might have made a joke to Savannah that Olivia and I used to date. And Liv got all uppity about it." She settled back into her seat with a frown.

"Oh." Farrah turned to Reagan. "Listen, you know we're all family here, but maybe Olivia wanted to tell Savannah she was into women herself—"

"Can we not talk about me like I'm not sitting here?" Olivia's voice rose and Savannah had no trouble hearing that.

Farrah pursed her lips. "I really doubt Savannah cares. She seems totally fine about those things—remember when Reagan hit on her?"

"It's not that. I don't actually care if she knows I'm gay or not," Olivia growled.

Savannah nearly laughed. They'd passed that getting-to-know-you phase a while back when Olivia was masturbating on the phone with her.

Olivia continued, "God, Reagan, stop pouting. It's fine."

"Why are you making this into such a big deal? I know you have a crush on her and all, but it's not like it's going anywhere, right?" Reagan uncrossed her arms and started tearing at the napkin in front of her, her eyes on the table.

A crush? She hoped it was more than a crush. But what she really wanted to know was the answer to Reagan's second question.

At first Olivia said nothing and Savannah swore Reagan looked hurt. Did Reagan have a thing for Olivia?

Olivia let out a sigh. She reached forward and stilled Reagan's nervous picking. "I'm sorry. It's been a long day, I think I'm just tired… or maybe just premenstrual, I dunno."

Savannah noted that she didn't quite answer Reagan's question.

"S'okay," Reagan mumbled and sipped her beer.

Savannah took the pause in conversation as an opportunity to return to the table. She lowered herself into her seat and thought about all the questions she had for Olivia. "Dessert, ladies?"

CHAPTER FIFTEEN

Olivia knew she had overreacted to Reagan's disclosure. She'd had no intention of telling Savannah about her history with Reagan. Ever. But it wasn't just that. It was more the fact that Reagan had inadvertently ruined her night's plans and announced that they used to fool around to the woman Olivia was having wet dreams about night after night. Sure, being angry at Reagan might be wrong, but she couldn't help it. She was pissed. But when Reagan started picking at her napkin and sulking like a child, she felt bad.

She knew she was misdirecting her anger in this moment. Plus, she'd practically put a spotlight on her feelings for Savannah. And that wasn't an obstacle she needed while they were still figuring things out between them. Still, Reagan was only being playful. She was just too tightly wound to appreciate it.

Once Savannah returned to the table, things eased back into normalcy. They shared a few desserts and made fun of Randal's outfits a few times before regaling Savannah with the story of how Randal had once lit his pants on fire at the launch of a design space when his untied shoelace got too close to a decorative tiki torch.

At some point during the destruction of the chocolate cake slice in front of them, Savannah's right hand moved to Olivia's knee and gently stroked it before pulling back. Olivia momentarily paused in her storytelling to sip her water. She hoped that she didn't give any hint that her heart lurched into her throat at the affectionate contact. She was explaining to Farrah the importance of social media when she slipped off her shoe and slowly dragged her foot along Savannah's calf under the table. She could dish it out, too.

Savannah nodded and followed along in the conversation, not pausing for a moment. Olivia was wondering if she'd accidently rubbed someone else's calf, when Savannah reached out to touch her again. Savannah shifted in her seat so her body was angled toward Olivia, and she traced the fingers of her left hand along her neckline. She tugged her shirt collar while she talked and exposed more and more of her neck and collarbone to Olivia's view.

Olivia was struggling to keep from staring. Savannah wiggled her fingers and shifted again, and this time Olivia felt Savannah's hand on the inside of her knee. Savannah stroked up and down before she reached for the check. Olivia felt like her face was on fire.

Reagan and Farrah were a few steps in front of them when they started to leave, engrossed in a conversation about the design space. Olivia stalled in order for Savannah to catch up with her.

"Not fair," she said as she reached out and tugged at the bottom of Savannah's shirt.

"I have no idea what you're referring to." Savannah's hand settled on Olivia's lower back and stayed there as they walked a few steps behind the other women.

Olivia warmed at the contact on her back. She liked when Savannah touched her. She felt very grounded and comforted by it, even when Savannah was teasing the crap out of her.

Savannah leaned close to ask in a husked whisper, "So, you and Reagan, huh?"

A shiver spread through Olivia, down her spine, back up to her thumping heart, as Savannah whipped out that secret sex voice weapon again, effectively rendering her powerless.

"Um, yeah, but it was forever ago. Like, years," she whispered back quickly, not quite sure why she felt the need to justify it with a time stamp.

Savannah looked at her. Her eyes trailed over Olivia's face and paused at her mouth before she said, directly to her lips, "Good."

"Why? Are you jealous?" Olivia bumped her shoulder into Savannah's.

Pink lips pursed into a lopsided grin as Savannah paused. "Jealous? No, not particularly. Curious though, yes."

"Curious?" Olivia asked as Savannah danced her fingertips at her lower back.

"Well, maybe *curious* is the wrong word." Savannah glanced at the two women in front of them and seemed to assess their distance before continuing. "Maybe *envious* is better suited for this situation."

Olivia felt that familiar tightening in her abdomen as she focused on the way Savannah licked her lips. "Envious of whom, exactly?"

Reagan and Farrah hit the elevator button in the lobby and continued their discussion as Savannah leaned close once more. She breathed right into Olivia's ear and shattered her attempts at composing her face into some semblance of a calm appearance.

"This is likely the only time you will ever hear me admit to being envious of Reagan, but I am. Envious." She paused. "And curious." She slid her hand from Olivia's lower back to squeeze her hip quickly before she stepped forward and held the elevator doors for Olivia.

Olivia let out a shaky breath as she walked past Savannah. She stepped into the elevator and put as much space between them as possible. She needed the space to think clearly again.

When Olivia finally got back to her room and settled onto her bed, she was sexually frustrated. Yet again. She noticed that her cell phone was illuminated next to her. She unlocked the screen and smiled at the awaiting text: *I had fun tonight, thx. Dinner again soon? Just the two of us?*

Olivia traced her fingers over the butterflies she felt in her stomach. She replied, *me too. Yeah, let's do that*

She typed another reply a second later. *soon.*

Savannah's response was immediate:. *ok, deal. Goodnight Liv.*

Olivia typed back a quick reply and let out a happy sigh as she lowered herself onto the bed again. Today had been a pretty good day.

❖

Olivia was exhausted. The past few days had been long and very busy. The skeleton of the design space was constructed, but they seemed to continually run into obstacle after obstacle. At first, the fabrics arrived in the wrong color, a shipping error. Then it was the water feature, a plumbing issue that required an unexpected redesign of the space to accommodate new piping. As if that wasn't enough hassle, Randal and Daniel came down with food poisoning that left them both out of commission for a few days. Thankfully, Reagan stepped in and teamed up with a member of the Phoenix crew, but they were shorthanded when they needed help. Savannah had been working overtime, there first in the morning and last to leave every night. Whenever Olivia saw her she was on the phone, typing furiously, or on the tablet with fingers flying over the touch screen, pulling up graphics and blueprints. Olivia hadn't seen her eat or drink anything besides her morning coffee since she landed in Phoenix four days ago. In fact, she hadn't spent a moment of alone time with her since Reagan interrupted their dinner plans.

They texted during the off hours away from the design space, but they were both swamped with work. It seemed like even in their periods of rest, they were doing something. Corrine had requested follow-up calls every few days to make sure they were on task. All other projects from Greater Image Design were backburnered, but not erased completely. Corrine had a small team still taking new clients and doing smaller projects, and she needed Olivia's input here or her creative design idea there. It wasn't that it was too much work, just a lot, crammed into a small amount of time. She'd gotten better at managing the various projects as the days progressed. She dealt with the Phoenix space in the mornings, took lunch calls from Corrine and fielded emails midday, before wrapping up with the Phoenix space at night. She felt as though she had gleaned some of her multitasking skills from watching Savannah. That woman was like a machine.

This morning, Olivia got to the design space early and caught the tail end of Savannah on speakerphone with someone named Annabelle, whom she assumed was her assistant. Savannah was dictating a memo for corporate while writing an email on her tablet. Annabelle commented here or there, agreeing with a *Yes, Ms. Quinn* or *No ma'am, not yet*. Olivia thought it was cute the way Savannah nodded in response to Annabelle's questions. She would pause when she realized that her assistant couldn't see her answer. It was sort of adorable how focused she was, but at the same time a little hot how much power she had. Savannah was a force to be reckoned with, but surprisingly patient, too.

Savannah corrected Annabelle half a dozen times about whatever they were working on. She would ask Annabelle to forward the file to her tablet, which she then tweaked on her end before sending it back to her assistant. But she was kind, thanking Annabelle for coming to work early, then giving her the rest of the day off. Her only request was that she be near her phone in case something came up, but she reiterated that she wasn't needed in the office. Olivia felt herself melt a little at the appreciative smile on Savannah's face when she ended the call. She seemed to pause in that moment, the fury and fast pace she was always exhibiting muted as she took a slow breath and sighed.

Olivia watched Savannah stretch in her seat, close her tablet, and put down her phone before she grabbed her coffee and walked toward the window overlooking the pond. Olivia felt like she was intruding upon a silent moment of tranquility, but at the same time, she appreciated seeing the quieter side exhibited by Savannah in this moment. When she and Savannah made eye contact, when they were alone, the world stopped. The quietness in those moments was what Olivia missed when the design space was crowded and bustling. It was the silent eye contact across the room and the secret smile that Olivia hoped for; her heart fluttered when they happened, those secret, stolen glances. The quiet moments. She wanted a chance to experience those moments with Savannah more, lots more.

She hadn't been able to sleep, and this morning, even though her body was tired, her mind wouldn't stop. She had gone down to the gym to hit the treadmill and burn off a little energy. In high school, she'd run cross-country. She ran for fitness and leisure in college, but never competed again. She had friends who ran marathons and did triathlons, but it wasn't for her. She liked the freedom running gave her. She liked the opportunity to lose herself in her thoughts. One of her favorite things about home was Central Park and running in the early mornings before work, or taking a midday jog through the park on the weekends when she could weave through picnicking couples or kids playing soccer with their parents. Today's run had been good for her. She'd rounded out almost four miles before she noticed that her iPod wasn't even on. Her thoughts had been consumed by a paramour, who at this moment was looking out at the pond, seemingly lost in her thoughts.

Olivia had made the decision this morning that she was going to ask Savannah to dinner. She hoped that tonight would be the night they could spend some quality time together. She decided that she would finally talk about that phone call and about their attraction. She wanted to feel Savannah against her again. She wanted to feel her lips on her neck and smell the way her perfume mixed so perfectly with her shampoo. Olivia wanted Savannah and she was tired of dancing around her desire. She needed to talk about it, and she needed to make sure it wasn't one-sided, because if it was, well, then she needed to know that, too.

"Good morning, Olivia," Savannah called from the window as she glanced over her shoulder with a smile before looking back out at the pond.

Olivia was surprised. She hadn't moved from her spot, hadn't made any noise. She cleared her throat and walked forward. "Good morning."

Savannah turned and nodded toward the water. "It's beautiful, isn't it? The pond, it's so quiet and calm looking."

"It is. This is a good location for the design space. The view is gorgeous." Olivia was half looking at the pond, half looking at Savannah. The statement was true of both embodiments of perfection.

Savannah kept her gaze out ahead of her. "How long were you here before I noticed you?"

"Not long. You seemed so peaceful—I didn't want to disturb you." Olivia was honest. She sipped her coffee and looked out the window with Savannah.

"You were watching me," Savannah stated quietly.

"I guess I was." Olivia didn't see any point in denying it.

"What were you thinking?" Savannah watched a small flock of birds circle the pond.

Olivia paused. She had been thinking about Savannah and how much she wanted to spend time with her outside of work and what that might lead to, which was hopefully less clothes and lots of kissing. She remembered her decision. She felt emboldened in the moment. "I was thinking about you. And dinner. And, yeah…"

Savannah turned toward Olivia. "Is that so?"

Olivia nodded. She could feel the skin on her neck heating up.

Savannah let out a soft sigh. "Well, I was thinking about you."

Olivia frowned. "You make it sound like that's a bad thing."

Savannah pursed her lips and examined Olivia. "It's not a bad thing, it's just a *thing*."

What the hell did that mean? She waited for Savannah to elaborate.

Savannah licked her lips. "Lately, it seems like I spend a lot of time thinking about you. It's distracting."

Olivia wasn't sure if she should be offended or flattered. From the slightly pained expression Savannah was trying to suppress, she felt like it was the beginning of a brush-off.

Savannah shook her head. "This is harder than I expected." She pinched the bridge of her nose and squeezed her eyes shut. "It's difficult. I think about you a lot."

The little bit of patience Olivia had left in that moment fizzled out. "Okay. Well, this has been, um, enlightening. I'll leave you to whatever you were doing." She turned and started walking back toward the sound of the morning crew that was arriving when a warm hand closed on her bicep.

"Wait," Savannah murmured and tightened her grip on Olivia's arm.

"Wha—?" Any protests Olivia was about to voice were quickly forgotten when Savannah spun her on the spot and pressed their lips together. Olivia closed her eyes as Savannah moved soft lips against hers. Savannah held her close with a loose hand still at her bicep. When the distant sound of construction supplies and men talking broke them apart, Olivia gasped and blinked in surprise.

Savannah glanced toward the sounds of the crew members trickling in before she looked back at Olivia. "What I was trying to tell you, obviously poorly executed, is that I think about you *a lot.*"

She was still so close as she continued, "I know we talked about this not happening and about setting boundaries and then we bulldozed those boundaries and then we danced around the wreckage but I can't stop thinking about you and that night on the phone. And it's distracting. Because I just always want to kiss you and I'm not sorry about that."

Olivia couldn't suppress the flutter that Savannah's words brought. She looked quickly left and right to make sure they were still alone before she rocked forward and pressed a quick kiss to Savannah's lips.

Savannah smiled into the kiss and moved her hand up to cup Olivia's cheek before they broke apart again. "You are the first thing I think about every morning and the last thing I think about every night."

Olivia sighed and sipped her coffee just to keep her lips to herself before she replied. "We ought to work on your delivery of heart melting phrases, because that almost got ugly."

Savannah looked smug as she countered, "Heart melting, huh?"

"Shut up." Olivia glanced toward the foreman who set his lunch pail down a couple dozen feet away.

They watched each other for a moment in silence, before Savannah added, "I'm not great at this"—she motioned between them—"but I want to try."

Olivia saw the almost embarrassed bashfulness settle on Savannah's face. Savannah Quinn was a champion of seduction, all hot phone sex voice and teasing touches. Who knew she was shy about regular relationship interactions. "That surprises me a little."

An unreadable expression passed over Savannah's face and she replied, "I'm sure I'm full of surprises."

"Well, then, I look forward to experiencing them. All of them."

A look of relief spread across Savannah's face as she stepped back.

Olivia became aware of the noise the rest of the crew brought with their arrival. They would have to continue this conversation later.

Savannah glanced once more at the pond before she looked back at Olivia. "Have lunch with me today."

"I'd like that."

"Good. Me, too. Let's talk a bit then, okay?"

"Sounds good."

"You look nice today, by the way," Savannah added before she turned toward the approaching foreman and slipped right back into her work mode.

Olivia let out a content sigh. Savannah had a way of giving her all kinds of butterflies, even if she didn't mean to.

CHAPTER SIXTEEN

The morning was hectic. A power outage put a hold on the morning construction of the panel wall. The electrical work couldn't be done, the tools wouldn't start, and the computerized panel was useless. Daniel and the construction foreman dismissed the crew shortly after lunch after they contacted the local electrical company and learned power wouldn't be restored until after normal business hours. And without electricity in the design space, Olivia's team was pretty limited. The overcast, gray day made it hard to work even by natural light, so everyone was eventually dismissed by one that afternoon.

Olivia was busy trying to make sense of some emails Corrine had sent her, squinting in the limited light coming in through the windows to survey the structural specs from Randal and Reagan to make the change resulting from the plumbing modifications for the water feature. It wasn't a big change, a few feet here or there, but it would determine the size of the matted canvas on the north wall and its proximity to the overhead lighting. This site had the option of light therapy for the person using the space, something not implemented in the Denver project. So special heated and infrared lights had to be placed beyond a certain distance from the art to not obscure the rays and color hues. They also had to figure out a way to keep this room partially shaded, which had been the plan for today until the power went out. Now they had to wait to see the room in all of its natural light stages on a bright day before installing the electronic panels to dim the space and calibrate the light therapy toggle settings. It wasn't necessarily a hard task, but it was something that required patience, focus, and *electricity*. All three were significantly lacking for Olivia today.

Thankfully, earlier in the week Farrah had made the fantastic suggestion to take digital images of the sun coming through the mostly glass walls at different points in the day and during different weather patterns. Laid out in front of Olivia on the drafting table were ten photographs, each labeled with time of day and each identifying the direction the sun was coming through the glass. She used these with the blueprint CAD program to help configure the art and furniture in the design space. The dividing walls were almost complete, but nothing could be finalized until the plumbing design was verified.

She cracked her neck and let out a heavy sigh as she repositioned the art on the north wall for the fifth time with an error resulting, again. She would have to have Reagan and Randal recalculate the dimensions. Something was wrong.

"Hey." A soft voice came from behind her and it was accompanied by an equally soft hand placed on her shoulder.

Olivia lightly touched the hand on her shoulder as she turned around. "Hey."

Savannah looked around the design space. Everyone had gone home for the day. Reagan had just left with Devon to have a late lunch, which Olivia assumed to mean cocktails at the bar down the street. It was getting stiflingly hot in the enclosed space since the air-conditioning wasn't working.

"It's hot. Why don't you pack that up and we head out to lunch?"

Olivia had gotten so wrapped up in the day she had forgotten about their plans. She shuffled the photos and papers into a folder and closed her laptop. She placed her work supplies into the soft, worn leather bag she'd used since she graduated from college. The leather was covered in scratches and dings from being tossed around. She'd had the straps repaired twice already; the buckles were tarnished, and the front zipper hadn't worked properly in years. She had been meaning to upgrade the bag and get something with more padding for her laptop. Something that was a little sturdier for travel to and from client sites. But she loved this bag. It reminded her of all the hard work she'd put in over the years. She remembered the pen that exploded in the inside pocket, the one that spread blue ink all over her first major proposal. She had been on the road to her client appointment and had to hop out of the cab at a copy center to try to fix it. She'd slathered the blue ink with Wite-Out and made fresh copies of the entire portfolio. She rebound it and hailed a new cab, and by some miracle she'd made it to the presentation on time.

No amount of scrubbing had taken the now slightly faded blue tinge out of the caramel-colored leather. The shape of the stain sort of looked like the state of New York, so she just joked about it being part of the bag's marketing strategy to people who inquired about it.

As Olivia organized the drafting table she noticed Savannah running her hands along the leather of her bag. Her fingers traced the fading color of the sturdy stitching along the top.

"This bag looks like it has a lot of history," Savannah said. "It's so soft and malleable but has a stoically defiant quality to it at the same time."

"It was a gift from my mentor, Albie Davis," Olivia supplied. "He gave it to me when I finished my internship, before I started working full-time for the company. It's falling apart and is impervious to any and all attempts at cleaning it. I'll need a new one eventually."

"It's beautiful," Savannah replied as her fingers danced along the marred surface of the satchel. She paused over coarse scratches and smoothed along oiled stains. "He has excellent taste."

"Had. He had excellent taste," Olivia said. "He died last year." She sighed and turned so she was leaning against the drafting table.

"I'm sorry." Savannah looked up at her apologetically. Her free hand reached out to brush against Olivia's. "Were you two close?"

Olivia entwined their fingers instinctually and watched Savannah's hand appraising the bag's surface. "He was the first person to really believe that I had a talent for this work. He encouraged me to pursue a slightly different path in college and spent long hours teaching me everything he knew. He recommended me for the job at Greater Image Design, and when he retired they promoted me to his position. He taught me the art of conflict resolution in the design space. He was always so levelheaded and soft-spoken, even with the neediest of designers or the most demanding clients. He helped me focus and breathe. He taught me to really feel the space, embrace its uniqueness, and accent those qualities in my design."

Olivia shrugged. "He was sort of like a father to me. My father died when I was younger. It was just my mom and my sister and me for the longest time. Just knowing that Albie was watching me and that he cared about my success, well, it made me confident enough to take chances. There is a little of him in every design I do, because he helped me to become who I am today."

Savannah soothed her thumb along Olivia's hand. "Well, you're fantastic at what you do. He must have been a great teacher to spot such a wonderful talent in you."

Olivia ducked her head. Compliments were usually well received by her, but coming from Savannah right now, they just felt like they were too much, too big. She didn't quite feel worthy of the praise. Maybe it was just the sincerity of the delivery that caught her off guard. "Thanks," she mumbled as she felt the reminiscence turn to sadness. This wasn't an emotion she wanted to feel right now. Not here. Not in front of Savannah. She tucked her chin and tried to still the tremble of her bottom lip as she turned away from Savannah.

"You don't have to hide from me." Savannah squeezed Olivia's hand and reached out to cup her jaw. "It's okay to be sad. I understand. You can talk to me about anything."

Olivia nodded. Her lip quivered and a few tears escaped. It had been a long time since she'd talked about Albie. Her team had stopped mentioning him to her because they said she would get this vacant, sad look and lose focus.

"It's okay." Savannah stepped closer to Olivia and caressed her cheek before pulling her into a gentle embrace. Olivia squeezed their entwined fingers and let herself sink into Savannah's hug. She stifled a sob into Savannah's neck as Savannah held her tighter. Her hands massaged up and down Olivia's back and Olivia melted into her. She sobbed quietly and let the feeling of Savannah's arms soothe her, calming the heavy tide that felt like it was crashing in Olivia's chest. She let herself get lost in that embrace.

"Thank you. I'm sorry," Olivia mumbled into the skin of Savannah's neck. She felt safe and warm here.

"Anytime. And don't be." Savannah's voice vibrated against Olivia's cheek, like a soothing rumble coated with honey.

Olivia wiped her eyes and laid her head back on Savannah's shoulder while she exhaled. She spent a moment to appreciate the feeling of being this close to her. She had envisioned it differently, a lot less tear filled. She let out an embarrassed chuckle as she rolled her eyes and pulled back. Savannah's hands slid down to her waist. "I must be a soggy mess right now."

Savannah smiled and leaned back. "You look beautiful."

Touched by the sincerity, Olivia found herself leaning forward, placing a soft, lingering kiss at the edge of Savannah's lips. She felt Savannah's breath on her face. Savannah's hands tightened slightly at her waist.

"Thank you," she breathed out as she kissed the same spot again, this time leaving her lips on Savannah's cheek.

Savannah turned her head and connected their lips as she pulled their hips closer.

Their lips moved against each other's slowly before Olivia sucked Savannah's bottom lip between hers and ran her tongue over it. Savannah's mouth opened, and what started as a soft, gentle kiss progressed into something much more as Olivia leaned back against the drafting table and pulled Savannah with her.

A soft chuckle escaped Savannah's lips as her grip on Olivia's hips got even tighter. She nudged Olivia to sit on the drafting table while she stepped between her legs. Savannah broke the kiss as she moved to Olivia's neck. She licked and sucked the soft skin below her jaw as her hands moved from Olivia's hips to her waist. Her thumbs slipped under the sweat-damp silk of Olivia's blouse and teased along the soft skin of her abdomen.

Olivia let out a pleased moan as she reclined on the table and spread her legs farther. She loved the hungry look in Savannah's eyes when she stepped closer, filling the space with her body. When Savannah's belt buckle pressed firmly against her crotch, she moaned again, but this time not from anticipation. This time it was from stimulation.

Savannah's mouth covered hers and soon Olivia found herself wrapping her legs around Savannah's hips and her arm around Savannah's neck, pulling her closer still. She rolled her hips ever so slightly and felt a wave of pleasure echo through her. The friction felt incredible.

"You are so hot," Savannah husked against Olivia's lips. She cradled the side of Olivia's neck and Olivia felt a drop of sweat bead its way from her hairline to her chest. She hadn't realized how hot it had gotten. She had gotten so caught up in the moment and the kissing that the excessive heat in the room had been momentarily forgotten.

"Sweltering," Olivia nearly moaned.

Savannah nodded. "I actually meant that your mouth and your body and your noises are hot, as in sexy, but I realize that it's like a million degrees in here and if we keep this up I will have you stripped naked and pinned to this fucking drafting table in like five seconds unless we leave."

Olivia contemplated this statement for a moment too long. Savannah's hand pressed against Olivia's chest and pushed her flat onto the table. A surprised gasp squeaked out of Olivia as Savannah pushed her silk shirt up to her chest, exposing her abdomen.

Savannah leaned down and pressed wet kisses below the bunched-up shirt as she made her way down toward the waist of Olivia's pants. She paused at Olivia's navel and circled it with her tongue. Olivia wrapped her hand around the back of Savannah's neck to keep her there. She felt Savannah grin against the soft flesh and move a few inches lower before she playfully bit the skin just above the button of Olivia's pants.

"Fuck." Olivia groaned and resisted the urge to lift her hips off the table as Savannah looked up at her with a mischievous glint.

"I'm hungry." Savannah opened her mouth and lowered her lips to the skin below her once again. And Olivia felt like she was going to explode, or burn up, or both when Savannah's tongue licked downward.

Before she knew what was happening, Savannah had her pulled back up to a sitting position and had pressed a blistering kiss to her lips. After a moment she gave her a cheeky grin and said, "Let's go eat."

Olivia was breathless and frustrated as Savannah helped her off the table. She was all kinds of tingly and wet in all the best and worst ways. The room was so hot she could see steam shadows coming off the windows behind them, but she doubted the temperature in the room was making her feel on fire right now. No, that was all the doing of the mischievous, smug-looking woman who held open the door to the design space for her. Lunch was the last thing on Olivia's mind as Savannah's hand settled on her ass when she walked by.

CHAPTER SEVENTEEN

It was significantly cooler outside the suffocating design space, but the Arizona heat was still making its presence known. Most of the local area businesses were without electricity, but Savannah found a deli not far from the design site that was running on an emergency generator. They ordered salads and large iced teas, and being the sole patrons, they got the prime seating in the shade behind the restaurant under some solar-powered fans with blades in the shape of large banana leaves. The building was painted in bright turquoise and orange, and looked almost Caribbean in the hot Phoenix sun.

Savannah moved the mandarin slice around her salad and dipped it in dressing before she slipped it between her lips. She caught Olivia watching her intently as she chewed and smiled through the motion. "So, tell me about your family. You have a sister?"

Olivia nodded and leaned back. "I have an older sister, Christine. She lives out in Pennsylvania, a few miles from my mother."

Savannah took another small bite of her lunch. "Is that where you're from? Pennsylvania?"

"Yeah, I grew up a little outside of Philadelphia, in a small town."

"Have you been in New York long?" Savannah watched as Olivia shooed away a fly from her salad. She moved a tomato around the plate like it was a toy before she finally forked the food and ate it.

"I went to school there and stayed there afterward. I've been a New Yorker for about ten years, I guess." She shrugged. "I like it. I feel like it suits me."

Savannah could envision Olivia cruising the busy sidewalks, seamlessly melting into the crowds, and hailing cabs like a pro.

"What about you?" Olivia tilted her head as she waited for Savannah's answer.

"I grew up in Southern California and I went to school out there before I finally ended up in Chicago." She didn't elaborate. The rest of the story wasn't very good.

Olivia frowned. "Any siblings? Do your parents live in California still?"

Savannah watched Olivia's frown deepen as she paused. Rarely did anyone inquire about her past life, so she rarely addressed it. "My mother left just after I was born and my father remarried a lot. I'm an only child, but I have four half siblings from three different women. We're not close. I haven't exchanged more than an email with any of them in months." Savannah shrugged. It was all she had known. If not for Cooper, she'd consider herself an orphan. "I am close to my youngest little brother, Cooper. He lives in Chicago. We see each other often."

"And your father? Do you talk to him?"

Olivia's questions were innocent. Savannah didn't love talking about her father, but she didn't want to keep anything from Olivia either. She felt her smile falter as she considered this question. "We don't talk. I've always been sort of…baggage in his quest to find a pretty, wealthy woman to live off of. Our relationship was always a little tense. When I was old enough to strike out on my own, I did. I probably talk to him on the phone three times a year, around holidays—that's about it. I haven't seen him in about a year, since he dropped Cooper off at school."

Savannah watched Olivia frown again as she mulled over this new information. She felt the need to clarify. "It's okay. I'm a firm believer that you can make your own family. Cooper and I get together for meals and hang out a lot. I'm grateful for him."

Olivia seemed to accept that. "I've always had a pretty good relationship with my mom and sister. We have a relatively small extended family, so it was always the Three Musketeers doing things together."

Savannah teased. "And which Musketeer were you?"

"Well, I was the youngest and a little troublesome, so of the true Musketeers, I was usually Aramis. But there's a lot of D'Artagnan in there as well." She laughed. "You know, I've never told anyone that story before."

"Not even Reagan?" Savannah hadn't meant to say that out loud.

Olivia raised an eyebrow at her. "Not even Reagan."

Savannah didn't want to talk about Reagan. She changed the topic. "And your family, they were okay with you dating women?" She was careful to walk this line gingerly. Even in the calmest of people, this line of questioning sometimes provoked chaos.

Olivia brushed a loose curl out of her face and tucked it behind her ear. She seemed completely unfazed. "Yeah, actually, I brought my first girlfriend home in high school. My mother didn't even blink. My sister had a harder time adjusting, but mainly because she thought I was going through some phase. She came around quickly, though." Olivia shrugged. "What about you? Did your father mind?"

Savannah tilted her head. "Well, I never really asked anyone's permission. I just sort of saw what I liked and went for it."

"Oh, yeah? Is that a trait of yours? Seeing what you like and pursuing it?" Olivia was flirting with her.

"I've been known to capitalize on an opportunity if it suits my fancy, yes."

Olivia vibrated with laughter and leaned back in her chair. Her expression was blissful. Savannah wanted to know what was going on in that beautiful mind.

"What are you thinking about?"

"I was just thinking that I'm very comfortable with you. Like this is a usual occurrence, sitting outside under a fan in a heat wave talking about my life."

"Yeah, I know what you mean." Savannah had felt from the moment she'd met Olivia back in New York that they had been old friends in a past life or something. She'd immediately felt a connection with Olivia. And she knew it was more than physical. But she wasn't ready to think about that just yet.

They spent a moment watching each other. Savannah felt like an easy calm was settling between them. The quiet felt nice.

Olivia crossed her legs and her expression changed. "I made a promise to myself on my run this morning that I was going to clear things up between us. But then there was kissing and groping and I got a little sidetracked."

Savannah wasn't sure where this was going.

Olivia continued, "I want to talk about earlier."

Savannah raised her eyebrow. "Which part about earlier? The part when I caught you watching me? Or the part when you were moaning on the drafting table?"

Olivia gaped at Savannah's reply. "Well, you don't mince words, do you?"

"We talked about how I pursue things I desire. So, no, I don't."

There was a blatant shift in their interaction—Savannah could feel it in the air.

She spoke first. "I liked that, earlier I mean. When you were watching me and when you were under me. Both times were enjoyable for me. So thanks."

Olivia fidgeted in her seat and Savannah loved it.

"Stop distracting me with your sex voice."

Savannah laughed. "My what?"

"You heard me." Olivia shook her head and crossed her arms.

"How would you know what my sex voice is? We haven't even crossed that delicious bridge yet." She licked her lips deliberately before she sipped her drink through the straw again.

"Jesus. See? That's exactly what I'm talking about." Olivia breathed out and looked away. A thought seemed to occur to her and when she turned back to face Savannah, her expression was taunting. "Well, that's not entirely true, is it? I mean, I seem to remember hearing all sorts of interesting things in that voice just a few weeks ago."

Savannah released the straw from her lips. "I remember that, too." She leaned forward and motioned Olivia to do the same. When Olivia shifted and leaned in, Savannah closed the distance and licked the shell of Olivia's ear. "That was on the phone. Imagine what it's like in person."

Olivia cursed as Savannah's lips made contact with her ear. She slumped back into her seat in defeat.

Savannah smiled. "You were saying?"

"I hate you." Olivia growled and pouted. "You're some kind of sex monster. I know it."

"Okay, okay. I'll behave. You were saying something about earlier…" She nodded in encouragement for Olivia to pick up where she'd left off.

Olivia narrowed her eyes as she asked, "What are we doing?"

"Well, at this exact moment we're having lunch."

"*Savannah*," Olivia whined as she rested her elbows on the table and let her head fall into her hands.

When Savannah didn't say anything, Olivia picked up her head and looked across the table. Savannah considered dodging the question but she decided against it. This felt like one of those turning point conversations where everything could and would change depending on what was discussed. She had been happily avoiding the truth for some time now, but after this morning, she knew there wasn't much time left for that.

She nodded and spoke softly, as if using a normal volume would drain the meaning out of the words. "I like you. And I want to experience all sorts of things with you. But I'm not sure how to make that happen considering our circumstances, and that makes me sad and frustrated and confused."

Without saying a word, Olivia stood from her chair and walked to Savannah's side of the table. She put her hands on the armrests of Savannah's chair and pushed her away from the table before she lowered herself onto Savannah's lap.

Savannah smiled and leaned back as Olivia looped her arms around her neck. "I like you, too. And I care less about the details, so let's worry about that later, okay? Because all I can think about right now is how much I want to kiss you."

Savannah beamed and connected her lips to Olivia's. She ran a hand up and down Olivia's back as the other lay across her thighs. A soft moan escaped when Olivia licked at her bottom lip and requested entrance. Savannah opened her mouth and tilted her head to deepen the kiss. Kissing Olivia was quickly becoming Savannah's favorite pastime. Savannah felt her heartbeat ramp up at the feeling of Olivia in her lap. She loved Olivia's weight on her legs, and her arms around her neck. Then there was the sensation of Olivia's lips kissing along her jaw—it was titillating. But more than anything, though, the soft little pants coming from Olivia's mouth drove her crazy. Her hands wandered, one under Olivia's shirt and the other tracing lazy patterns on her thighs. Both moved higher with each kiss.

"Savannah," Olivia murmured into Savannah's lips once she made her way from sucking at Savannah's jaw. "You're the best kisser ever."

She whimpered when Savannah took her bottom lip between her teeth and gently bit down before licking the area to soothe it.

"It's easy wanting to kiss you. Those lips, Liv. You have the best lips." Savannah breathed against Olivia's mouth. She sucked each of Olivia's lips between hers and savored the fullness of them. Just as Savannah's hand crept a little higher up Olivia's shirt, a soft buzzing in Olivia's pocket drew Savannah's attention and broke the impromptu make-out session.

"Ignore it." Olivia leaned back in and pressed a searing kiss to Savannah's lips.

Olivia's hand closed over hers and pulled her palm up to her bra. Savannah groaned at the feeling of Olivia's full breast in her palm and Olivia's tongue in her mouth. She massaged the tissue and felt Olivia's nipple pebble under her palm. She circled it with her thumb and Olivia shifted in her lap, pressing her lips harder against Savannah's. Her kisses were getting more and more aggressive.

Savannah cupped Olivia's breast through her shirt once more before she rolled Olivia's nipple between her thumb and forefinger. She kissed her back and dominated Olivia's tongue as she teased with her fingers. This was escalating too quickly. How was it that she kept finding herself in these situations with Olivia? Too turned on to think clearly and too wet to deny her attraction.

She slowed the kiss and nuzzled Olivia's nose before she breathed against her lips in short, staggered breaths. "Baby, we need to slow this down or we're gonna make a scene."

Olivia's lips were kiss-plump and red when she pulled back. Savannah regretted putting a stop to their make-out session but Olivia nodded and frowned. She knew it was the right decision. It still sucked, though.

"One could argue we already did." Olivia leaned forward and tucked her head against Savannah's neck.

It was oppressively hot, even under the fan, but Savannah couldn't care less. She would have kissed Olivia until the sun went down if she could. Granted, she doubted they would just keep kissing, at the rate her heart was thumping out of her chest. No, she was right to stop them.

"I know." Savannah pressed a featherlight kiss to Olivia's forehead before reclining her head onto the back of the chair. She closed her eyes and let her heart rate calm down. There was nothing more Savannah wanted than to feel all of Olivia under her fingers, but the timing just wasn't right. This wasn't where she wanted that to happen, not like this, in the dead heat, outside in the open. No, she wanted Olivia all to herself and with significantly less clothes involved. "If we let this happen, we need to be careful. We need to take things slow and keep it between us."

She felt Olivia sit up in her arms. She was quiet and Savannah worried that maybe she'd said something wrong. She was about to open her eyes when she felt Olivia's lips brush against hers.

"Okay. I want that. I want this to happen. I want you."

Savannah opened her eyes to find Olivia watching her expectantly.

"We have to take this slow, though, Liv. I mean that. I want this to work, I do. I want you, too, but it's got to be slow."

Olivia nodded in agreement. She kissed Savannah once more before she untangled herself from her lap. She stood and extended her hand to pull Savannah up with her.

The impish smile on Olivia's lips brought a soft chuckle from Savannah. "What are you smiling about, beautiful?"

"Oh, nothing," Olivia teased. "It's just that you called me *baby* earlier, that's all."

Savannah entwined her fingers with Olivia's as they walked away from the table and disposed of their trash. "You're right. I did."

As they walked toward the parking lot, Olivia stopped and turned to her. "So, when you say we should take it *slow*…like, how slow do you mean? Because I have to be honest with you—there's been lots of not so slow stuff happening between us and I'm about ready to bust. Like, all the time. I'm always *right there* and it's making me a little crazy."

"Always?" Savannah knew what she meant.

"Pretty much." Olivia nodded. "So just putting that out there."

"Message received."

"Great." Olivia smiled and Savannah was grateful they were on the same page.

CHAPTER EIGHTEEN

The heat subsided as night approached even though it was still predicted to be close to a hundred around noon the following day, but at least the power was back on in some areas. Savannah insisted on taking Olivia out to dinner that night, and although it took them a while to find a county with electricity, they did eventually find one about forty-five minutes from the hotel. Olivia felt like the drive gave them a chance to get a little more acquainted without the physical distractions they kept seeming to run into.

"Favorite movie from your childhood?" Savannah stroked her thumb along Olivia's hand. She'd reached across the console and taken Olivia's hand after the first five minutes of driving. Olivia loved it.

"*Goonies.*"

"*Goonies*?" Savannah sounded skeptical.

"Yes, and before you criticize that decision, know that I will judge you forever for not liking an underdog story about precocious teenagers trying to save their town and their families by participating in the ultimate adventure—"

"Of finding a hidden pirate ship with treasure." Savannah nodded seriously.

"Exactly." Good. They were on the same page. "What about you?"

"My favorite movie, or my favorite movie from my childhood?" Savannah tickled Olivia's palm before resuming the gentle stroking from before.

"Both." Olivia wanted to know all the things. All. The. Things.

"Um, as a little kid, I loved, loved, loved *Pippi Longstocking.*" Savannah looked shy in her response.

"Pippi was legit. Excellent choice." Olivia was totally on board with this. "Any particular reason? I mean, aside from the awesomely badass female heroine aspect and all."

"She was a redhead," Savannah replied simply.

Olivia wasn't sure what that had to do with anything. "Okay?"

Savannah laughed and looked over at her. Her gray-blue eyes shone as she said, "There weren't a lot of red-haired characters that got leading roles or decent characterization when I was a kid. I don't think I would have phrased it that way if you'd asked me at the time, but I probably would have told you that I liked her independence and cool style. She was the adventurous and fearless daughter of a buccaneer captain and she had really awesome red hair."

"Like you." Olivia squeezed Savannah's hand.

"Well, duh." Savannah flicked on the blinker and they pulled into the parking lot of a quiet little restaurant not far from the highway ramp.

"Okay, and your favorite adult movie?"

Savannah didn't hesitate for a second. "*Clue.*"

"As in you'll give me a clue?" Olivia was lost.

Savannah scoffed. "Tell me you're joking."

"I'm joking." She wasn't.

"Good. I was really—" Savannah put the car in park and gaped at her. "Wait. You really don't know what I'm talking about, do you?"

"Not a clue."

Savannah gave her a look. "Not funny."

"Really? I thought it was pretty perfect." Olivia pulled Savannah's hand up to her lips and kissed her knuckles. "Okay, clue me in…"

"You're the worst." Savannah sighed and pulled her hand away, substituting her knuckles with her lips. "But you're gorgeous and funny, so I'll let it slide."

"You're too good to me." Olivia savored the kiss before she exited the car and rejoined their hands. "But you'll tell me about the movie at some point, right? I don't want to be clueless forever."

"You're dead to me." Savannah shook her head and held the door open for Olivia to enter the restaurant, wrapping her arms around Olivia's waist as they stepped through, laughing together.

All throughout dinner, Olivia was taken by how attentive Savannah was. And sweet. Savannah was very, very sweet. It wasn't that she hadn't anticipated her to be—just Savannah was so controlled and serious at work, she hadn't thought about what it would be like to date her. Truthfully, she'd spent more time dreaming about fucking her and being fucked by her than thinking about dating her. But she never thought either would come to fruition. And here she was, on an actual date with her. She was still holding out hope for the sex part, but the dating part was plenty exciting all by itself. It felt too good to be true. She smiled at every word Savannah uttered. She felt like she could listen to that soft, husky voice all day long and never get bored.

They were sharing an appetizer and wine when Olivia's phone began buzzing again, much like earlier. She pushed it aside until it buzzed again a few minutes later, this time more insistently, refusing to be ignored. Olivia opened her purse to make sure it wasn't an emergency and apologized to Savannah for the interruption. Savannah seemed unfazed and motioned for Olivia to answer it.

Olivia looked down at the screen and immediately felt an annoyed wave roll through her. It was Reagan. She had called five times in the last forty-five minutes. Reagan was a woman of few words via the phone, favoring a text to a phone call. A phone call meant one of two things usually: she was drunk and feeling chatty, or she was drunk and locked herself out of her room/apartment/whatever. It wasn't uncommon for Olivia to be on the receiving end of some drunken rant from Reagan. It *was* uncommon for her to ignore it. Which she considered. Seriously. Instead she texted a quick reply telling her she was out to dinner…and immediately hated herself for it. That was more information than she had wanted to share. She didn't have a problem with Reagan knowing something was going on with Savannah, but she'd intended to wait until she had an idea of just how serious things were. Or how casual things were. That was still to be determined.

"Everything okay?" Savannah quirked an eyebrow as the waiter placed their entrees on the table.

Olivia frowned. "Yeah, it's fine. It was Reagan. Sorry."

"It's not a problem. Really. I'm not like that," Savannah assured her.

"That may be the case, and I'm glad it is, but still, it's rude. I don't want to be checking my phone when I'm on a date with a beautiful woman." Olivia tried to ward off the angry feelings she was having toward Reagan and her terrible timing, again, but it was a struggle.

The waiter placed their entrees down and Olivia's stomach growled. She didn't realize how hungry she was. "This looks amazing."

"Agreed." Savannah thanked the waiter and began cutting her food.

Olivia tasted her pasta and let out a soft moan of appreciation. "This is so good. Like, super good."

Savannah laughed.

"What?"

"Nothing. You're all kinds of adorable right now." She forked a piece of her dinner and held it out to Olivia. "Would you like to try mine?"

Olivia leaned forward to taste Savannah's bite. Savannah used the flat part of the utensil to catch a little sauce threatening to drip down Olivia's chin and brought it to her lips while she waited for Olivia's opinion. "Ooh, that's good too."

Savannah chuckled and accepted Olivia's offer to try hers. "That is good."

"I know, right?"

"Splitsies?" Savannah offered and Olivia was in love.

"You read my mind." This woman was perfect. It was decided.

By the time dessert came to the table, Olivia had mustered up enough courage to ask Savannah about her dating history. "So, I'm pretty thrilled about it, but why are you single?" She paused. She'd just assumed Savannah was single, but what if she wasn't? "You *are* single, right?"

Savannah choked on her water. She cleared her throat in a light cough and she nodded. "Yes, I'm currently single. You can relax."

Olivia let out a nervous sigh. She forked the key lime pie in front of her, more to occupy her hands than anything else. "Good. Me, too."

"That's makes all the kissing less complicated, doesn't it?" Savannah sipped her water.

"Seriously though, why are you single? You're the complete package. Is there something I should know? Are you a serial killer?" She figured it was a little late in the game to get that last bit of intel, but she had to try.

"If one was a serial killer, would one answer that honestly?"

Savannah made a valid point.

Olivia pouted. "That sounds like something a serial killer would say."

Savannah reached her hand out to graze her fingers along Olivia's cheek before she tapped her protruding lip. "I'm not a serial killer. And I don't know anything about this complete package you're talking about, but I like to think I'm a pretty decent partner." She pulled her hand back and brought a piece of dessert to her mouth.

Olivia scoffed. "Really? Are you being modest? Or do you have no idea?"

Savannah raised her eyebrows in confusion.

"Okay, I'll break it down for you. You're gorgeous, I mean like unbelievably attractive. And you have excellent taste—I love your dress, by the way. You're, like, the most efficient person I have ever met. Your eyes are this hypnotizing stormy blue and that voice...don't even get me started. And you play the piano like some magical, musical unicorn. Are you even for real?" She looked around playfully. "Maybe you should pinch me so I know I'm not hallucinating that you are actually taking me to dinner, because this dream would suck to wake up from."

Savannah scrunched her nose and shook her head. "This is not a dream. And I am not a unicorn. There are plenty of things about me that are not as wonderful as you might think. I promise you." She took Olivia's hand in hers and squeezed it lightly before she fed the last bite of key lime to Olivia.

Olivia didn't believe her for a second. She gave her a skeptical look while she chewed.

"I was in a serious, long-term relationship a few years ago that ended badly." Savannah looked off into the distance, her expression sad. "I was lost for a while. I spent a long time trying to figure out what went wrong and if I could have done more. Eventually, I realized that it had less to do with me and more to do with her and her needs that couldn't be met by me. But that took a long time to learn. I beat myself up about it and dragged some bad habits and baggage into my next relationships. They all suffered a similar fate because of it."

"What happened the first time?"

Savannah paused. "She cheated on me. And then she left. She just packed up and walked out of my life like we hadn't been together for almost a decade."

"Savannah." Olivia squeezed their joined hands. "I'm so sorry."

A soft sigh escaped Savannah's lips and Olivia noticed she looked everywhere but her face.

Olivia considered her next question carefully. She didn't want to push Savannah too far, but she wanted to know what she was getting into. "And the last relationships? What about them?"

Savannah leaned back a little. "Gwen broke my heart. I think for a while that ruined my sense of stability. It hardened me in a way I wasn't expecting. I didn't give all of myself away again, not for a long time.

I think I was subconsciously trying to protect myself, so I never let things get too serious. I think I was afraid of planting roots."

"Is that how you are? Do you flee?" Olivia was a roots person—they'd already discussed that. This information bothered her. She knew her attraction to Savannah was far beyond physical and bordering on something else. She traced her thumb along the back of Savannah's hand to encourage her to answer and to keep herself from letting go.

"No. My nature is not to run. I want a house and a family and a dog and PTA meetings. I always wanted what I never had growing up, stability and affection and a home. I think I took the breakup with Gwen so hard because it felt like I was destined to be alone forever. A traveling nomad as it were, like I was in my youth. My father bounced from wife to wife with me as his unfortunate baggage." She paused. "I don't want that life, though. I do want to plant roots somewhere. I'm not hard or cold or distant, but sometimes I forget that. Sometimes it's easier to be something you're not."

Olivia nodded. She could understand that. It made perfect sense to her. "You're not though—cold, I mean. You're sweet and thoughtful and caring. And in the small amount of time I've known you, you have been nothing but warm and welcoming. I always feel so important when I'm around you, like you care what I have to say. You're so attentive to my movements and my words. It's like there is no one else around, even in a crowded room. I feel special around you." Olivia ducked her head to catch Savannah's eyes. "I like you. All of you. And I want the good and the bad. I'm sorry you were hurt. But I'm here to listen if you ever want to talk about it, or, umm, not talk about it. And I will kiss it better, I promise." Savannah rewarded her with a hearty laugh. It was a nice reprieve from some of the tension that had formed.

"Olivia Dawson, you are something else." Savannah leaned across the table and pressed a soft, lingering kiss to Olivia's lips before she settled back in her seat. "So, cat's out of the bag on my less than spectacular dating history. What about you? How is someone like you not married with a family yet?"

"Well, New York can be a hard town to date in. I've had my fair share of dating nightmares, but I haven't really had the opportunity to meet someone I felt a real connection with. The longest relationship I've been in was about a year, and that was dysfunctional, at best. I seem to only find someone I can stand for a few months before I need a change." She paused. Gosh, that made her sound awfully fickle. "That sounded bad. I mean, it's true, but, I—" She took a breath. "I want a family and a house and a fish tank and vacations at the beach and inside jokes and…I just haven't found the right person."

Savannah laughed. "I get it."

"I like this." Olivia motioned between them. "I like the taking it slow approach. It's nice. Don't get me wrong, I really, really want to not take it slow with you, like, *really*, but I appreciate getting to know you and the romantic aspect of it. Maybe that's what I've been missing all along."

"Agreed." Savannah finished her glass of wine. "And just so you know, I really, really want to not take it slow, too."

Olivia basked in the new information. She was definitely falling for Savannah Quinn. There was no avoiding it.

CHAPTER NINETEEN

A nnabelle's voice over the speakerphone read faxes aloud for Savannah to hear as Savannah anxiously tapped her foot. For whatever reason, her email had been down since before her date with Olivia the other night. She wasn't receiving the emailed copy of any of the faxes from corporate, and she was losing her patience with her boss, who was no help whatsoever.

Savannah sighed. "Thanks, Annabelle."

"Sure thing, Savannah. Need anything else?"

"No, no, that's fine. Can you put me through to Mr. Dodd?"

"You got it."

"Bye, Annabelle. Thanks again."

A booming laugh came across the line. "Savannah! How are things in…wait, where are you these days?"

"Phoenix. And things are fine. Well, sort of, the email's down again."

"Oh, yes, yes, Phoenix, right." He was unfazed by her obvious irritation. "I'll let my admin know to contact IT and look into the problem. So, what's new with you?"

Savannah sighed. She didn't want to make small talk with him. She wanted him to fix the goddamn problem so she could wrap up this project. The process had been bumpier than the Denver site. She only had two more days to finalize the space before Olivia and her team started to break apart. They were under a crunch, and she needed her email to be working, now.

"Not much, Ken. Just trying to wrap up these deadlines." She paused, deciding to take this opportunity to bend his ear about their progress. "I sent over the midterm review of this installation with some extra information before the email server went down. There have been a lot of obstacles along the way, but the Greater Image Design team has been truly incredible."

"Indeed, indeed. I'll make sure the forms get to the correct people." He sounded like his attention was elsewhere. Like on another planet, like he usually seemed to be.

"Thanks, Ke—"

"You know, Savannah, I think you ought to take some time for yourself." He bowled through her and offered his unsolicited advice. "I know we worked out a deal to give the crew from Greater Image Design some time off afterward at that hotel and spa we partner with, and I think you should take a few days there, too."

Savannah's brow creased. She hadn't considered this, mostly because it hadn't been offered to her. She'd heard rumblings that some of the team were taking an immediate break, but she wasn't sure about the others. Savannah had assumed she would just fly back to Chicago to prepare for the next project. She hoped to iron out some details so it would be less stressful than this installation had been.

"Savannah, are you there?"

She shook her head. "Sorry."

"I mean it. Take a few days to yourself before you fly back, okay?"

Savannah considered it for a moment. "Okay, I'll think about it."

"Great. See you when you get back." Ken disconnected the line before she had a chance to say good-bye.

She pulled up her calendar. If she got creative, she could move some appointments and reschedule a few conference calls. She'd left a little void in her schedule in case the project ran long. They were on pace to finish on schedule. They were ahead by half a day, which she still couldn't believe considering how many issues they'd had. She redialed Annabelle and set the plans into motion. The idea of some time off was exciting.

She leaned back in her seat and looked over the drafting table at the view before her as she waited for the morning crew to arrive. Thoughts of Olivia danced around her head. Yesterday had been an eventful day for them. It'd started with the little make-out session in the design space, then lunch with more kissing, then dinner with a side of kissing and groping. She let out a contented sigh as she remembered the way Olivia's lips felt on her own. She had savored the taste of Olivia's mouth and the cute little pout she made when she didn't get her way. It was all too adorable to ignore.

She pulled out her phone and texted Olivia a quick good

morning message before she approached the builders. Today was the installation of the solar panels. All the partitions were constructed, the lighting fixtures installed, and after this, the only thing left was to test the electronics and furnish the space with furniture and plant life. Savannah was excited to wrap up this project, but she realized that completion would also decrease the amount of time she would be able to spend with Olivia. The thought settled heavily in her chest—she had a hard time envisioning her days without Olivia in them. She could feel herself growing attached and that scared her. Although they had agreed to *casually* date, it was only a matter of time before it became something more, or fizzled out to something much less. Either of those conclusions was overwhelming to her in that moment. She stood and straightened her skirt. Those thoughts would wait for another time.

After a productive meeting with the site crew, Savannah glanced up at her reflection in the bathroom mirror. She clipped her hair up off her neck and turned on the water. She looked tired. She could see her fatigue at the edges of her eyes today. She closed them and let the warm water trickle down her fingers from the tap.

"Hey." Soft lips breathed into Savannah's ear as she washed her hands at the sink. A warmth settled in her chest. Olivia was exactly the person she wanted to see right now.

She smiled and kept her eyes closed as she leaned back a bit into Olivia. She tilted her neck to allow Olivia better access to the skin below her ear. "Hey."

Olivia hummed against her neck and dragged her lips down slowly before tracing lazy patterns with her tongue. "You seem tired. Something been keeping you up?"

"It's been tricky sleeping." Savannah let her head fall back as she focused on Olivia's mouth. She was being truthful. She'd been waking up to steamy dreams involving the succubus attached to her neck at this very moment. Their dinner earlier in the week had only intensified her feelings. They'd been dancing around each other the past few days. Olivia's team had divided so only the designers and Savannah were left in the work space. It was easier for her to sneak away and have little private lunch meetings with Olivia, but their evenings were still busy with tying up the loose ends. Tomorrow was the launch to the representatives and they would be departing shortly afterward.

Savannah hadn't had the opportunity to talk with Olivia like she had hoped she would be able to.

Savannah reached out and shut off the faucet as she opened her eyes. Olivia looked great, as usual. Olivia's hands came around Savannah's waist and Olivia bit down on her neck. Savannah reached up and slid her hand into Olivia's hair. She held Olivia's mouth against her, and her clit throbbed when Olivia's tongue lavished attention on her neck. She turned her head to catch Olivia's lips and let Olivia lead for a moment or two.

"This is a hello I could get used to." Olivia nipped at her lips as she turned in her arms.

"Me, too." She sucked on Olivia's tongue for a moment before she pulled back and took the opportunity to trace the perfect lines of Olivia's face. She brushed back a few rogue curls from Olivia's forehead and decided to ask the question that had been on her mind all morning, since her call with Ken. "What are your plans for next week?"

"I'm going to take advantage of the offered trip and stick around for a while." Her voice was soft. Almost contemplative. "What about you?"

Savannah tightened her arms around Olivia's waist and rubbed her thumbs along Olivia's back. "I was thinking the view around here was rather nice." Her gaze trailed up and down Olivia's front before fixing back on the bright eyes in front of her. "So I'm going to soak it up a little longer."

"I like the idea of getting to spend some quality time together. You know, maybe enjoy the, uh, sights." Olivia's lilt hinted to anything but that.

"I can't think of a better way to spend a vacation." She meant that.

The sound of the bathroom door opening broke them apart as a construction worker shuffled into the stall behind them. Savannah smiled as Olivia kissed her quickly before she slipped back out into the design space. She let out a contented sigh and saw her happier, much more awake self reflected in the mirror before her. It was just another day or two until she could relax and maybe get Olivia alone, for some uninterrupted getting to know you time. Her smile broadened as she stepped back out to work, feeling newly invigorated to wrap this project up.

CHAPTER TWENTY

So, tell me everything." Olivia could hear the smile on her sister's face.

She snorted at the playful interrogation attempt. "There's nothing to tell, Christine."

"I don't believe you for a second. You haven't taken a vacation in forever. Obviously something or someone is involved."

Olivia ignored her sister and changed the subject. "How was Mackenzie's week?"

"She's doing great. She brought home this macaroni art project the other day that looked exactly like the Eiffel Tower. Maybe I ought to cut back on the nightly readings of the *Madeline* books—I think she's becoming obsessed with France..." Her sister trailed off. "Stop trying to distract me. Tell me it's Savannah, the hot corporate chick. You're vacationing with her, aren't you?"

Olivia made a mental note to send her niece the next four books in the series and a matching beret just to hear Christine's reaction. She decided there really wasn't any point in avoiding the topic any longer. "We're not vacationing *together*. We are on vacation in the same place and might see each other during that time. But—"

"But you're not *together*. Right. Like anyone believes that," Christine replied.

"We're dating. But we're taking it slow. So this is like an opportunity to get to know each other outside of work." Olivia chewed her bottom lip as she keyed into the hotel room at the resort. The design space had wrapped up without any problems and was unveiled, on time, to the VIPs a week ahead of schedule as planned. She had been invited to the launch party and spent the entire night shaking hands and receiving compliments on her team's work. The next morning, she'd checked out with her team, firing off a quick text to Savannah to ask her to dinner that night once they had both checked into the vacation resort. She was met with a smiley face and a *sounds good, babe* that made her inwardly swoon a little. They hadn't spoken since, and it was late afternoon by the time Olivia got to the resort. She might have lingered in the lobby looking for Savannah, hoping to see her sooner rather than later, but she didn't find her.

"Dating? That's progress. When did that come about?" She could hear her niece singing what sounded like French in the background.

Olivia shifted the bag on her arm, cradling the phone on her shoulder and as she set her suitcase against the wall. The card reader kept flashing red when she swiped her room key.

She frowned as she tried again. "Uh, a little over a week ago? I can't remember. I feel like we talked about it like a dozen times before we finally agreed. There was a lot of kissing in between conversations. It's kind of a blur."

"Kissing? Is that all?" Christine didn't pull any punches.

"So far." Olivia omitted the groping and straddling that also occurred. No reason to spill all her secrets.

"What's she like?"

"She's perfect. She's gorgeous and smart and single and perfect. She has the world's sexiest voice. Did I mention she's gorgeous?"

"Twice, actually." Christine chuckled. "Why are you grunting in frustration while you sing her praises?"

"Oh, sorry," Olivia said. "My fucking room key won't work and I have a date with her later. I kind of wanted to relax a little beforehand."

"And by *relax* you mean rub one out and take a nap, right?" Leave it to her sister...

"Jesus, Christine. Get your mind out of the gutter." Olivia grimaced, because she was thinking exactly that, but she would never admit it. Ever.

She let her forehead thump forward onto the door in frustration before she swiped her key card once more. The door unlocked and she stumbled forward, pushing the door open as she walked in. "Anyway, as I was saying, she's gor—"

Her progress into the room was halted when a hand gently landed on her arm. She looked up to find Savannah scantily clad in a tiny bikini and sporting a surprised look on her face.

"Oh, shit," was all Olivia could get out before the phone slipped off her shoulder and hit the ground. Her eyes were glued on Savannah's chest and abs, and she licked her lips reflexively.

"You were saying something?" Savannah flashed a smile, her eyebrow cocked.

Olivia just gaped. This was the least amount of clothing she had ever seen on Savannah. It was...mesmerizing.

Savannah glanced down at the dropped phone and reached to retrieve it. A tinny voice called out from the forgotten object. "Liv? Liv?"

"I think someone's looking for you." Savannah held out the phone to Olivia, nodding for her to take it.

Olivia closed her fingers around it while she continued to closely examine the smooth plane of Savannah's exposed stomach as she stuttered out, "What are you doing in here?"

Savannah cocked her head to the side and a confused look crossed her face. "It's my room." She paused and asked through a smile. "The real question is, what are *you* doing here?"

A frown settled on Olivia's face as she stepped back from Savannah, looking back into the hallway at her abandoned suitcase. She glanced at the key card envelope in her hand. The envelope was labeled *Room 475*. She looked up at the door, her eyes widening as she read the door number out loud. "457...oh."

Savannah followed Olivia's gaze between the door and the envelope and her smile broadened. "Our date isn't until later. Eager much?"

Olivia felt the blush creep up her face. She had been eager—maybe that was why she had been so distracted while talking to Christine. Oh, shit. Christine.

"Liv!" Christine's voice sounded far away.

Olivia shook her head and brought the phone back to her ear. "Sorry, Chris." Savannah waved her into the room, pulling her suitcase in from the hall and shutting the door behind her.

"I thought you died. What happened?" Christine asked.

"Um, wrong room. I gotta go." Her eyes remained focused on Savannah's body as Savannah moved toward the bed. Olivia ended the call before Christine could ask more questions.

Savannah motioned for her to sit on the bed and she complied because she didn't know what else to do. Because she couldn't contain her leering. Like a creep. She nervously ran her hands down her thighs to rest on her knees before wiggling her fingers a bit. "Um. Hi." Olivia watched Savannah close a folder on the desk to her left before turning and leaning against it, facing Olivia and wearing an amused expression, and little else. "So, do you always parade around your hotel rooms in a bathing suit or…?"

The soft chuckle from Savannah's lips made Olivia shudder. "No, you caught me about to head out for a swim."

"Oh, I'm sorry. I should go," Olivia sputtered, feeling embarrassed as she glanced over to the luggage that Savannah had dragged in for her.

"No, please. Stay." Savannah stepped away from the desk and placed a hand on Olivia's forearm as she continued, "I was just going to burn off a little excess energy before dinner, but…"

"But?" Savannah sat next to her on the bed. Olivia moved her hand to cover the one Savannah had resting on her forearm. She was always amazed at how soft Savannah's skin felt. She was always so warm. She let her fingers trace swirling patterns on the back of Savannah's hand while she waited for her answer.

"But I would be more than happy to burn off that excess energy with you, instead." Savannah's voice dipped into that danger zone as she leaned toward Olivia and brushed Olivia's hair off her shoulder, exposing her neck.

Olivia's head felt foggy as the implications of Savannah's suggestion settled low in her stomach. A warm buzz spread through her chest to her limbs as Savannah inched closer.

"And how do you propose we do that?" Olivia closed her eyes at the feeling of Savannah's breath on her neck.

"We could"—Savannah pressed a featherlight kiss to the skin below Olivia's ear—"take a walk." She moved her lips a little higher and pulled Olivia's earlobe into her mouth, sucking softly before she added, "Or we could…get wet together."

A shudder rippled through her body. She took in a deep breath as Savannah nibbled on her earlobe, tugging a bit before letting go with a wet popping noise. When she opened her eyes, she saw the lust on Savannah's face as her tongue slid along her bottom lip.

"You mean, like, go for a swim together?" Olivia decided to play along with Savannah's taunting. She had a feeling she'd be rewarded for her efforts.

Savannah traced her finger along Olivia's collar and pulled the fabric from her skin while dancing her fingertips along the flesh under her collarbone. "Of sorts, sure." Her eyes sparkled. "Either way, you are far too overdressed. Don't you agree?"

Olivia watched the fingers playing with her shirt. She nodded and tried to slow her breathing as those nimble fingers started to unbutton her blouse, painfully slowly, one button at a time.

Savannah finished unbuttoning her shirt and grasped both sides, sliding up the fabric until her hands loosely held the shirt collar. Her thumbs traced Olivia's exposed collarbone and Olivia whimpered at the touch. Savannah leaned forward and brushed her cheek along Olivia's before she whispered, "It'd be a shame to get this shirt wet, right?"

"Fuck." Olivia breathed out as Savannah's lips made contact with the shell of her ear. A breathy chuckle accompanied the gentle disrobing by skilled hands, and then the blouse was discarded by the side of the bed. Before Olivia could react to the sudden rush of cold on her newly exposed skin, Savannah had moved onto her lap, a thigh on either side of her legs. She looked down at Olivia's cleavage with a hungry stare and motioned for Olivia to scoot up the bed with a firm nod.

Olivia moved up the bed as Savannah stayed over her. She settled at the top of the bed, resting on her elbows as she looked at Savannah through her eyelashes. Her heart thumped in her chest.

"I like you, on my bed, half naked." Savannah purred as she crawled up Olivia's body, pausing when their faces were just inches apart to blow cool air across Olivia's lips.

Savannah's dark red hair was pulled into a sloppy bun. Loose strands hung along the side of her face, taunting Olivia to brush them aside. She reached forward, her left hand skimming along Savannah's hairline before pushing the errant strand behind her ear. Savannah let out a sigh and Olivia flattened her palm along Savannah's jawline, lazily stroking her thumb along Savannah's cheek.

Savannah turned her head and kissed Olivia's hand. Her tongue brushed along Olivia's palm and Olivia shuddered again. Savannah kissed the tip of each finger and asked, "Are you nervous?"

Olivia let out a slow, shaky breath as she considered the question. She wasn't exactly nervous—excited, yes, but nervous, well, maybe a little. She debated how she would express that feeling to Savannah, her concerns melting with each successive press of Savannah's lips to her skin. She wanted this. She wanted to be with Savannah. She wanted to feel Savannah's skin against hers. She wanted to taste her mouth and she wanted to feel her. Everywhere. But she was a *little* nervous. After taking in another slow, deep breath, she nodded.

Savannah pressed one final kiss to Olivia's index finger before she pressed Olivia's hand to her chest to feel the rapid beating of her heart. "I am, too."

The quiet admission and the patient look of affection from Savannah helped dissolve the remaining concerns Olivia had as she leaned forward, pressing their lips together with a smile. Savannah laughed into the kiss and pushed Olivia back to the comforter while her hand held Olivia against the increased cadence of her heart.

Savannah gently lowered herself onto Olivia, trapping Olivia's hand between them, as she carefully distributed her weight along her. They kissed quietly for a few moments, playfully nipping at each other's mouths until Savannah slid her tongue along Olivia's, deepening the kiss and increasing the continuous pulse felt against Olivia's palm.

Olivia moaned into the kiss and her hips bucked up against Savannah's involuntarily when Savannah shifted her weight. Olivia's hand slid out from between them and up into Savannah's hair, pulling it from the loosely tied bun so she could thread her fingers through the silky locks.

Savannah groaned and sucked on the skin along the column of Olivia's neck as she dragged her palm over the upper curve of Olivia's left breast, settling along her side as her thumb gently grazed the smooth satin of Olivia's bra. Olivia whined in frustration and a velvety chuckle vibrated against Olivia in response, winding that feeling in her lower abdomen just a bit tighter.

Olivia let out a contented sigh when Savannah used her knees to push Olivia's legs apart, slipping between them and settling her stomach against Olivia's jean-clad crotch with a hard roll of her hips. Savannah's pressure was everywhere and nowhere, and it was driving Olivia crazy. Her kisses were teasingly deep before she skirted away. Her hand massaged and stroked the side of Olivia's breast but didn't palm it the way Olivia was dying for her to. No, Savannah seemed very well aware of every roll, every press, every movement she made, and she deliberately denied that last little bit Olivia's body was requesting.

Olivia groaned as Savannah bit lightly over her pulse point. Savannah's hand continued to gently scratch and caress along the side of her chest, breezing a thumb over her nipple just to dance away. She rolled her hips against the seam of Olivia's pants and Olivia felt like she was going to explode if Savannah didn't touch her. If she didn't fuck her right fucking now.

"Savannah, please," she begged and pulled Savannah's hair to bring their lips together. She settled her hand on Savannah's hip, encouraging her to continue her movements.

Savannah smiled into the kiss and her previously teasing touches accelerated as she palmed over the satin of Olivia's bra again, massaging the flesh of her chest before rolling a pert nipple between her fingers. Olivia mewled and bucked her hips, rolling them harder against Savannah's stomach as her fingers scratched along Savannah's scalp and shoulders.

"You feel so good," Savannah said against Olivia's lips as her hands worked their way from Olivia's chest to her back and unclasped and discarded her bra. "Let me see you," she implored as she leaned back to appreciate Olivia's now naked torso.

Olivia warmed under the admiring gaze. She settled her hands on Savannah's thighs and smoothed up and down the skin as she let Savannah appreciate her chest for a moment. A contented sigh escaped Savannah's lips when Olivia's hands trailed up and cupped Savannah's breasts through the skimpy bikini top still clinging to her skin.

Savannah moaned at the sensation, her hands coming up to untie the bathing suit top and pulling it off before gently closing around Olivia's hands and encouraging a more forceful massage. Olivia slid one hand up from Savannah's chest to grip her neck and tug her down until Savannah's hard nipples were rubbing against hers, sending shockwaves to her lower abdomen. They kissed deeply, hands exploring each other, before Olivia's frustration won out. She hooked her thumbs under the fabric of Savannah's bikini bottoms and guided them down and off her narrow hips.

"I need to feel you. I need to touch you." Olivia grunted against Savannah's lips as she tossed the discarded scrap of fabric aside.

Savannah's hand slid along the waist of Olivia's pants before deftly unbuttoning the jeans and pulling down the zipper. "Take these off."

Olivia complied, assisting Savannah as she worked the skintight jeans off her legs, kicking them to the floor before she leaned up to kiss Savannah again. Savannah's hands settled on Olivia's, halting their attempts to remove the satiny fabric of her underwear, instead shooing them away. "Let me."

Olivia paused and swallowed, feeling suddenly vulnerable as

Savannah pressed a chaste kiss to her lips and slowly dragged the final article of clothing away from her damp sex. She felt her face flush at the soft moan Savannah let out while taking in the view in front of her. The reverence of that look made Olivia shiver and burn up at the same time.

"You're so beautiful," Savannah drawled in that soft, lusty tone as she continued to gaze affectionately at Olivia. She reached out and caressed Olivia's inner thigh before she leaned forward and kissed the flesh before her.

A soft whimper escaped from Olivia's lips as she closed her eyes and let the feeling of Savannah's warm mouth wash over her. She felt like her heart was going to explode out of her chest when Savannah's tongue slid along her sex, her nose lightly brushing against Olivia's clit and sending sharp vibrations through her core. Olivia gripped Savannah's hair, holding her against her as she continued to gently kiss and lick along Olivia's slit, winding her up tighter and tighter.

"Oh God, you feel incredible," Olivia said between panting gasps.

Savannah swirled her tongue over Olivia's clit, as her hands wandered up from Olivia's hips to palm at her breasts. She plucked and twisted Olivia's nipples as she continued to taste Olivia's arousal.

Olivia felt herself climbing quickly and arched her back on the bed, focusing on the rising pressure in her abdomen. Savannah's mouth was magical. She was officially convinced, as if she needed any further evidence of that fact given how mesmerizing it was just kissing her. She felt herself begin to tremble when Savannah suddenly paused her affections.

Olivia let out short, frantic breaths as she surveyed Savannah with confusion.

"Show me," Savannah encouraged in that low, teasing tone. "Show me how you touched yourself when you were on the phone with me."

Olivia felt a deep blush settle over her already flushed cheeks when she realized what Savannah was asking. She wanted to see Olivia masturbate. Well, then.

As if she sensed Olivia's hesitation, Savannah climbed up her body and nudged Olivia's head to the side. She leaned close and whispered, "Do you remember? Do you remember how I told you to imagine me over you? To imagine me breathing against your neck and palming your breasts? Do you remember…wanting me there?"

Every detail of that phone call came rushing back to Olivia. She nodded as she trailed one hand down her abdomen, and hovered it over her swollen clit.

"That's it, baby. Just like that, show me." Savannah looked down at Olivia's hand before she leaned forward and pressed her lips to Olivia's neck.

Olivia trembled at the sensation of Savannah kissing her neck and lowered two fingers to press against her pulsing clit. Savannah continued to work along her neck, nipping and sucking on the skin, nibbling at her earlobe as Olivia replicated the motions from that night—a night she frequently replayed in her mind.

"Tell me, Liv, are you as wet for me now as you were that night?" Savannah asked as she bit down on Olivia's earlobe. Olivia moaned and nodded as her fingers continued to work against her clit. Savannah spread her hand across Olivia's shuddering stomach and slid her hand up to massage and tease Olivia's breast. "I wanted so badly to be over you. To touch you. Licking you. That night...Liv, God, you make the sexiest noises."

"Fuck." Olivia cried out as she felt herself fly back to the precipice again. Savannah's lips on her skin, her hand working at her breast, those dirty whispered notions, it was getting to be too much for Olivia to resist. "Oh, Savannah, I..."

In a quick motion, Savannah returned her lips to Olivia's and pressed a hard kiss against her mouth as she slipped a hand between them and through Olivia's wetness to pause at her entrance.

"Yes, oh yes, please..." Olivia begged. She needed that last little bit to push her over the edge.

Olivia let out a loud moan of approval as Savannah thrust two fingers into her and began moving her fingers in and out in a steady rhythm. Olivia clenched around her and scratched down Savannah's back. Savannah pressed one last firm kiss to Olivia's lips as Olivia froze in ecstasy, her eyes squeezed shut and her body shuddering under Savannah's as her release consumed her.

Olivia collapsed against the bed as Savannah slowed her thrusts, easing her down slowly before pulling out. Savannah pressed a lingering kiss to the edge of Olivia's mouth as Olivia caught her breath and slid both her hands up to cradle Savannah's back and pull her close. She hummed happily.

"Oh, yeah?" Savannah kissed along Olivia's jaw.

"Mm-hmm. Yeah. Wow." Olivia laughed and turned her head to connect their lips in a slow, lazy kiss as she rolled to her side and slipped her leg between Savannah's.

Savannah gasped.

Olivia smiled into the kiss and nipped at Savannah's lip before she pushed Savannah onto her back and climbed over her. "Oh, yeah?" she parroted.

"Mm-hmm. Yes, absolutely." Savannah's laugh was stifled by a moan as Olivia pressed into her again.

Olivia danced her hand down Savannah's abdomen as she said, "Now about that excess energy…"

❖

Olivia stretched out on the bed and let her muscles adjust as she rolled to her side, her gaze falling on the soft curve of Savannah's back. Her bottom half was covered with a sheet as she propped herself up on her elbows and scanned through her tablet.

"What're you doing?" Olivia asked.

Savannah let out a happy sigh as Olivia's fingers walked up her spine. She pushed the tablet aside and tilted her head to look at Olivia on the pillow next to her. "Nothing. Well, looking at work stuff."

"You know the rule, no work this week," Olivia chastised while she scratched the skin on Savannah's back, making soothing circles as she scooted a little closer.

They hadn't made it to dinner that first night, or breakfast the next morning. After Olivia had accidently stumbled into Savannah's room, she hadn't bothered to leave. Her suitcase and belongings mingled with Savannah's in the comfortably large suite. There had been multiple instances in which one of them almost scandalized the poor guy delivering room service. By the week's end they had emerged long enough to hit up the pool twice, grab dinner at the bar, take in one quick tour of the city, and ignore all emails, texts, and calls that weren't of an urgent nature. Every moment she had spent with Savannah had been wonderful, but she thought that these quiet moments were her favorites.

"I know. I was just trying to figure out the accommodations for Chicago."

"Hmm?" Olivia shifted in the bed and pulled back the sheet, scooting under it to lay her front against Savannah's naked back. She pressed soft kisses to Savannah's shoulders and sucked on the skin as Savannah's voice vibrated against her lips.

"I live in Chicago. So there isn't really any point in booking a hotel room for me. I'm sort of struggling with room arrangements."

"I don't follow. What's the problem?" Olivia mumbled into the warm skin at the base of Savannah's neck.

Savannah let out a slow breath before she turned under Olivia and linked their hands together. She kissed Olivia and added, "Well, I was kind of hoping I would see more of you than just at the work site. And not staying in the same hotel with you made me sort of sad, I guess."

Olivia frowned as she realized why Savannah seemed so focused on the tablet before. Savannah had to plan out the details for the next installation; those details included all the other people they had blissfully forgotten over the past few days. Olivia had gotten so used to waking up in Savannah's arms that she'd almost forgotten that outside of this week, she might be expected to sleep alone. She wasn't sure she was ready to resume normal life again, and the prospect of booking a room without Savannah in it was extremely unappealing in this moment. "Oh, I see."

"Yeah."

"Well…" Olivia considered her next question carefully. She didn't want to scare Savannah off, but at the same time, she needed some clarification to understand where this thing between them was going. "We're dating, right?"

"Yes, we are." Savannah raised her eyebrow as she waited to see what Olivia would say next.

"Well then, since that makes you my girlfriend, I want to spend as many of my nights with you as I possibly can."

"Mm-hmm, I like your thought process, girlfriend. Please, continue." Savannah pressed soft kisses along Olivia's neck.

"Savannah. That's distracting," Olivia deadpanned and pulled her neck away from the warm lips currently sucking it.

"Sorry."

"You're not."

"I'm not," Savannah agreed.

Olivia laughed. But she knew they needed to talk. Really talk. "So we're really doing this, huh?"

Savannah seemed to consider this. "We are."

"And we're on the same page still, right?" As the final installation loomed, Olivia was acutely aware that their blissful bubble from this past week had popped. Their relationship had an expiration date—or, she hoped, maybe it didn't. It had occurred to her more than once that if Greater Image Design secured the long-term contract with New

Horizons after this last trial, then she and Savannah might be able to see each other in both a personal and professional capacity. She could dream, anyway.

Savannah nodded. "I want to make this work, Liv. Let's stick with the original plan and do our best to keep this"—she gestured between them—"between us and not let it interfere with our working relationship. Regardless of the outcome on this last site, I want lots more of this in my life. I want lots more of you."

Olivia didn't feel like she had the right words to reply, so she settled for kissing Savannah instead. She hoped Savannah knew what she meant to her.

A thought seemed to occur to Savannah and she blinked up at Olivia. "Stay with me."

"What?"

"Stay with me. Let's not book a hotel room at all in Chicago. Stay with me, at my house."

Olivia looked down at Savannah and smiled. "Stay with you? At your house, in your space, for the duration of the Chicago gig?"

"Yes." Savannah nodded confidently. "At my house, in my bed, with me every night."

Olivia cupped Savannah's cheeks and kissed her. "I'd love to."

CHAPTER TWENTY-ONE

Chicago

Olivia's back hit the kitchen cabinets as Savannah pushed her hips up onto the granite countertop. She had been amazed at the simple, uncluttered existence Savannah inhabited. Her place was all clean lines and contrasting whites with dark cabinets inlayed with glass. Her kitchen was gorgeous, a thought that was quickly abandoned when Savannah's hand slipped under her skirt and ran through her wetness.

"I've been dying to touch you all day." Savannah's lips sucked at her pulse point as Olivia hooked her ankles around Savannah's hips and pulled her closer.

"You and me both. Mm, Savannah, yes." Savannah pressed two fingers against her opening before gliding inside easily. Olivia had been riled up and wet all day long.

Savannah massaged her tongue along Olivia's and silenced her mutterings. She loved how Savannah knew just how she liked to be touched. She loved feeling Savannah inside her. It was so distracting working with her in such close quarters and not being able to touch her the way she wanted to.

"You're so wet."

"Today was torture." Olivia tucked her head into Savannah's neck as Savannah increased the pace of her thrusts. It seemed like every interaction she had with Savannah at work today ended up in some unexpectedly sexual way. Shortly after lunch an overpacked elevator resulted in Olivia's ass positioned squarely into Savannah's hips with Savannah's breath hot on her neck. It was innocent enough, but that position had triggered a memory of the night before when she found her face pressed against Savannah's shower tiles with that same hot breath along her ear and neck. Her focus was shot for the remainder of the day. She'd been desperate to feel Savannah against her and she had a hard time keeping her mind on anything but that.

Savannah turned her head to press her lips to Olivia's, and Olivia let out that familiar sharp breath and whimper. Savannah slowed her movements and eased Olivia through her orgasm. Savannah pressed affectionate kiss after kiss to Olivia's mouth and jaw before she pulled her into a hug.

"Mm, hey." Olivia nuzzled close, pressing her ear to Savannah's chest. She felt herself warm at the rapid pace of Savannah's heart.

"Hey, baby."

Olivia scooted to the edge of the counter and wrapped her legs around Savannah again, her muscles trembling slightly as Savannah's hands soothed up and down her back. Savannah touched her in such a soft and delicate way, particularly after their lovemaking, and her touch made Olivia feel precious. She let herself bask in the way Savannah held her close, a protective strength combined with a softness that she didn't think she could explain to anyone with words alone. She'd tried and failed to explain it to Christine during their weekly gossip phone calls, which, of late, all seemed to end with Christine mocking her playfully about being a romantic and a sap. Olivia wasn't bothered by Chris's teasing, though. She was happy to have someone to share it with. She had never experienced feelings like these before in a relationship.

"You know what my favorite thing about you is?" Olivia breathed the words across Savannah's collarbone, her lips lingering on Savannah's smooth skin.

"What's that?"

Olivia's hand slipped from around Savannah's back to press along the wet mark left by Olivia's sex on the front of Savannah's dress shirt. She toyed with the buttons briefly before she moved the offending fabric from Savannah's stomach. "That I know without even touching you that you are just as wet from fucking me as I am from being fucked."

"Maybe you should double-check, just to be sure." Savannah's head dropped back when Olivia's teeth skimmed the base of her throat.

"Oh, I plan to do more than just check." Olivia tugged down Savannah's zipper with urgency as the sound of a key in the lock of Savannah's front door behind them halted her movements.

"Hey! Sav? You home?" a male voice called out from behind a large laundry bag, blocking his face from view. The unmistakable giggle of a woman accompanied the sound of the door swinging open and hitting the wall in the foyer. "Crap! Amber, watch the door."

"Oh fuck." Savannah groaned as she whipped her head in the direction of the intruders. She gripped Olivia's wrist and shuffled forward, quickly adjusting Olivia's clothing as the thump of the laundry bag hitting the floor was followed by a—

"Whoa! Jesus! Sorry!"

Olivia felt her eyebrows shoot up to her hairline as she looked over Savannah's shoulder at the athletically built flame-haired man who was desperately trying to cover his eyes as well as the eyes of the short blonde next to him. "Um, Savannah?"

"Shit, uh, sorry." Savannah cleared her throat and nodded toward the fidgeting form behind her. "Olivia, this is my poorly timed and inconvenient little shit of a brother, Cooper."

"Hey, it's not my fault you didn't answer any of my calls or texts warning you I was coming by." He glared at her before glancing at Olivia and covering his eyes again. "Sorry, Olivia. Ah, it's, uh, nice to meet you...God, this is awkward."

"Why don't you take that stuff to the laundry room and give us a sec. Okay, Coop?"

"Um, yeah. Okay. C'mon, Amber." Cooper grabbed his laundry bag and Amber's hand, and disappeared down the hall in the direction of Savannah's guest room.

Olivia leaned back and took in their position: Savannah was pressed tightly between the legs Olivia still had wrapped around Savannah's hips, and the top three buttons of Olivia's shirt were undone and her cleavage exposed—there was no way Cooper had misinterpreted what they were doing. Olivia glanced back down the hallway at his retreating form. Her commentary came fast and hissed. "Seriously? That's how I meet your brother? With my hand in your pants?"

Savannah's normally calm, collected face was flushed as she stepped back and helped Olivia off the counter. "I know, I'm sorry... I'm going to kill him."

The sudden lack of composure etched on Savannah's face warmed Olivia a little. She placed her hands over Savannah's frantic attempts to fix her clothes and added with a chuckle, "Baby, chill." She tucked Savannah's shirt back into her pants and gripped her hands as she ducked her head to make eye contact, biting back a laugh at the mortified expression on Savannah's face. "I just meant that I was hoping to make a better first impression is all. It's fine."

Savannah palmed her forehead and pinched her brow as she exhaled slowly, her head shaking. "I know, just, fuck, I—ugh. No, just let me kill him. I'll make it quick."

"Well, take care of the other witness while you're at it, 'kay?" Olivia laughed and rolled her eyes.

"Oh, Amber? Nah, she's cool—wait, you were hoping to make a good first impression on Cooper?"

"Savannah," Olivia said, "of course I wanted to make a good first impression on your brother. He's important to you. And you're important to me."

Savannah's shoulders relaxed and she pulled Olivia into a hug, pressing their lips together. "I'm important to you, huh?"

Olivia was momentarily preoccupied by Savannah's tongue in her mouth before she remembered they had company. She pulled back and playfully shoved Savannah's shoulder. "Stop that."

"Stop what?" Savannah's eyes twinkled as she ducked down and captured Olivia's lips with hers.

Olivia hummed and savored the moment just a bit longer. "Stop all of that." She motioned toward Savannah's mouth and lips. "It's distracting."

Savannah sucked her lips into her mouth and nodded.

"And yes, you are important to me," Olivia supplied as she pressed a kiss to Savannah's lips, her forehead resting on Savannah's as they breathed each other in.

Savannah's hands cupped Olivia's cheeks as she kissed her once more. "You're important to me, too." She smiled and glanced toward the noise of Cooper's footsteps pacing in the hallway. "I'm excited for you to meet Coop. I think you'll like him."

"You might as well put him out of his misery and call him in. I think he may be treading a hole into your beautiful wood floors."

Savannah called over her shoulder, "Coop, it's safe to stop scuffing up my floors now."

Olivia laughed and shook her head as she stepped back from Savannah's grasp and reached into the cabinet to grab some wineglasses. A drink was definitely called for in this moment. "Savannah, dear?"

"Yeah, Liv?" Savannah's attention was directed toward the glare

Cooper was giving her as he stuck out his tongue when he bent down to grab his backpack, abandoned by the door. Amber was toying with her phone and looking down as she strolled into the kitchen.

"Go change your shirt. There's sex all over it," Olivia whispered as she sipped the red wine currently occupying her glass. She laughed as Savannah's hand flew to cover her abdomen before she darted out of the kitchen, leaving Olivia with her brother and Amber, whom she assumed was his girlfriend. "So, can I interest you two in a drink, or six?"

❖

"So, anyway, that's how Sav here almost ruined my senior prom," Cooper said with an exaggerated eye roll.

"Until I saved it from being a total dud at the last second, so you're welcome, you ungrateful creep." Savannah threw a dinner roll at him.

He caught it without flinching and shoved it in his mouth before he added, "Whatever. You had to almost ruin it to save it, hence the now infamous phrase—"

"Nice save, Sav," they said in unison with their glasses raised.

Olivia shook her head and cleared the dishes with Amber's help while the siblings teased each other at the table.

"They get along really well." Amber smiled as she handed the dirty dishes to Olivia. "I wish I got along with my little brother that well."

Olivia took the dishes and loaded them into the dishwasher, rinsing them as she went. "Yeah, they do. Does he see her often?"

Amber leaned against the counter and cocked her head to the side, an amused look on her face. "Um, you know, when she's around. Savannah travels a lot for work, so he usually stops by here to do his laundry every few weeks and they make a dinner night of it. We weren't expecting her to be home today."

Olivia cleared her throat awkwardly and glanced back toward Amber. "Yeah, I gathered that much."

Amber held Olivia's eye contact for a moment before she said, "She must really like you."

Olivia leaned against the kitchen island behind her and crossed her arms. "Why do you say that?"

Savannah's cell phone rang and she excused herself from the table mouthing an apology as she walked out to the balcony for privacy. Cooper stretched in his seat and sauntered over, pecking his girlfriend on the lips as he hopped up to sit on the counter.

"What are we whispering about?" He wrapped Amber in a hug.

"I was just telling Olivia that Savannah must really like her." Her attention was drawn to the buzzing noise of the dryer. "Be right back."

Amber wiggled out of Cooper's grasp and trotted toward the laundry room as Olivia took the wineglass from his hand and put it in the top rack of the dishwasher.

"She's right, you know," he supplied quietly, his gaze following his sister's pacing on the balcony.

"Mm? About what?" Olivia closed the dishwasher and yawned.

"Savannah doesn't introduce us to anyone she's dating. Ever. Not since the whole Gwen debacle." His brow furrowed as he watched his sister's pacing form. "Savannah went quiet for a long time after that. We've been working on our relationship for a while now, but I can't remember her being this happy in forever. So Amber's right—she must really like you." He shrugged and grabbed an apple out of the bowl next to him, biting into it loudly as Savannah reentered the living room from the balcony with a look of annoyance on her face.

Savannah rubbed her temple for a moment before she shot a playful glare at her brother. "Coop, off the counter."

"Oh, what? Now there are rules as to who can be on the counter? Because I distinctly remember seeing Olivia sit here without any complaints from you in the not too distant past," he mumbled around the apple chunk still in his mouth.

Savannah strode over to her brother, taking the apple from his hand and biting it before shoving it back into his mouth and silencing his attempt at a complaint. "And aren't you lucky that's all you saw?"

Cooper winced and hopped off the counter, shoving Savannah's shoulder as he shuddered. "Gross, Sav. Fucking gross."

Savannah laughed and shoved her brother toward Amber, who was waddling into the room with a precariously stacked pile of clothes in her arms.

Olivia stepped close to Savannah and wrapped her arm around Savannah's hip as she rested her head on Savannah's shoulder. She stifled another yawn. "You're no better than he is."

Savannah scoffed and feigned mock offense. "He started it."

Olivia shook her head and pressed a soft kiss to the underside of Savannah's jaw, nuzzling close.

Cooper and Amber shuffled their now clean clothes into the laundry bag and walked to the front door, hugging them both and thanking them for the impromptu dinner night. "It was nice to meet you, Olivia." Cooper gave her a genuine smile as he grabbed Amber's hand and pulled her toward the door.

"You guys, too."

"Bye." Savannah waved and let out a quiet sigh as the door closed.

"He's hilarious. And she's really cute. I'm glad I got a chance to meet them." Olivia yawned again.

"Yeah, me, too." Savannah pressed a kiss to Olivia's temple. "Let's get you to bed."

Olivia nodded without resisting and laced her fingers with Savannah's as they walked down the familiar hallway toward Savannah's bedroom, shutting off lights as they went. She smiled at the domesticity of the whole night: dinner with family, dishes washed, laundry done, and now walking hand in hand with her girlfriend to her bedroom. It was nothing that she was expecting, but she was pleasantly surprised nonetheless.

After washing up, Savannah slipped under the covers and held the blankets back for Olivia to join her. Olivia cuddled close as strong arms wrapped possessively around her shoulders. She lay there for a moment soaking up Savannah's warmth before she remembered the annoyed look on Savannah's face from earlier. "Hey, who called you earlier?"

Savannah's fingertips paused before continuing their gentle circles along Olivia's arm. She sighed. "It was a work call. I have an early meeting tomorrow morning with Ken."

"Do they usually call you after hours?"

"More often than I'd like, unfortunately."

Olivia nodded and frowned at the sad tone in Savannah's response. She lifted her head and looked at her while she gestured playfully between them. "You know, taking a little work home with you sometimes isn't so bad."

Savannah smiled and pressed her lips to Olivia's. "This kinda work after hours is never a bother, trust me."

Olivia opened her mouth to deepen the kiss when a yawn interrupted her again, for the third time tonight. Savannah pulled back and cast Olivia an amused look. "Tuckered out, Liv?"

Olivia nodded sheepishly. "As much as I want to return the favor from earlier, I think I need to sleep."

"Rain check?"

"Definitely." Olivia kissed Savannah before closing her eyes and drifting off to sleep.

CHAPTER TWENTY-TWO

Olivia looked down at their linked hands on the center console of Savannah's car as they pulled up to the hotel. They had gotten into the routine of having breakfast together and carpooling to work these past few weeks. Except instead of actually going to the work site, Savannah would drop Olivia off at the hotel before work started on some days just so she could meet up with her team and keep up appearances. Olivia had been surprised when Savannah had sheepishly admitted that she had still booked a hotel room for her. When she questioned it, Savannah had been almost nervous in her explanation: she wanted Olivia to still have freedom to come and go as she pleased from Savannah's place, but also wanted her to be able to spend time with her team without having to lie about where she was staying.

They had agreed to keep the relationship a secret until the final project was complete since Savannah was concerned that her involvement with Olivia might look like favoritism during the New Horizons deliberation phase regarding a long-term future contract. At first, Olivia had felt the concern unwarranted. The work her team had done was exceptional and didn't need favoritism to earn a positive evaluation. But she could appreciate Savannah's perspective. And she would be lying if she didn't admit that part of her was glad that no one knew about their relationship either. The fewer people that knew, the less complicated it was. Right now, it was just her and Savannah and amazing sex and sweet, tender moments and living in the present. She would ignore the future for as long as possible.

"Sorry this is so early." Savannah interrupted Olivia's daze.

"Don't worry about it," Olivia replied. "I should probably make some attempt to appear like I'm staying here."

"Maybe we should stay here one night, you know, to make sure the bed is comfortable." Savannah expression was mischievous.

"Why? You plan on having me stay here when I come to visit after the project is over?" Whoops. So much for ignoring the future.

Savannah held her gaze. "I hadn't thought much about life after the project was completed, to be honest." She frowned and glanced at the clock on the dash.

Olivia felt her shoulders sag at the thought. She had only been joking when she had initially replied to Savannah, but this was a reality for them, one she hadn't considered.

Savannah's frown deepened the longer she looked at the clock. "I have to get to the office, but I think we should probably talk about this more. I'll call you when the meeting gets out and maybe we can go out to dinner somewhere tonight. What do you think?"

"Yeah, that sounds nice. Hey, we'll figure it out." Olivia said it more for herself than for Savannah.

Savannah's smile didn't quite reach her eyes as she nodded. She leaned across the console and cupped Olivia's jaw, pressing her lips to Olivia's. "I'm going to miss you today."

"I know what you mean." Olivia abandoned their hand hold and pressed one hand over Savannah's heart, the rapid beat against her palm mirrored by her own. "Call me later."

Savannah nodded and rested her forehead against Olivia's before she pulled back. "Have a good day, Liv."

Olivia exited the car with a small wave and watched Savannah drive off in the direction of her office. She adjusted the purse on her shoulder and rummaged for the room key as she walked toward the entrance of the hotel and right into a surprised looking Farrah.

"Good morning, Olivia."

"Farrah. Uh, hi."

"Having trouble breathing?" Farrah arched her eyebrow and waited.

"Hmm? Why would you say that?" Olivia asked, suddenly feeling a little short of breath.

"Well I imagine that Savannah was just giving you lifesaving maneuvers because you aren't feeling a hundred percent, right? I mean, why else would she be giving you mouth-to-mouth if you weren't short of breath?"

"Shit. Uh, fuck." Olivia mumbled, "How much did you see?"

Farrah's amused expression softened. "Not much. Just two people sharing what appeared to be a very familiar and intimate exchange outside a hotel at"—she glanced at her watch—"seven in the morning."

Olivia sighed but made no attempt to lie. Farrah was no fool. "Yeah."

Farrah smiled and stretched her neck before she adjusted her workout shirt. "As much as I'd love to get all the details out of you now"—she looked back at Olivia with a genuine smile—"I have to get my power walk in before the team meets back here in an hour. That gives you plenty of time to wipe her lipstick off your mouth."

Olivia's hand reflexively went to her lips as Farrah laughed and turned to go, pausing to add, "You two make a beautiful couple, Olivia. Good for you."

Farrah walked off as Olivia stood there in a daze. "I'm going to get so much shit for this, I can already tell…"

❖

Savannah unlocked the door to her office and glanced at the empty chair outside her door. Annabelle wasn't due in for another hour and a half. She flicked on the light and dropped her purse and jacket on the chair across from her desk as she settled heavily into her seat. It wasn't like Ken to call a meeting this early with such short notice. She powered up her tablet and checked her voicemail while her fingers traced along the file in front of her labeled Greater Image Design. She liked to keep hard copies of all her projects and assignments in her workbag just in case something like this popped up. She had crawled out of bed early, careful not to disturb Olivia, so that she could skim through their projections and check the deadlines again. Something about the tone in Ken's voice last night had put her on edge, and she wanted to make sure she covered all her bases.

Savannah exited the voicemail menu and scanned over her emails once more before she packed up her tablet and portable keyboard. As she slid it back into its case, her attention was drawn to a small Post-it stuck to the back of her tablet that she must have overlooked before. In looping, carefree script was a message from Olivia, signed with a heart. *Cash in that rain check after work? Call me.* Savannah smiled as she traced the shape of the heart with her finger and let herself wonder what the symbol meant to Olivia. She tapped the heart twice and sighed before she folded the note and tucked it into her pocket. As she headed toward Ken's, she let herself wonder what that heart shape meant to her, too.

Ken's admin was sitting at her desk with a focused look when the chime of the elevator alerted her to Savannah's arrival. "Early morning, Savannah?"

Savannah paused and looked at her curiously. "I have a meeting with Ken. I assume he told you."

She bristled and straightened her back at the implication that her boss had made a decision without informing her. "No. He didn't mention it. But that does explain why he wanted me here so early." She frowned. "I'll let him know you're here. Hang on a sec."

Savannah nodded and looked out at the view; the city skyline was gorgeous at this time of the day. She was rarely in her office to appreciate her own view, although it was nothing compared to Ken's panoramic paradise. Her daydreaming was cut short by his admin's return. "Mr. Dodd said to head over to conference room seven." She nodded her head toward the end of the hall. "He said that everyone else is waiting."

"What? Who is waiting?"

She shrugged and pinched her lips together. "I don't know, Savannah, I didn't even know you were having a meeting."

Savannah's eyes narrowed as she considered the new information, and her voice was flat when she spoke again. "If I'm not out by eight forty-five, would you please call down to Annabelle and tell her to push back my nine o'clock call to right before lunch?"

"Yes, ma'am." She jotted down the note.

Savannah turned and strode toward the conference room, the clicking of her heels echoing off the blank walls as she went. The rest of the office doors on this floor were still closed—it was barely seven thirty in the morning, after all. She took a deep breath and paused outside the conference room door before stepping inside.

Four unfamiliar men looked up at her; the one in the glasses with the ill-fitting suit jacket's eyes lingered on her pencil skirt for a moment longer than was socially acceptable. She made it a point to look directly at him when she spoke. "Good morning, gentlemen."

He swallowed and redirected his eyes to the papers in front of him as Ken's booming laugh sounded behind her in the doorway. "Savannah, making friends already, I can see."

She stifled the desire to shrug his hand off her shoulder and offered him a false smile. "Ken."

He motioned for her to sit at the other end of the conference table and introduced her to the group in his usual obnoxiously jovial way. "Savannah here is the best of best, gentlemen. You are very lucky to be in her audience today."

Savannah took her seat and crossed her legs as she waited for Ken to explain why this meeting was happening.

"Anyway, Savannah, I wanted you to meet our new associates. James and Alvin Pearson, and…I'm sorry, what's your name?"

The other two men introduced themselves and smiled at her warmly, but Savannah couldn't have cared less. The one Ken had identified as Alvin, the one with the glasses and the wandering eye, seemed nervous and his fidgeting was distracting. Savannah directed her attention back to Ken and cocked her head to the side. "I seem to be missing something. You said *new associates?*"

"Oh yes, yes, excuse me." Ken spread his arms in a grandiose gesture, his jolly, fat face shaking with his movements. "They're part of your new team."

Alvin cleared his throat and looked more uncomfortable. James's attention was fixed on Savannah's face. He seemed to be watching her reaction closely.

"Let me explain," Ken continued. You see, Savannah, this project you've been working on has gotten us a lot of positive attention. The big shots who run this joint want to expand and do it quickly. James and Alvin will be observing the Chicago launch and are looking to take over the design reins from this point forward."

Savannah didn't believe her ears. She glanced back at the two men, pausing to hold James's gaze as she responded with blatant sarcasm. "Take over? Now that the pilot projects are almost done, you want to take over?"

Alvin nodded and whispered something to James, who looked back at Ken with a frown.

The smile on Ken's face disappeared and his happy facade slipped away. "Savannah. The Pearson brothers will be taking over after the Chicago launch. They're going to install the concept in our sites nationwide and begin pitching it in Europe. I wanted to give you the opportunity to meet with them today so you can begin planning the next project site with them immediately."

Savannah was reminded of the rumors that, in his youth, Ken Dodd had been a vicious businessman who dealt many decks at the same time. "You're severing our relationship with Greater Image Design?"

Ken's face was impassive. "They were contracted to complete three job sites within a six-month time period. They have completed their contractual obligation and have been appropriately compensated for that work. This is the end of their partnership with us."

Savannah felt her blood pressure begin to rise. This morning she had checked and double-checked the dates of all the evaluations she'd submitted regarding Olivia's team and the project outcomes. They were all in on time, early even, and all had the necessary supporting documentation showing Greater Image Design's incredible work and success at every turn during these pilots. Olivia's team had knocked this audition process out of the park. Savannah knew that Olivia had been specifically sought out for her ingenuity with modern green space design. "So let me get this straight—after you used them to engineer and perfect this project, you're going to put all their hard work into the hands of someone else and toss them to the side?"

Ken's masked face twitched, and his eyes narrowed. "Ms. Quinn, I'm sure you meant to phrase that question another way."

James scowled while Alvin seemed to sink farther into his chair. The other two men shuffled their papers and looked flustered.

The realization settled in her stomach like a stone: Ken and New Horizons never had any intention of pursuing a relationship with Olivia's team outside of having them do all the grunt work on the front end. That's why he had always been so dismissive of the reports she had agonized over all these months. Greater Image Design was never the endgame for him. That fucking snake.

Savannah's lip curled in response. "No, Mr. Dodd, I believe my question was appropriately worded. I can see the answer I was searching for is blatantly evident on the faces of the Brothers Grim, here."

Ken leaned forward in his chair. "Savannah—"

James cleared his throat and interrupted. "I can see you are uncomfortable with this discussion, Ms. Quinn. Perhaps a later time would be better to approach these details."

"Where are the next sites?" She ignored James and kept her eyes locked on her boss.

"San Francisco, New York, and Miami, then some European partnerships begin," Alvin squeaked out next to her as he avoided raising his gaze from the papers in his hand.

"I suppose you expect me to travel to all those sites, too? Walk them through every site detail from the first three locations?" she asked, even though she already knew the answer.

Ken leaned back in his seat. "You are expected to complete the duties of your position, yes. You will meet your new team on Monday and leave at the end of next week for San Fran." He paused and pressed the tips of his fingers together. "It would behoove you to wrap up Chicago and take a few days off to prepare yourself. I will have my admin get all the logistics to yours after today's meeting."

Savannah made sure her face remained emotionless as she pushed out of her chair and stood. "I assume since you are giving me more unsolicited vacation advice that this meeting has come to a close." She glared at Ken before directing her attention back to James and Alvin. "You'll like what you see at the launch party. There's no team more qualified or talented than Olivia Dawson's. You have some mighty big shoes to fill. Good luck with that."

She reached the elevator in what seemed like fifteen steps. She was shaking with anger as she pressed the button to her office floor. Her temples throbbed and she felt nauseous as she imagined the look of hurt on Olivia's face when she would hear the news. She slammed the *door close* button just as the sound of Ken's false laughter approached.

She exited the elevator and charged around the corner to her office, pausing in front of her admin's desk. "Annabelle."

Her administrator looked startled and immediately stopped what she was doing. "Good morning, Savannah."

"Get Legal on the phone for me, immediately. Cancel my morning calls. Page Corrine Baylor in New York and make sure no one, I mean no one, interrupts me until further notice."

Annabelle's eye widened. "Yes, Ms. Quinn."

Savannah paused in the doorway of her office, her voice low when she spoke again. "Thank you, I appreciate your help." She meant that. She was going to need all the help she could get.

"Of course, Ms. Quinn."

❖

Olivia checked her phone for the fifth time in the last twenty minutes. Savannah had not returned any of her texts and it was almost noon. It wasn't as though she expected constant communication from Savannah during their workdays, but she had been a little on edge ever since her run-in with Farrah, and she wanted the reassurance of Savannah's voice in her ear to quiet the noise in her brain.

"Why do you keep checking your phone? Do you expect it to start doing tricks?" Reagan asked around her coffee cup.

Olivia chewed the inside of her cheek to keep from blushing. She felt guilty keeping this from Reagan, but the last thing she wanted was to fuel Reagan's curiosity. "No, ass. I was just waiting for an email from Corrine about the projects back home," she lied.

"Hmm, I almost forgot about those." Reagan frowned. "I'm looking forward to being back in the Big Apple. All this traveling is a drag."

"Is that because you haven't found any hot ladies to keep you company here yet?" Farrah appeared over Reagan's shoulder. "I hear Chi-town has quite the gay scene."

"Did you just say Chi-town?" Reagan scoffed. "You've got to be kidding me."

"What?" Farrah's brow furrowed. "Am I not allowed to use slang?"

"No," Olivia and Reagan replied in unison, breaking out into laughter.

"Well, whatever." Farrah sighed. "Devon and I are almost done with the last of the art installations." She motioned toward the room behind them. "We'll be finished here soon—having all these extra hands really helped move this site along."

Reagan nodded and made an exaggerated fist pump.

Olivia gave a small smile, making eye contact with Farrah briefly before looking back at the schedule in her hands. This installation had been the fastest and smoothest of all three sites. They had hit a nice rhythm with their local workforce and did not encounter any of the setbacks they'd had in Denver or Phoenix. It should have brought Olivia great satisfaction, but it didn't.

"Since this is the final stop on our world tour," Reagan joked, "I say we go out with a bang."

Olivia added without looking up, "New Horizons has the launch party scheduled in two days. Once they showcase the room to the rest of corporate, there will be a reception afterward."

"Uh, okay. But that's *their* party. I think we should do something as a group. One last hurrah, you know?" Reagan encouraged.

Farrah smiled at Reagan's infectious enthusiasm. "It might be nice to do something as a small group, Liv. Have Savannah come—let's do something together before the big official party."

"Yeah, exactly. Listen to reason, Liv." Reagan pulled her into an aggressive one-armed hug before she skipped away and exclaimed to the rest of the group. "Olivia's planning a dinner, guys. Get ready for some overpriced filets!"

Olivia rolled her eyes and sighed.

"How about you and I get a coffee?" Farrah said quietly by her side as Olivia checked her phone again.

Olivia nodded and grabbed her purse. She followed Farrah out of the work space and to the vendor on the corner outside the busy downtown building.

Farrah handed Olivia her coffee and sat on the bench, motioning for Olivia to join her.

Olivia closed her eyes and leaned her head back, basking in the warm sunshine.

"So, you and Savannah, about how long?"

Olivia sighed and slouched into the seat. "Since Denver."

Farrah did a double take and gaped. "You've been seeing Savannah since the beginning?"

"Well, no. Sort of. Yes? It's complicated." Olivia sipped her coffee and watched the cars zoom by.

"And?"

Olivia looked over at Farrah with a confused look. "And what?"

"Listen, I have two teenage daughters. I know that vacant, dreamy look I saw this morning when she drove off. I know all about that embarrassed blush you're sporting now. And I have known you for a very long time, Olivia, so does she know how much she means to you, or not?"

The forwardness of Farrah's statement should have made Olivia laugh, but instead her eyes welled with tears and her chest tightened. "I don't know. Yes?"

Farrah took her hand and squeezed it. "Does she make you happy?"

Olivia nodded and wiped her eyes.

"Why are you so sad if she makes you happy?"

"Because in a few days we'll be back in New York and everything will change and God, why hasn't she texted me today?"

Farrah stroked along Olivia's hand in silence for a moment. "Olivia, she's probably busy wrapping up loose ends at the office."

Olivia's lip quivered, and she tried to silence the sob in her throat. Farrah's rationale didn't give her any comfort. It just reaffirmed the fact that their time together was running out.

"Aw, Liv, don't cry." Farrah pulled her into a motherly hug. "Shh, sweetheart. It'll be fine."

Olivia nodded and hoped Farrah was right.

CHAPTER TWENTY-THREE

Olivia was alone, waiting for Savannah to meet her, when she finally got the opportunity to look around the project space with a proud smile. She took a moment to admire the way the photographs of the Chicago skyline complemented the canvas painting she'd finished earlier today after Christine had talked her off the ledge. By the time Savannah had finally texted her late in the afternoon with a promise of a date after work, she had already left a few frantic calls and texts for Christine, even though Farrah had assured her she wouldn't mention anything to anyone about what she had seen. She had felt foolish calling and texting her sister like some panicked teenager, but when Savannah was unreachable and Farrah caught them kissing and the realization set in that the project was almost over, she freaked out. Christine had listened to her and completed her sisterly duty of telling Olivia to snap out of it and get it together.

Once she had hung up the phone she was able to silence her panic and put all her energy into the signature piece that would be the focal point of the room: a vibrant and passion-filled red and orange abstract that, when positioned above the photographs of the skyline, looked like the sun was either rising or setting, depending on the angle.

"It's beautiful, Liv," Savannah's husky voice supplied as her arms looped around Olivia's waist from behind. She pressed a kiss to a spot below Olivia's ear. "This might be my favorite one yet."

Olivia melted into Savannah's embrace and hummed in agreement. There was something so deliciously seductive and evocative about the color swirls in the canvas. She was proud of the outcome. She turned in Savannah's arms and pressed their lips together in a slow kiss. "Just give me a few minutes to freshen up and I'll be all set."

Savannah pulled Olivia close to her once more and kissed her again before playfully slapping Olivia's ass as she walked away.

❖

Savannah was admiring the canvas when the smell of Olivia's perfume brought a smile to her face.

"So, all this secrecy is exciting," Olivia said, "but where are we going?"

"Well"—Savannah turned with a wink—"I am taking you to one of my favorite places in Chicago."

"Ooh, sounds delightfully vague," Olivia deadpanned as Savannah laughed.

"Shh, good things come to those who wait." Savannah looped her arm with Olivia's and tugged her to the door, casting one last glance at the burning sun image on the wall.

A half hour later, Savannah inhaled the smells of freshly popped corn and cotton candy combined with the gentle lapping noise of Lake Michigan as they walked under the ornate archway of Navy Pier with the sun setting in the distance. She'd kept their destination a secret for the whole ride from the office to here, a smile etched on her face as Olivia asked more and more questions the closer they got to their destination. Olivia had squealed with excitement when the Ferris wheel came into view.

"This was one of the places I was hoping to see while I was here," Olivia said as they wove through the crowds of people. "It popped up on every must-see list when I was researching Chicago."

Savannah chuckled. "Well, what kind of girlfriend would I be to deny your need to experience Navy Pier?"

The cheers of the crowd around a street performer nearby preempted Olivia's response. She turned to watch him breathe fire as he spun a flaming rope above his head while balancing on a large ball. The crowd that had formed around him clapped and tossed money into his tip bucket while another performer played the accordion nearby, the beat egging on the fire-eater to increase the pace of his spins. As the rope twirled faster and faster into a large circle, the performer jumped off his ball and somersaulted through the flaming hoop, landing perfectly on the ball positioned on the other side. Olivia cheered and clapped, the glow of the flames reflecting off her face in such a way that Savannah felt her heart rate increase just a bit.

"Did you see that, Savannah?" Olivia's smile was blinding. "I can't even walk in a straight line and that guy just jumped through a flaming hoop and landed on a ball. A freaking ball!"

Savannah nodded and tugged on Olivia's hand, pulling her toward the array of carnival games that faced out toward the water. Music played over the speakers that ran along the pier, and children laughed as parents won them stuffed animals. Savannah pulled Olivia to her favorite food vendor and pointed out the many choices, whispering suggestions into Olivia's ear and punctuating her words with softly placed kisses along Olivia's jaw.

They ended up with a little of everything: sausage with peppers, a famous Navy Pier Chicago hot dog, funnel cake with cinnamon and sugar, and a large, freshly squeezed lemonade to share. Savannah led them to a bench near a fountain whose spray danced in a choreographed show with colored lights to the soft music piped through the pier. Olivia sipped her drink and settled into Savannah's side on the bench as they watched the dinner cruise ships that were returning to dock. It was a warm night with a gentle breeze, and the sky was clear of clouds, the stars starting to twinkle as the night settled above them.

Savannah used her thumb to catch the powdered sugar along Olivia's bottom lip and sucked her thumb clean while Olivia watched with a giggle. Olivia rested her head on Savannah's shoulder and they watched a little girl run by with her mother chasing after her, a balloon tied to the child's wrist whipping in the wind.

"I spoke with Christine today," Olivia said quietly as Savannah pressed a kiss to her top of her head.

"Oh, yeah? How is she?"

"She's good." Olivia paused. "I had a little bit of a meltdown today and called her."

Savannah pulled back and waited until Olivia made eye contact with her. She had spent the better part of the day talking to the legal department and playing phone tag with Olivia's boss, Corrine. Legal had advised her that Ken's moves were within the parameters of the original contract between Greater Image Design and New Horizons. They also warned her that she was not to mention anything to Olivia or her team because they were still working on the current installation. That both relaxed and infuriated Savannah. She wanted to tell Olivia herself, as she felt her boss's behavior was a betrayal. But part of her was glad that she was forbidden to be the messenger. Still, she felt like a coward, like she was somehow part of the betrayal. So she took a risk and reached out to Corrine. She realized that doing so could very well put her own job in jeopardy, even though Corinne wasn't technically part of Olivia's team. But she wanted to make sure Olivia had support when the news broke, that no one would blame her for losing the contract. Corrine had been grateful for the heads-up, which offered little consolation to Savannah. She still felt awful about it all.

"What happened?" Savannah asked. "Is everything okay?"

"Farrah saw us kissing outside the hotel this morning."

Savannah was relieved that was all that was wrong. Afraid she would betray her emotions, she directed her focus to the water in front of them. "Oh."

When Savannah didn't continue, Olivia said, "We talked about it over lunch, and she promised me that she wouldn't tell the rest of the team."

"Are you okay with that?"

"That she saw us or that she's sworn to keep it a secret?"

"Well, both, I suppose."

Olivia was quiet. Savannah's gaze followed a seagull swooping low above the water's edge. Olivia's hand gently cupping her chin broke her trance.

"I'm not ashamed of kissing you or anyone knowing about it. No." Olivia leaned forward and connected their lips, the taste of sugary sweetness evident on her lower lip as Savannah sucked it between hers.

Savannah let herself enjoy the kiss, leaning into it and running her hands through Olivia's hair affectionately, before a thought occurred to her. "Why did you have a meltdown, then?"

Olivia pulled away from the kiss and ran her hands through her curls, brushing them out of her face, her expression almost pained. "I realized that being with you makes me very happy, Savannah. And our time together is running out. You said so yourself this morning. Having Farrah see our connection and comment on it makes it that much harder to imagine not waking up with you every day. Not seeing you at work. It's so much more real when other people know."

Savannah frowned and nodded. She had felt a similar apprehension when Cooper had called her at work to tease her about meeting Olivia for dinner the night before. It was his call that had inspired her to bring Olivia here tonight. She wanted to share all the important things in her life with this woman—she wanted lots of hearts on hidden Post-its. Savannah reached into her pocket and pulled out the message from earlier, showing it to Olivia with a shy grin as she kissed the heart on the note and placed it into the breast pocket of her jacket. She looked at Olivia's slightly teary eyes and admitted, "I'm having a hard time accepting the fact that in a few days you will be hundreds of miles away." Savannah took Olivia's hand and entwined their fingers as she held Olivia's gaze. "I meant what I said that day at lunch. I want this to work. We'll figure it out, Liv."

Olivia nodded and wiped her eyes with her free hand. "Farrah thinks we make a cute couple."

"Farrah has excellent taste. I knew I liked her." Savannah kissed Olivia's smiling lips once more before nudging her with her shoulder. "Enough sad talk. Ready for Phase Two of our date?"

"Aye, aye, Captain." Olivia saluted as Savannah led her back to the lights and sounds of the carnival area.

CHAPTER TWENTY-FOUR

A ll right, Liv, we gotta be fast. All the good horses get scooped up first," Savannah instructed as they impatiently waited in line at the carousel.

Olivia nodded and narrowed her eyes in the direction of two little boys. "Which way should we go? Left or right?"

"Definitely left. If we go counterclockwise we can head off the foot traffic and get to Pegasus before one of them does." Savannah pointed her chin at the rowdy teenagers at the front of the line.

"Pegasus, huh? A winged horse? Why is he so special?" Olivia questioned while playfully jostling Savannah as the attendant walked toward the entrance gate to let them onto the ride.

"Oh, you'll see." Savannah smirked as she grabbed Olivia's elbow. "Ready?"

"Ready."

When the attendant opened the gate and put the two little boys in front of the height chart, Savannah tugged Olivia toward the left and jogged between the chariots and multicolored horses to the far side of the carousel.

Olivia's laughter alerted the teenagers of their approach and Savannah pulled her along faster as she practically launched Olivia onto the horse as one of the guys ran toward them.

"Oof!" Olivia huffed as she attempted to get settled in the seat. The teenagers complained quietly as they moved in front of them to a pair of chariots a few horses away.

Savannah waved at one of the guys who glanced back over his shoulder with a frown.

"I mean, Pegasus is pretty awesome and all." Olivia wiggled into the seat and ran her hands along the smooth white porcelain of the horse below her. "But what's the big deal? And why aren't you getting on one?"

Savannah positioned herself behind Pegasus's right ear in front of his wing and looped a braided strap around her waist. She took care to make sure Olivia's feet were comfortably and safely placed in the leather stirrups, and then she faced Olivia. She motioned for Olivia to lean forward so she could whisper something into her ear as the horses around them started to fill up. "Pegasus is the fastest and most beautiful of all the horses. Even though he is one of the lowest at the start, he moves the most during the ride. And I'm going to stand to make sure you really get the full effect."

Olivia leaned back and gave a confused look to Savannah as the lights above them flickered and the music began. The carousel started to rotate forward and slowly the horses around Olivia started to move up and down. When Pegasus began to move she noticed what Savannah had mentioned—his movement was faster and off beat with the horses and chariots around them. She gripped the gold pole a little harder for stability as the carousel lurched forward. Halfway around the first rotation, Savannah shifted forward and her right hand, hidden from public view by Pegasus's ornate wing, cupped Olivia's sex on one of the fast descents.

Olivia's eyes widened and she hissed as the heel of Savannah's hand connected with her clit. The pressure from the horse's sculpted saddle held Savannah's hand against her firmly as Pegasus sped up even more. Olivia moaned.

"Shh," Savannah said. "Enjoy the ride, Liv."

The lights flashed around her as the carousel slowly sped up. The singsong haunting music paired perfectly with the rise and fall of the horses while Savannah's hand cupped her possessively, sending sparks through her with every alternate beat. Pegasus rose and fell faster than the other horses, and Olivia felt Savannah stroke her fingers along the crotch of her pants while she pressed harder against Olivia's clit as the carousel hit its maximum speed.

Olivia's hips rolled forward of their own accord as she locked eyes with Savannah, grinding into Savannah's hand with every movement of the horse as the background blurred around them. She released one hand from the pole to caress discreetly across Savannah's chest, the pebbling of Savannah's nipple under her touch and the lustful look in Savannah's eyes that accompanied her low moan spurring Olivia's movements to become more erratic.

Savannah bit her bottom lip as Olivia pinched her nipple through her shirt. Soon, Olivia felt the telltale flush working its way up her neck. Savannah must have noticed because she pressed her fingers against Olivia's opening, penetrating as far as the fabric allowed. Olivia rolled aggressively against her palm and whimpered at the sensation.

"Just like that, baby. Come on," Savannah encouraged, her left hand reaching out to grip tightly around Olivia's thigh, her nails digging into the sensitive skin there.

The carousel lurched again and reversed directions. Pegasus's motion jerked at the change, driving the heel of Savannah's hand harshly against Olivia's clit and catapulting her over the edge. She closed her eyes as she felt the blood drain from her face and neck, the flashing lights making her feel dizzy. Olivia felt Savannah's hand gently squeeze her sex once more through her pants before it slid up to rub comfortingly along Olivia's belly, grounding her.

As the ride slowed and the music began to fade, Olivia blinked her eyes open and grinned at the adoring look Savannah was giving her. "Whoa."

Savannah's grin outshone the carousel lights as she wiggled out of the rope holding her in place and shifted under Pegasus's wing to help Olivia slide off the horse and into her arms. She pulled Olivia into a snug embrace, her arms looped around Olivia's waist as she kissed her passionately on the lips. "Mm, you taste like funnel cake, baby."

Olivia smiled but did not break the kiss as she started to regain feeling in her legs. She wobbled a little as the ride came to a full halt.

Savannah held her tight and waited as the rest of the riders made their way to the exit. "You almost ready?"

Olivia nodded and nuzzled against Savannah's chest for a minute as she caught her breath. "Okay, I'm good."

Savannah stepped back and ushered Olivia toward the exit. Olivia saw her glance at the clock on the operator's podium. "Good, because we have to hurry to the Ferris wheel and we'll get there a lot faster if I don't have to carry you."

❖

Savannah pocketed her phone as they stood in line for the Ferris wheel. Olivia was reading the sign explaining the ride's history as she nestled her ass into the crook of Savannah's hips.

"Did you know that this Ferris wheel was modeled after the very first Ferris wheel from 1893?"

"Let's hope they used more updated technology when they built it."

Olivia rolled her eyes and elbowed Savannah in the ribs. "It's over one hundred fifty feet tall and is supposed to have the best view of the Chicago skyline in the whole city."

Savannah felt her eyes bulge.

"Wait, are you afraid of heights?"

"Only when I'm hanging in a car by some cables from the largest moving wheel in the Midwest."

Olivia gave her an exaggerated pout and pressed a quick kiss to her lips before resuming her position cradled by Savannah's hips. She leaned back and rested her head on Savannah's shoulder as the line moved forward infinitesimally. "I promise to keep your mind off the height while we're up there."

Savannah kept her eyes straight ahead. "Oh, yeah? And how do you plan on doing that?" Her fingers gripped Olivia's hips a little tighter.

Olivia tipped her head up to kiss the skin below Savannah's jaw. She sucked lightly as she slipped a hand between them and mirrored Savannah's previous ministrations.

"*Liv,*" Savannah groaned out, the wetness from her playtime with Olivia on the carousel sticking to her panties as Olivia pressed against Savannah's skirt with her hand discreetly between them. Savannah knew that to the naked eye it would appear that Olivia's back was innocently pressed against Savannah's front in a casual embrace, even though this was anything but innocent at this point.

"I can feel how hot and wet you are, Savannah," Olivia teased as she pressed her ass into the back of her hand. She punctuated her taunt with a gentle bite to Savannah's jaw which Savannah answered with a moan and closed her eyes in response.

"Hey, you two there. Yeah you, the two ladies looking cozy." A male voice sounded off to Olivia's left, jarring her hand out from between them.

Savannah's eyes blinked open and she squeezed Olivia's hips twice as she turned toward the voice. "Hey, Coop."

"Cooper!" Olivia exhaled. "Jesus, you scared me."

"Sorry, Liv." Savannah liked that he used Olivia's nickname like they'd known each other forever. It felt right. "I just came to see if you guys were ready."

"Ready for what?" Olivia glanced up at Savannah, who took the opportunity to edge away from her in an attempt to take a deep breath.

"To ride on the greatest amusement ride of the Pier, duh," Cooper replied as he pulled them out of line. Savannah laughed when Olivia finally noticed his bright yellow polo shirt with *Navy Pier Staff* embroidered over the left chest. "As my special guests for the evening, you two get to go right to the front of the line."

Cooper brought them to the front, passing them under the security tape to the operator's entrance. He whispered something into the ear of the attendant, who nodded and cycled down the next gondola. Olivia noticed the caution tape at the entrance and looked back at Savannah with concern. Savannah was equally concerned.

"What's with the caution tape, Coop?" Savannah questioned.

Cooper leaned close and whispered, "I had to make sure you two got a romantic setup, so I put this tape on with the false warning that it can only safely hold two people."

"It is just a *false* warning, though, right, Cooper?" Olivia asked, sounding nervous.

"Yeah, duh. Like the park people would let an unsafe gondola go around." He shook his head and laughed as he ushered them into the car. "Now, you two ladies have fun."

Savannah glanced back at him as he closed the door and waved, tapping the car's door to signify it was ready to move.

Savannah was trying not to panic. She kept her attention directed straight ahead out the opening of the gondola as they slowly lifted off the platform. She was only aware that Olivia had turned to face her when Olivia took her hand.

"You've been on a Ferris wheel before, right?"

Savannah blinked and nodded, careful to make as little movement as possible. "Yeah, but it's been a while."

The car moved up another few feet and a gentle breeze rocked them lightly in the air.

Savannah sucked in a sharp breath and gripped the seat with her other hand. Olivia leaned forward and pressed her lips to Savannah's clenched jaw. "So, Cooper was in on your little date night plan, huh?"

Savannah's eyes closed at the sensation of Olivia's warm lips. "Mm-hmm. He's the one who told me about that great Pegasus detail."

Olivia chuckled as she sucked on the skin of Savannah's neck. "Well, I definitely appreciated that intel."

Savannah shuddered at the cool breeze coupled with the hot mouth moving along her neck. With her eyes closed, she could ignore the height change as the gondola rose again.

Olivia leaned closer and connected her lips with Savannah's. Savannah opened her mouth to deepen the kiss and Olivia took the opportunity to shift over and straddle Savannah's lap. "Now, about that promise I made to you about keeping your mind off the height…"

Olivia's hands ran through Savannah's hair, gently clasping behind her head as Savannah exhaled into Olivia's mouth. She kept her eyes closed and her hands firmly on Olivia's waist as she focused on the deliberate rocking of Olivia's hips in her lap. Her arousal increased with every body roll, with every stroke of Olivia's tongue against hers. "Fuck, Liv, you taste so good."

Olivia sucked Savannah's bottom lip between hers before she bit down lightly. She broke the kiss and waited until Savannah opened her eyes and looked at her. "I'm willing to bet you taste even better."

The gondola shifted higher and Savannah glanced warily over Olivia's shoulder as they swayed a little more. Before Savannah could panic, Olivia wiggled off her lap and lowered herself to her knees.

"Eyes down here, babe," Olivia commanded as she pushed at the hem of Savannah's skirt, guiding it up her thighs.

Savannah's head dropped back, but her eyes remained focused on Olivia as Olivia clucked her tongue and cooed as she pushed aside Savannah's thong.

"Aw, babe, you are so, so wet. Is this all for me?" She fluttered her eyelashes and leaned close, stopping just short of connecting her lips with Savannah's sex.

When Savannah only nodded in response, Olivia said, "What's that? I can't quite hear you."

"Yes, Liv. It's for you."

Olivia's lips pressed a whisper of a kiss to the immediate left of where Savannah needed it.

"Good." Olivia looked up to ensure she had Savannah's full, undivided attention, before she dragged her tongue along Savannah's slit.

Savannah moaned at the warmth of Olivia's mouth on her sex and dropped her hands to cradle Olivia's head and neck. Olivia's dedicated tongue worked quickly, easily winding Savannah back up as her nose bumped repeatedly into Savannah's engorged clit.

The soft hum of the music that was pumped into the gondola momentarily stuttered as their car rose a little higher, causing Savannah's eyes to widen, but still she kept her gaze on Olivia. Olivia rewarded the action by slipping lower and thrusting her tongue as deep into Savannah as her position would allow.

Savannah tightened her grip on Olivia's head as she increased her pace. Olivia's left hand held up Savannah's skirt while the other pressed hard and fast circles over Savannah's clit, all while her tongue continued thrusting in and out.

Savannah felt her thighs begin to quiver as Olivia curled her tongue and dragged it over the inner ridge of Savannah's pulsing sex. She licked Savannah's clit, and Savannah couldn't hold eye contact any longer. She shuddered and moaned, her eyes closing automatically as her orgasm shot through her. Olivia slowly lapped at Savannah's wetness until Savannah pulled her up to kiss her lips.

Savannah mumbled between kisses, tasting herself on Olivia's tongue and sighing. "You are something else, you know that?"

"See? I promised I would distract you. Just look at that view." Olivia adjusted Savannah's thong and skirt before she snuggled up close to Savannah and pointed to the city skyline outside their swaying car.

Savannah kept her eyes on Olivia's face, watching the shimmering light reflect off her beautiful hazel eyes. "It's a great view."

She watched a blush settle on Olivia's face when she caught Savannah looking at her. She leaned forward and pressed their lips together just as a loud popping noise went off in the distance, jarring Olivia back with a gasp.

Savannah laughed, her gaze still on Olivia and not on the skyline. "What's better than the perfect view of Chicago's skyline on a clear night than some fireworks?"

Olivia cuddled close to Savannah and rested her head in the crook of Savannah's neck. "It's perfect."

Savannah wrapped her arm around Olivia's shoulder and dared to look out at the view in front of them. They watched the fireworks in peaceful quiet for a few minutes. The view was unbelievable—the clear night sky, the warm air, it *was* perfect. Savannah didn't feel afraid of the height with Olivia's arms wrapped around her waist; in fact, she barely registered the car's movement as the fireworks wound down.

Olivia shifted next to her as the fireworks ended and she clapped, her smile wide. She looked over at Savannah and Savannah tried her best to process all the things that had happened today. She had so many emotions bubbling under the skin, but she mostly felt happy.

"I meant it when I said it, Savannah. It's perfect." Olivia echoed her feelings. "You're perfect."

Savannah shook her head and opened her mouth to reply but was silenced by Olivia's lips on hers.

Olivia pulled back. "Meeting you, this job, this opportunity, it's been the best experience of my life. Thank you."

That familiar sinking feeling from earlier settled in her stomach and Savannah tried her best to keep a smile on her face as she nodded. "You make me happy, Liv."

"Me, too." Olivia held her hand tightly as the reminder of their limited time together came to the forefront as the gondola swayed down to the landing.

"How was it, ladies? Everything you hoped for and more?" Cooper asked as he helped them out of the car and onto the platform.

"It was awesome. Thanks, Coop," Olivia gushed.

"Great. Well, as payback for me securing you the best car with the longest unobstructed view of the fireworks, you two can buy me dinner since this is the end of my shift." He smiled as Savannah playfully shoved him.

"C'mon, you troll." Savannah yanked him by the hand, taking Olivia's hand with her other one. "Call Amber to meet us and we'll make a night of it."

Olivia laughed as he did a little jig and nodded in the direction of the exit to a waving and excited Amber. "Way ahead of you, sis."

Savannah rolled her eyes and kissed Olivia's cheek, happy to have a distraction from the chaos that undoubtedly awaited them in the morning.

CHAPTER TWENTY-FIVE

"All right, all right. I want to propose a toast to the hardest working group in all the land." Reagan made a grand sweeping gesture with her arm and everyone cheered.

The Greater Image Design team and Savannah raised their glasses as Reagan cleared her throat to continue. "This has been one hell of an adventure. Thanks for all the great experiences. And all that sappy shit. Bottoms up!"

The table cheered and Reagan started nodding her head to the beat of the music on the dance floor behind them. "This is my jam! Let's burn it up!" She tugged Devon out of the booth and reached blindly for Olivia.

"I'll meet you there, lush." Olivia batted her hand away and shooed her toward the dance floor.

"When did you get so old?" Reagan stuck out her tongue before leaving.

"That's our cue to go, gentlemen. Ready?" Farrah stood from the table and looked over at Randal and Daniel, who only nodded in reply. "Savannah, will we see you in the morning before the flight?"

"You bet," Savannah replied as she embraced Olivia's colleagues. Farrah held Savannah close and whispered something into her ear. Savannah nodded in silent reply as Farrah released her and waved.

Olivia waited until her coworkers had left before pulling Savannah back into the booth by her hand, cradling it in her lap. "What was that about?"

"Oh, you know, just Farrah telling me to make sure you make your flight."

"Why do I feel like it was more than that?" Olivia gave her a skeptical look.

Savannah shrugged. "I guess you'll never know."

Olivia looked out at the dance floor and watched Reagan twirl Devon in dramatic fashion. "The launch went well."

Savannah nodded. They had planned to a do a dinner before the launch party, but things got a little hectic last minute with the final touches on the space. They'd settled for drinks after the party ended, but it was late and they all had early flights. Well, everyone except Savannah. "It really tied up nicely, didn't it?"

Olivia looked over at Savannah, whose expression was serious. "You were awfully frosty to that Dodd person tonight."

"Was I?" Savannah looked at the contents of her glass.

"I would say you were borderline, uh, rude, actually." Olivia bit her lip as she waited for Savannah's reply.

Savannah glanced up. "Oh. You heard all that, huh?"

"Yes." Olivia waited for Savannah to continue, frowning when she didn't. "Is something wrong?"

Savannah looked at her for a moment and swallowed. "No." She paused. "Yes—"

"Whoa. You two look very, very, very serious over here," Reagan said a little too loudly, drawing attention from the booth next to them. She leaned across the table and pointed to their closeness, narrowing her eyes. "You're looking awfully snuggly, too. Wassup with that?"

Olivia shifted a little away from Savannah and reached for her glass. "It's loud in here, Reagan, and some of us prefer to talk instead of yell. That requires a bit of closeness." Reagan had the worst timing ever. Always, it seemed.

"You're cranky," Reagan said with a pout. "Savannah, come dance and bring that ball and chain if you dare. It's last call!"

Savannah chuckled and nodded. "I'm all over it."

Reagan wiggled. "That sounds kinky."

Olivia's eyes widened as Reagan stared at her for a moment before Savannah took Olivia's hand and pulled her out of the booth, "C'mon. Let's enjoy the end of the night."

❖

Savannah had spent the entire car ride to the airport trying to figure out what to say to Olivia. She knew that once Olivia got settled back in New York, New Horizons would inform them that they didn't plan to renew their contract. She had done everything in her power last night to keep Olivia's mind off the conversation that Reagan had interrupted at the bar. They had an intense and passionate night at Olivia's hotel room, both of them barely sleeping before the alarm clock went off. It had been a memorable time with slow kisses and soft caresses punctuated by sincerely whispered intentions. All of it made this moment that much harder. She wasn't ready to say good-bye to Olivia yet. She certainly wasn't ready to do it with an audience.

"We're here, folks. Thanks for visiting, come back soon." The driver of the shuttle pulled up to the curb and started unloading their luggage on the sidewalk in front of their terminal. Savannah held Olivia in place as the others trickled out to get their belongings. Farrah tossed them both a knowing look as she corralled the guys and Reagan toward the departure doors.

Olivia was watching her coworkers head toward the entrance when Savannah took her face in her hands.

"I promise I will see you soon. Thank you for last night, Liv. For all the nights."

Olivia leaned forward and kissed her. "I'm not ready to leave yet."

Savannah pulled back and blinked. When she spoke, her voice was soft but her expression was serious. "Then stay."

"Stay?"

Savannah nodded. "Stay. Forget about the flight. Stay with me."

Olivia hesitated. "Savannah. I can't just stay. You know that."

Savannah let out a heavy sigh. "I know."

A gentle tap on the glass by the driver broke them apart. He stood with Olivia's bags on the sidewalk and pointed to his watch. It was time to go.

Savannah squeezed Olivia's hand before she slipped out of the seat and through the door. She spoke to the driver, who nodded and walked around the van to the driver's seat, flicking on his hazards.

Olivia adjusted the purse on her shoulder as she stepped toward Savannah's open arms and melted into them.

"I'm going to miss you." Savannah kissed Olivia's ear and squeezed her so tightly she was afraid she might hurt her. "Be safe."

Olivia pressed her face into Savannah's neck and nodded. "I'm going to miss you, too."

Savannah pulled back and kissed Olivia with as much passion as she could muster. "Good-bye, Liv."

"Bye."

And just like that, Olivia was out of her arms and headed toward the terminal. The finality of the moment made Savannah queasy.

❖

Farrah gave Olivia a sad smile as she plopped into the seat next to her. "I was a little worried you weren't coming."

Olivia frowned. "Me, too."

"Seriously?"

Olivia nodded and looked out the gate window at the taxiing planes. Her heart felt heavy and she was pretty sure if Farrah asked her any more questions she might cry right on the spot. She glanced down at their boarding passes and panicked when she realized Farrah was in a different row.

"You're not sitting next to me this flight, Liv. I can see if it's one of the other guys. Maybe Reagan?"

"Oh." Olivia was pretty sure this was what it felt like to be kicked while you were down. It wasn't that she minded sitting with anyone else. But it would be a lot easier to quietly cry the entire flight back to NYC if the person next to her had some idea why she was so melancholy. Plus, Farrah always made her feel protected in that motherly way.

The agent behind the check-in counter spoke into the PA. "We are now boarding rows twenty and higher."

"That's us, c'mon, Liv." Farrah pulled her arm and guided her to the door.

Olivia boarded on autopilot. She settled into her seat and stared at the tray table for a few minutes.

"I'm in the window seat, Liv." Reagan's face was blank.

"Sorry." Olivia stood and shifted so Reagan could pass in front of her.

They sat in silence during takeoff and the initial ascent into the air. Reagan adjusted the air flow above Olivia's head but looked out the window without saying anything. If Olivia was being honest with herself, she kind of enjoyed the quiet. Had Farrah been her seatmate they would undoubtedly be talking about Savannah and Olivia's broken heart and blah, blah, blah. She closed her eyes and let the quiet sounds of conversation around her lull her into a restless sleep.

Light turbulence and the sound of the seat belt light dinging on above her woke Olivia from her doze. Her mouth felt dry and her head throbbed. She was regretting the lack of sleep from the night before until she remembered what had taken up the time. Savannah had been so soft and gentle with her last night. It was like she was trying to preserve the memory of Olivia's skin, her smell, her taste. She'd been so attentive that Olivia had practically had to pin her to the bed to return the favor. She'd always felt Savannah's attraction for her, but last night, she swore she could feel Savannah's love for her. So much so, that at the airport she had to stop herself from saying the words to Savannah before they broke apart. She had been overwhelmed. There were few instances in her life when she had expressed true love to anyone, particularly a romantic partner. Her dating record wasn't great—Christine always told her that she lacked vulnerability. But under Savannah's intense gaze last night and today at the airport, Olivia *had* felt vulnerable. She felt downright fragile. And at the moment, a little broken, too.

She became aware of Reagan's eyes on her.

"Why didn't you tell me?" Reagan's voice was low, annoyed.

"What?" Olivia blinked and turned toward Reagan's voice.

Reagan looked around and over at the sleeping stranger to Olivia's right, her eyes flicking between Farrah and Devon, both of whom were across the aisle and one row ahead of them. She looked down at her hands and crumpled the napkin on the tray table in front of her. "I saw you, you know."

Olivia was confused. "Saw me what?"

Reagan grunted and turned in her seat to face Olivia more fully. "I saw you kissing Savannah at the airport."

Olivia became aware of the warmth in the plane at that moment. She didn't reply. She didn't break eye contact. She was just still.

Reagan said, "You hadn't come into the terminal, and it was getting late. Farrah told me to give you a minute, but I shrugged her off. When I went to get you, I saw you." After another minute, Reagan scoffed. "Earth to Olivia. Did you hear me?"

"Yes. I heard you." Olivia turned away from Reagan and stared at the seat back again.

"And?"

"What do you want me to say?"

"Oh, I don't know, how about, *Sorry Reagan, must have slipped my mind to tell you I was fucking Savannah Quinn, my bad.*"

Olivia whipped her head toward Reagan and hissed. "Lower your voice, Reagan."

Reagan raised an eyebrow. "So you *are* fucking her? That wasn't a denial, Liv."

When Olivia didn't reply, Reagan continued, "Well, that explains all those moon eyes you've been throwing in her direction. I just thought you had some unrequited crush."

Olivia thought about their night last night and her heart ached. This was definitely more than a crush. In fact, it felt positively crushing.

"So, are you, like, in a relationship or something?" Reagan pressed her again. "How's that going to work? You gonna rack up your frequent flyer miles just to scratch the itch, Liv? We both know you can't hack that kind of life."

Olivia bristled at Reagan's statement. The words stung because they were true: Olivia had a terrible track record when it came to relationships. But she didn't need Reagan pointing that out, not now, or ever. Her eyes welled with tears. "I don't know."

Reagan frowned and sighed. "Don't cry, Liv. I didn't mean to come at you so aggressively. I just…I guess I was hurt you didn't tell me. You tell me everything. I didn't, I just…Sorry."

That only made Olivia cry harder. She had not done right by Reagan during all this. She was an absolute mess. "What am I going to do, Rea?"

Reagan handed her the tiny napkin square she'd been fiddling with and shrugged. "Well, why don't you start from the beginning and catch me up to speed?"

Olivia nodded and took a deep breath. She was in for a bumpy ride.

CHAPTER TWENTY-SIX

Olivia saw Corrine shifting papers in front of her when she came through the doors of the coffee shop. She signaled for the barista and smiled as she sat in the booth next to her.

"Hey, Corrine." Olivia was sure her face reflected the restless sleep of the night before. She and Reagan spent the remainder of the flight discussing her disaster of a personal life. Savannah had texted her later that evening, but she had fallen asleep before having the chance to reply. The phone call from Corrine this morning asking her to meet her at the coffee place near the office had caught her off guard, seeing as it was a Saturday.

"Hey, Olivia. How was the flight?"

"Bumpy." Olivia accepted the cup the barista brought over and added the extras from the bowl in front of her. "So, what's so important that it couldn't wait until Monday morning?"

Corrine hesitated. "Listen, I got the final pictures from the Chicago launch and everything came out great."

"I know—it was pretty seamless," Olivia said.

"I really want to commend you on the job you and the team did. It's great that even given the obstacles and environmental challenges you faced, you pulled off such a smashing success."

"Why do I get the feeling that a *but* is coming next?" Olivia leaned away from Corrine and sipped her coffee, pulling back when the too hot liquid touched her tongue.

"With all that being said, I just wanted to give you the heads-up that although the people at New Horizons loved the final product, they will not be contracting with us to continue with the project."

Olivia was mid-sip, after blowing on her cup to cool it down, when Corrine concluded. She choked on the liquid and Corrine patted her back to help her. "What?"

"We completed our contract with them and they've decided to go another route moving forward." Corrine's tone was diplomatic.

"You've got to be kidding me." Olivia was shocked. "We hit every angle they wanted, we made impossible timelines work, Randal and Daniel both almost quit on me during this process, and don't even get me started on Reagan...They just...Corrine, did we get fired?"

"Fired? No. Of course not, Olivia." Corrine looked scandalized. "We were perfect. So perfect they have decided to replicate the installations nationwide and internationally."

"But without us. That's what you're saying?" Olivia felt blindsided.

"Correct." Corrine looked uneasy. "It's still a huge win for us, Olivia. Greater Image Design is being recognized by all the major interior design magazines and architectural journals for the work we've done with New Horizons. The positive press we'll get from this will really boost our business. I've already got two interviews scheduled for next week that I want you to headline. This is big for us, Olivia."

"Then why do I get the feeling like we've been cheated somehow?" Olivia pushed the nearly full cup away from her. She sat there for a moment before something dawned on her. "When did you find out?"

Corrine looked remorseful. "I received the formal notice on Friday, while you and the team were flying back."

Something about the guilty look on Corrine's face made Olivia's stomach roll. She took a stab in the dark. "And when did you get the informal notice?"

"Wednesday." Corrine looked pained by the detail.

"Who told you?" Olivia pressed, fearing that she already knew.

"I don't know that that's important." Corrine tried to dodge. "What's important is that we really aced this one and I wanted you to know that I am truly grateful of all your hard work."

"Thanks for the vote of confidence." Olivia slid out of the booth and grabbed her purse. "Was there anything else, Corrine?"

"Oh. Uh, no. I just wanted to let you know in person before our debriefing Monday with the rest of the group."

"Thanks." Olivia hesitated before she turned to go. "Thanks for letting me know ahead of time."

Corrine nodded. "Of course, Liv. I know this project was important to you."

Olivia sighed and headed toward the café door, reaching into her purse for her phone.

❖

Savannah answered on the second ring. "Hey."

"You knew, didn't you?"

Savannah could hear the hurt in Olivia's voice. She'd expected a call like this but had hoped for it to be on Monday so she could find a way to break it to Olivia over the weekend.

"Savannah?" Olivia was impatient.

"I'm here."

"It was you. You told Corrine. You knew, didn't you?"

"Is that what she told you?" Savannah's fingers dragged over the edge of her desk as she listened to the sounds of Manhattan in the background of the call.

"No. She wouldn't tell me anything," Olivia said. "But my gut tells me it was you. She was far too calm and far too informed to have just heard the night before. Tell me."

"Tell you what, Liv?"

"How long did you know?"

Savannah weighed the pros and cons of the situation. She didn't want to lie to Olivia. But she also didn't want to come across as the bad guy. Last night had been miserable for her. When Olivia didn't text her back, she'd thought something bad had happened. She found herself a little shocked by how much the prospect of that sent her into a panic spiral. Of course, she just checked online to see that her plane had landed safely, but still, she found herself missing Olivia more last night than ever. "I found out at the emergency meeting Wednesday morning."

Olivia raged. "The fuck? Why didn't you tell me, Savannah?"

"I couldn't, Liv."

"That didn't stop you from telling Corrine. So that's bullshit."

"It's not—" Savannah tried to defend herself. "I didn't want you to be blindsided. I wanted someone there to protect you."

Olivia's angry cluck in response spurred Savannah to try to explain further. "It was a matter of my job on the line. Ken didn't like how upset I was at the meeting, and that's why I was so cold to him that night at the party. He had the legal department inform me that if I told you prior to the formal announcement, I could expect to be out of a job."

"So, you put your own career aspirations ahead of doing the right thing?" Olivia's reply was bitter.

"Olivia." Savannah backtracked. "I did what I could to help soften the blow. I did the best I could with what was given to me."

The line was silent except for the bustling sound of the city in the background on Olivia's end. Savannah felt helpless.

"That was rude. I'm sorry. I'm just..." Olivia's voice trailed off. "I guess...I guess I thought...Well, it doesn't matter what I thought, does it?"

"Liv." Savannah wanted nothing more than to be there. She hated that this was happening on the phone. But she hated herself even more for letting Corrine deliver the news. It just felt wrong. After their last night together, even being away from Olivia for a night had felt wrong. She felt so out of control in this moment. This was more than she felt equipped to handle.

Olivia said, "We knew all along this was a slippery slope. That was the whole reason we resisted in the beginning, right? There were no guarantees. I know that. I knew that. And yet, I can't help but feel betrayed. You should have told me, Savannah. I would have rather heard it from you." Olivia let out a heavy sigh and something inside Savannah broke.

"Olivia, I—" Savannah's heart felt like it was in her throat. Her eyes burned and her chest felt tight. How had they reached this point? How had she fallen so hard and so fast for this woman? The thought of disappointing Olivia made Savannah feel sick.

"I need to reevaluate some things, Savannah. I need some time." Olivia's voice sounded far off, distant. "I'm sorry. I have to go. Good-bye, Savannah."

Olivia was gone before she even had a chance to process what had happened. Her stomach rolled, and she thought she might be sick. She dropped her head between her knees as the room spiraled around her. Everything was ruined and it was all her fault.

CHAPTER TWENTY-SEVEN

New York City

"Okay, team, new project on the books." Corrine sashayed into the room with a wide grin. She handed out folders and laminated binders with bright pictures on the covers and each creative designer's name on the binding.

Reagan groaned. "Corrine, seriously, why does my binder always look like a Lisa Frank reject?"

"Because you need a little light in your life, and it brings me great joy to put hologram stickers of little monkeys on your stuff. Besides, Olivia suggested it."

Reagan kicked Olivia's chair, causing her to snicker. "Way to throw me under the bus, Corrine."

"All right." Corrine called the meeting back to order. "We've really been crazy busy this past month and half and I just want to reiterate how proud I am of you guys really going with the flow." Corrine smiled when Devon and Reagan high-fived. "Those three pieces in the beginning of last month's marketing push really propelled us into a new level of work, and the client inquiries have been rolling in."

Olivia nodded and flipped open her date book as Corrine continued to address the group. Since she had gotten back from Chicago things had been sort of a blur. There were interviews to be given, consults to complete, and the projects that had been running while they were away needed to be tidied up and finished. Work started piling up and the decision was made that new hires should be sought out to manage the influx. When Olivia wasn't working with the team, she was scheduling late night interviews with Corrine to expand their workforce. It had been sort of a marathon these past six weeks. She was grateful for the distraction, eager to put New Horizons and Savannah Quinn far behind her.

"Okay, so, Olivia, are you ready?" Corrine brought her back to focus.

"Yes." Olivia leaned forward and pulled out a few papers from her bag. "As you guys know, we've been busy interviewing some new talent to help lighten up the load around here." Her statement was met by cheers and a few groans. "Listen, I know some of you are excited and some of you aren't, but we're too busy to keep up this feverish pace without some sort of burnout."

She handed a few papers to the group and pointed at them. "We've narrowed it down to three candidates, but we only have space for two at the moment. I want you guys to read over some of our notes from the interviews and scan their résumés to tell me what you think."

"Wait—no head shots?" Reagan asked.

"Reagan. No." Olivia glared at her.

"I'm just saying—"

"Anyway," Corrine interrupted, "the important thing here is that we want to make sure the people we choose will be a good fit with this team. Initially, they will be trained by the other groups on the basics, but I really want them to join your team in the future. So we care about your input."

They chattered amongst themselves before coming to agreement on two candidates. Farrah made the recommendation that the third candidate, who was the youngest and least experienced of the final choices, be offered an internship for the time being. They expected to have a third position to fill eventually, and this way they could train this person for the job. Olivia smiled and remembered her position here as an assistant to Albie, so many years before. How things had changed in that time.

"Great, so that concludes our meeting for today." Corrine clapped, her pixie haircut bouncing as she hopped out of her chair. "Any exciting plans for the weekend?"

"Birthday party and sleepover at my house for the twins. Kill me now," Farrah said.

"Date with a cute boy from Soho. If I'm late Monday, it's because I'm recovering," Devon said with a sly smile.

Reagan smirked. "I plan on crashing your gay boy rave—where's this date?" She laughed as Devon shoved her.

The rest of the team filed out chatting and laughing, leaving Corrine and Olivia.

"Anything good happening with you, Liv?" Corrine closed the door and checked to make sure it was locked.

"Yeah, Christine and my niece got here a few days ago and we're going to do some touristy stuff before they leave tomorrow."

"Well, there is no place like New York City in the fall. Have fun."

"Thanks." Olivia gave her a genuine smile. Although work had been busy, she had been ecstatic when Christine had offered to come by and hang out. She had spent the better part of two weeks crying into the phone to Christine about not securing the long-term New Horizons project, but if she was being honest, it was mostly about Savannah. At the end of the day she really just wanted a hug from her big sister and a chance to spoil her niece. That made everything feel right in the world.

"Olivia! Your phone is ringing!" Christine called from the kitchen.

Olivia let out a playful groan to make Mackenzie laugh. "All right, Mom!"

Mackenzie giggled and whispered, "Maybe if we ignore her she won't bother us."

Olivia nodded conspiratorially. "It's our only chance to avoid her wrath when she sees that we got paint on your shirt."

Mackenzie nodded and then looked confused. "What's wrath, Auntie?"

"It's what befalls your aunt in about two seconds when I get ahold of her for getting your nice new shirt dirty," Christine supplied from behind the couch with her hand on her hip and a frown on her face.

Olivia gave her an innocent grin. "Her *I Heart NY* shirt wouldn't be complete without a little stain here or there. It adds character."

Christine raised her eyebrow and pointed the sauce spoon in Olivia's direction. "You, kitchen, now. And bring the shirt so I can try to get the stain out before it sets." She turned to Mackenzie. "Go wash up for dinner and put on your pj's, please."

Mackenzie scampered off and Olivia let out a contented sigh. She had needed this. "Oh. My. God. This all smells so good."

"Olivia, I know you don't like to cook for one, but your pantry was like a bachelor's sad discarded leftovers. I left the Fresh Direct bill on the fridge for you," Christine said.

"You are too kind." Olivia was grateful someone else was in charge of the decision making. She had never quite embraced cooking like Christine had. Her nights were usually filled with takeout or popcorn and wine on the couch watching *Friends* reruns. Christine had been impressed she even had place settings for four. Olivia had scoffed. She wasn't a total savage, after all.

Olivia walked Mackenzie's shirt to the sink and turned on the warm water. "It's water-based paint, so it should come out."

"Not if you plan on washing it like that." Christine bumped her out of the way and took over, handing the spoon to Olivia. "Stir the sauce while I try to work a miracle over here."

"God. You're more like Mom every day," Olivia teased and did as she was told.

"So, are we going to talk about her or what?" Christine asked, her eyes still on the stained shirt.

"Talk about who?" Olivia blew on the spoon to cool its contents before tasting the sauce.

"Whom," Christine corrected. "Savannah."

Olivia looked over at her sister as she shrugged and put the spoon in her mouth and mumbled a response.

Christine took the spoon from Olivia's hand and pulled it out of her mouth. "Let's try that again with less mumbling and talking with your mouth full."

"I take it back—you are becoming more like Grandma than Mom." Olivia pouted and leaned against the counter as Christine resumed cooking and laid Mackenzie's shirt out to dry.

Christine ignored the jab. "She was calling your phone when you were in the other room. Unless you know someone else with the contact *Savannah don't answer she sucks*, which is very mature, by the way."

"What do you want to talk about?" Olivia examined her manicure.

"I take it she's still calling and trying to reach you?" Christine turned off the burners and faced her sister.

"Apparently."

"Olivia, less with the vague, more with the sisterly sharing, please." Christine reached out and took Olivia's hands in hers. "What's up?"

Olivia's shoulders sagged. "She really hurt me, Chris. I mean it, like bulldozed my feelings. I don't have anything to say to her."

Christine frowned and pulled Olivia into a hug. After a moment or two she leaned back and brushed her sister's wild curls from her forehead. "It sounds like the situation sucked for everyone involved, Liv. I'm not saying she made the best choices, but from the way you described her and spoke about her so brightly during better times, I can tell she was important to you. If she's trying to reach you after all these weeks, maybe you should give her a chance."

Olivia leaned forward and rested her head on her sister's shoulder. "I don't know, Chris. Maybe it's best I just count this as a life lesson and move on."

Christine rubbed along her sister's back. "When you love someone, it's not always so easy to just give up and walk away, Liv."

Olivia squeezed her eyes closed and let out a heavy sigh. "I know. Love sucks."

The vibration of Christine's chuckle shook Olivia's head as the sound of little footsteps came into the room.

"Ready for dinner, Mommy!"

Christine replied. "Grab your cup and have a seat. We'll bring dinner over."

Olivia smiled as Mackenzie made her way to the almost too high chair and struggled to get on it before settling in comfortably. She had missed this so much.

"All I'm saying is, maybe think about what you had and if you think it's possible to have it again." Christine set the serving platter on the table. "You deserve to be happy, Liv. Savannah made you happy. Just think about it."

Olivia nodded. What did she have to lose? "I'll think about it."

❖

"Yes?"

After the fourth ring, Olivia's voice startled her. Savannah shot forward to grab her phone and fumbled to take Olivia off speaker. "Hey."

"Can I help you?" Olivia's tone was quiet and emotionless.

"Uh, yeah, sorry, I wasn't expecting you to pick up." Savannah was so nervous her palms were sweating.

"Well, you called me. I can hang up if you'd like."

"No! No, uh, I didn't mean to yell." Savannah palmed her forehead and took a deep breath. "I'm glad you answered. How are you?"

"I'm good." There was a long pause. "How are you?"

"I'm okay." Savannah wasn't sure when she would have another chance at this so she leaped. "I want to talk to you, Liv."

"We are talking."

"Not like this. Can we meet up?"

Olivia laughed. "Savannah, unless you invented a teleportation device, that seems highly unlikely."

"Sorry, Liv. I should have been clearer. I'm in New York. Can I buy you some coffee? And catch up?"

"Wait, why are you in New York?" Olivia sounded surprised. Then annoyed. There was definitely a tone of annoyance there.

"It's complicated. And long-winded." Savannah tried again. "How about that coffee?"

"I don't know, Savannah." Olivia's voice sounded hesitant. "I'm just getting comfortable with the idea of talking to you on the phone."

"Oh." Savannah deflated a little before she thought about what Olivia said. "Well, I could get used to the idea of you getting comfortable talking to me on the phone."

"We're just talking, Savannah."

"Absolutely," Savannah agreed easily. "I'm happy to hear your voice."

"Yeah. Me, too." That was all the encouragement Savannah needed to make her believe she had a chance at winning Olivia back.

CHAPTER TWENTY-EIGHT

"You seem chipper today," Reagan said behind dark sunglasses.
Olivia shrugged. "No more than any other day."

"Nope, I don't believe that for a second." Reagan pulled her glasses down a bit and winced at the brightness before pushing them back over her eyes. "You getting laid or something?"

Olivia rolled her eyes and signaled for the waiter. Reagan had been an absolute saint in helping her get over the Savannah betrayal she'd felt. When Corrine informed the rest of the team that they would not be working with New Horizons in the future, Reagan had taken the information in stride. The rest of the group had mixed emotions. Everyone was happy to be done with traveling, but they'd felt a little used at the same time. Farrah and Reagan had both looked at Olivia intently when she had remained stone-faced during the debriefing. Farrah had approached her immediately after the meeting, but Reagan had given her a little more space until she'd caught Olivia crying in the bathroom after giving a magazine interview later that day.

It had surprised her how patient and understanding Reagan was about the whole thing. She knew Olivia was equally if not more devastated about what had happened with Savannah than about just losing the contract. That talk on the flight back to NYC had really helped rebound their friendship. She was grateful for Reagan in her life.

"What can I get you, ladies?" the waiter asked with a smile.

"Mimosas and bacon," Reagan replied gruffly.

"Don't mind her, she just got out of rehab and is a little cranky."

"Oh, well, we have a lovely assortment of non-alcoholic beverages if you'd like—"

Reagan held up her hand and shook her head. "Stop right there, Sparky. She's being sarcastic. We'll take two mimosas, an order of blueberry pancakes for Funny Girl over here, and I will have the Heart Attack Combo plate with white toast with butter and extra bacon. Thanks."

"You're no fun," Olivia teased and she sipped her water as the waiter walked away.

"Don't poke the bear that you dragged out of hibernation early on a Sunday for some godforsaken reason."

"So, who's the lucky girl leaving hickeys on your neck?" Olivia poked Reagan's neck from across the table with her fork.

"Olivia, forks are for eating, not poking." Reagan batted her hand away and looked off to the left. "Uh, no one in particular."

"Mm-hmm. Didn't catch her name, huh?"

Reagan twisted her mouth to the side before reaching to sip her water. "No, she has a name."

"So, I should ask old lady Cranston next door? I'm sure she turned off her hearing aids to avoid the repetitive chorus of her name last night, given the looks of that bite mark on your collarbone."

Reagan adjusted the collar of her shirt and grinned. "She knocked a picture off the bathroom wall last night. That old lady is going to put a hole in the plaster one of these days."

"That old lady is your landlord. Talk about not poking the bear, Rea."

"Yeah, yeah. We have an understanding. I do all the annoying maintenance stuff and pay my rent on time. She shuts off her hearing aids on Friday and Saturday nights."

"Don't forget Wednesday nights," Olivia pointed out. "You had a pretty legit got-laid grin at the meeting Thursday morning."

Reagan blushed. "Yeah, that's true. Fair point."

"So," Olivia pressed again, "who is this frequent bed buddy?"

"Oh, uh…" Reagan looked around and mumbled something Olivia couldn't hear.

"What?"

"Hannah." Reagan dared to push her sunglasses up on top of her head as she waited for Olivia to reply.

"Hannah?" Olivia gave her a confused look, "Wait, *Hannah*, Hannah? Like, stage five clinger Hannah? My Hannah, Hannah?"

"I didn't see your name branded on her anywhere, Liv," Reagan said with a sly smile. "Trust me, I gave a really thorough check."

"Ew, Rea." Olivia grimaced. "Too much info. Brunch hasn't even been served yet."

"Anyway." Reagan cleared her throat. "I ran into her at a bar a few weeks after we got back from Chicago and she was sort of complaining about you a little, sorry."

"It's fine, please continue."

"So, one thing led to another and we sort of ended up naked."

"You tell a riveting tale, Reagan. Maybe you should have become a writer."

Reagan gave her a look. "Well, the girl is a little intense, I will give you that, but she's great in bed."

Olivia nodded in agreement. "That's a fair point."

"I don't know, I kinda started to like her. I mean, she's direct, you know? It's kind of nice to be so desired." Reagan shrugged. "It's still new, but it's working at the moment."

"Good for you, Reagan."

"Are you mad?"

"No. I can see it actually. I can see how you two might actually work. She's a nice girl, Rea. She was just a little too much for me at the time."

"Yeah, okay, cool. I was kinda afraid you were gonna blow your stack."

Olivia rolled her eyes as the waiter brought the food over. "Why would I freak out? I'm the one who ended it."

"I know, but still, I probably should have told you about it sooner."

"Thanks, Reagan. I appreciate that." Olivia was touched at Reagan's sensitivity. It was easy to overlook it sometimes, but Reagan had always proven that she had Olivia's best interests in mind over years of their friendship, even if it was sometimes hidden under crude language and sexual advances.

"All right. So, spill," Reagan mumbled between loud chomps on her bacon. "Why Sunday brunch so fucking early?"

"Reagan, it's two p.m."

"Yeah, like I said, early. It's Sunday. That is a day of rest and recovery. What's up?"

Olivia cut a piece of pancake and popped it into her mouth. "This place has the best pancakes."

"Liv," Reagan tried again, "what's up?"

Olivia sighed and put her fork down. "So, let's say you owe me for the Hannah thing and I need your advice on something—but you owe me, so be nice."

Reagan nodded and chewed her toast. "Okay, go."

"I've been talking to Savannah on the phone every night for the last week and she's in town and wants to meet tonight. And I said yes and I'm freaking out."

Reagan choked on her bite and started coughing, drawing the attention of the table next to them. Olivia pushed Reagan's water glass closer as Reagan gagged and sputtered.

"Jesus, Liv! Wait for me to swallow before you punch me in the throat, will ya?" Reagan wiped tears from her eyes with her napkin as she tried to glare at Olivia. "For fuck's sake. A little warning next time."

Olivia raised her hands in defeat. "Reagan. C'mon. I'm serious."

"Serious about what? Trying to kill me?" Reagan scowled and pushed her plate away. "I think I lost my appetite."

"*Reagan.*" Olivia pouted. "What do I do?"

"Well, it sounds like you already decided what you're going to do." Reagan leaned back and rubbed her forehead with her hand. "What do you want me to say, Liv?"

"I don't know, Reagan, how about *You're making a big mistake, Liv*, *This is a supremely bad idea, Liv*, *Cancel your plans, Liv*, *Your tits look great in that shirt, Liv*—anything would suffice."

"Okay, first off, your tits do look great in that shirt. Is that a new bra?" Reagan winked. "Secondly, I don't know if I think it's a bad idea."

"Really?"

"Really."

Olivia was dumbfounded. She'd been counting on Reagan to talk her out of the meeting tonight. "I guess I—What? Really?"

"How many mimosas have you had, Liv?" Reagan picked up Olivia's glass and went to drink it before Olivia reached out and grabbed it back. "I'm not sure your ears are working. I was just looking out for you."

Olivia gulped down the rest of her drink and signaled the waiter for two more. "I guess I figured you would be the voice of reason here."

"When have I ever been the voice of reason? The voice of bad decisions, dangerous choices, inappropriate suggestions, yes. Reason, no. But I'm flattered."

Olivia frowned and rested her head heavily on her hands.

Reagan leaned forward and said, "Look, I'm not the biggest fan of Savannah. Mainly because I know she hurt your feelings. And at the end of the day, you're my best friend and I feel protective of you. But I remember how happy you were when you two were together, even if at the time I didn't know you were together. You were happy, Liv. And your creative side shone like it did when you were younger. So I think if your gut says go, you should go."

Olivia looked at Reagan through her fingertips before she lifted her head and chuckled. "Reagan, have I told that you never stop surprising me?"

Reagan beamed. "No. But is my reward you buying brunch?"

"Ha-ha, yeah, Rea, this one's on me."

Savannah had gotten used to being confident and in control. It was something altogether unfamiliar for her to be nervous and jumpy. But tonight, she was definitely feeling the latter. She checked her phone again for the time, to make sure she wasn't late. Okay, not really. She knew she wasn't late. She checked it to make sure that if Olivia did stand her up, she would know just how long she had been sitting here in a frantic panic.

"Hey."

Savannah turned toward the sound of Olivia's voice and smiled. "Hey, you."

Olivia slowed to a stop in front of the coffee shop where Savannah was sitting on a bench and hesitated.

Savannah stood and took a tentative step toward Olivia. She reached out and ran her fingers along the hand that held Olivia's purse close to her side. When Olivia didn't pull back, Savannah got a little bolder and tugged at Olivia's fingers until they slackened their hold, and she entwined their fingers. "I'm glad you came."

Olivia nodded, her eyes watching the way their fingers clasped together.

"Walk with me." Savannah guided Olivia from the front of the coffee shop.

"Not in the mood for a little caffeine?" Olivia allowed herself to be led down the sidewalk toward Central Park.

"I'm feeling pretty energized." Savannah paused. "But we can grab a cup if you want."

"No, I'm okay. So, where are we going?"

"I'm not sure, to be honest." Savannah ran her thumb along the back of Olivia's hand. "I'm sure we'll know it when we find it."

The night was clear and cool. They walked in silence along the gas lamp lit paths of the park, winding their way past vending carts and children playing soccer on illuminated fields to a bench facing a small duck pond. Savannah nodded toward the bench and they sat down, hands still entwined.

Savannah looked out at the water in front of them and pulled Olivia's hand into her lap, gently tracing her fingertips along the lines of Olivia's palm. She let out a soft sigh and faced the woman she had missed so much these past seven weeks. "I'm so sorry, Liv. I'm not, I don't—" She struggled. "I'm sorry."

Olivia frowned. "Savannah…I—"

"Wait." Savannah paused and centered herself. "Hear me out—really, I'm sorry. There were at least a dozen times I could have talked to you or tried to warn you or, I don't know, done more than I did. But I was selfish and I wanted to enjoy every minute I had with you since I knew the project was ending and you were leaving, and I just—fuck, I'm sorry."

Olivia blinked. "Savannah, I get it."

"You do?" Savannah couldn't believe her ears.

"I get it. I get that you were in a tough spot. I just, I guess a part of me felt like I should get preferential treatment in that case." Olivia frowned as she spoke. "That sounds ridiculous when I actually say it out loud."

Savannah surveyed Olivia's face closely before she asked what had been on her mind almost constantly for the last week they had been casually speaking. "Why didn't you take any of my calls or emails? I tried to reach you for weeks. What changed?" She held Olivia's hand and quickly followed up with, "Not that I'm complaining."

"I couldn't talk to you, Savannah. I couldn't stomach the thought of what you had to say."

Savannah took a chance and released Olivia's hand, reaching to cup Olivia's jaw. "And what were you so afraid of hearing?"

Olivia didn't answer her, but she didn't turn away or shrug her off either.

"Tell me," Savannah implored as she leaned closer to Olivia.

"There's that sex voice again, kryptonite." Olivia sighed as she leaned into Savannah's touch. "I guess I was afraid you would tell me that we had a good run but that you had no intention of pursuing this relationship beyond the end of the project. And I don't think I could have handled that."

Savannah moved so her knees were pressed against Olivia's, her body facing Olivia's fully as she asked, "And now?"

Olivia furrowed her brow in confusion. "And now what?"

"Can you handle it if I tell you I have every intention of pursuing this?" Savannah pressed her thumb against Olivia's lower lip while she waited for an answer.

Olivia's eyes closed and she shuddered.

"Can you handle it if I tell you that these last few weeks have been the most difficult of my life because you weren't in them?" Savannah brought her lips to the edge of Olivia's mouth, pausing before she gambled and placed a long, slow kiss to Olivia's lips.

To her delight, Olivia responded earnestly. Her hand threaded into Savannah's hair and Savannah let herself be consumed by the passionate familiarity of Olivia's mouth on hers.

Savannah broke away from the kiss and rested her forehead on Olivia's. "Can you handle it if I tell you I love you?"

Olivia blinked, then her mouth opened slightly, but she said nothing.

A pit formed in Savannah's stomach when Olivia did not respond. It wasn't that she expected to hear it back. She hadn't even expected to say it aloud. "Because I do, Liv. And I'm not sorry about that. But if it's more than you can handle, I understand."

Savannah's attempt to pull away was halted by Olivia's lips on hers. Olivia mumbled between kisses. "It's not. I can handle that. Stop seducing me and kiss me."

"Gladly."

CHAPTER TWENTY-NINE

Olivia awoke to the smell of coffee and the soft sound of music coming from her kitchen. She glanced over at the clock and let out a lazy sigh. It was Monday, but she was in no rush. She had warned Corrine via email a little after midnight not to expect her until late.

"You're up." Savannah's voice was soft and playful from Olivia's bedroom doorway.

"Why are you all the way over there?" Olivia whined and impatiently pulled back the covers, motioning for Savannah to join her.

"I was making coffee, babe." Savannah crawled into bed, her warm lips caressing Olivia's jaw. Olivia had surprised herself when she asked Savannah to come in after their date last night. She'd had every intention to toss Savannah to the curb, until she saw her, that was. And then all those feelings rushed to the surface. And then the L-word showed up and the train jumped off the tracks and she found herself wrapped in familiar long limbs, breathing in her favorite perfume like they had never been apart.

Olivia turned her head to expose her neck to Savannah's lips. "Coffee sounds like heaven right about now."

"Mm-hmm," Savannah hummed into the skin over Olivia's collarbone.

Olivia let herself bask in the affection for a moment before she asked, "What's your schedule today?"

Savannah sucked on Olivia's clavicle briefly before she rolled onto her back and pulled Olivia onto her T-shirt clad chest. "I have some meetings in the early afternoon, nothing too important. What about you?"

"We have a conference call over lunch, and I have some interviews later." Olivia closed her eyes at the sensation of Savannah's fingers running through her hair. They had made it a point to avoid talking about work; it still felt a little taboo to know that Savannah was in New York working on the project that they had previously worked on together. Olivia had conflicting feelings about it.

"Do you have any plans later?" Savannah scratched lightly at the nape of Olivia's neck. "I was hoping to make you dinner."

Olivia lifted her head and rested her chin between Savannah's breasts as she looked up at her. "Nope, no plans. What are you making me?"

Savannah's forefinger tapped Olivia playfully on the nose before she leaned down and kissed her. "Well, you'll just have to wait and see, I guess."

Olivia pouted against Savannah's lips. "No fair."

"Now, now, Liv. You know how I feel about that pout." Savannah mirrored Olivia's pout before adding, "What do you say about a quick breakfast before I head back to my hotel and get changed for work?"

"I think the outfit you have on now is pretty great." Olivia's gaze dragged over the soft cotton track and field shirt from college that Savannah had borrowed last night. She'd been impressed that she'd managed to spend time with Savannah that didn't involve nakedness. She wasn't quite sure she was ready for that type of intimacy just yet, and Savannah seemed to be on the same page. Savannah was affectionate but still respectful, like she was worried she might cross a line or something. It was reminiscent of when they first got together, and Olivia found it endearing.

"Well, I can't disagree with you there. I like wearing your clothes." Savannah wiggled out from beneath Olivia and looked down at her barely covered behind. "Your shirt makes my ass look fabulous."

"It really does." Olivia nodded in agreement, appreciating Savannah's assets as she led Olivia out of the room toward the kitchen.

❖

"I wasn't expecting to see you today," Reagan whispered to Olivia as Corrine addressed the rest of the group members in the conference room.

Olivia pretended to pay attention to Corrine's words. "Why's that?"

"Uh, didn't you have a date with Savannah last night?"

"It was coffee, not a date." Olivia watched Corrine point to the graph on the wall.

"Yeah, okay—coffee, date, whatever," Reagan said. "So?"

"Any questions?" Corrine's voice drew them back to her presentation. When no one spoke she said, "Okay, great work, guys. Olivia, I will meet you in conference room B for that interview in a bit."

"Sounds good." Olivia made an attempt to stand when Reagan's hand landed softly on her forearm, halting her progression.

Reagan gave her an expectant look.

"Fine." Olivia sighed and sat back down. "It went well."

"The vagueness of this conversation is killing me."

Olivia shrugged and looked out the window.

"Hannah does this thing with her tongue that is unreal."

Olivia whipped her head toward Reagan and grimaced. "Ew, Reagan."

"Well, I had to say something to get you to look me in the face," Reagan said. "So, what's up? Why so evasive with the gossip?"

"Why so curious?"

"You're deflecting. Your game is weak." Reagan leaned back and crossed her arms. "I'm going to go ahead and Sherlock this for you because you're taking too long."

Olivia furrowed her brow. "What?"

"Well, if it had gone badly, you would have come into work earlier with red, puffy eyes and been a real *b-i-t-c-h*, if you know what I mean."

"Hey—"

Reagan held up her hand. "Nope. No peanut gallery comments until the case is presented."

Olivia suppressed a smile and nodded.

"Thank you, Watson. Now, as I was saying, if it had gone badly, you would have been entirely impossible to work with and there would have been lots of weeping and references to *Sleepless in Seattle*."

Olivia rolled her eyes. "Rea—"

"Tut!" Reagan warned. "No speakie." She cracked her neck. "So the way I see it, your coffee talk must have gone pretty well because you didn't get here until noonish and you have a hickey on your neck."

Olivia's eyes bulged and her hand went to below her right ear as she panicked about the extra attention Savannah paid to that area before she went back to her hotel.

"Bingo, bango. Case solved." Reagan gloated and brushed invisible dust from her shoulder. "And way to give yourself away. There's no hickey there, amateur."

"I hate you."

"You love me." Reagan grabbed Olivia's water bottle and took a swig.

"She told me she loves me."

Reagan spat the contents of her mouth onto the top of the conference table.

"Reagan." Olivia pushed her chair from the table to avoid the mess.

"Olivia. I thought we talked about you trying to kill me. It's rude." Reagan wiped her mouth with the back of her hand and shook her head as she looked forlornly at the now empty bottle. "Man, I was really thirsty…"

Olivia shook the files in the air in an attempt to dispel the droplets as she whined, "It was my water."

"Well, don't leave me hanging. What did you say back?" Reagan leaned forward, resting her elbows on her knees.

"Um, nothing." Olivia picked at the edge of the folder.

"Oh." Reagan paused before she ran a hand through her tousled hair. "I forgot about that."

"Forgot that it was my water? Because you totally owe me one."

Reagan shook her head with a frown. "I forgot how that makes you react. You know, for some sappy, chick-flick loving hopeless romantic, you get worse whiplash than me when someone drops the love bomb. It's a conundrum."

Olivia opened her mouth to argue when a knock at the open door caught her attention. "Savannah?"

"Hey, ladies." Savannah leaned against the door frame dressed to kill in a power suit with just the right amount of cleavage exposed. "How are things?"

Reagan shot Olivia a look before she stood up and strode over to her old colleague. "Savannah Quinn, what brings you to the Big Apple?"

"Oh, you know, I guess I just missed you."

A look of recognition settled on Reagan's face and her jovial expression changed. "Work. You're here on business. Our business."

"Reagan," Olivia warned as she stood. "Let's not start this."

"It's okay, Liv." Savannah straightened up and turned to Reagan.

"Yes, I'm here for a new project." She sighed. "I'm sorry things ended the way they did."

Reagan surveyed her with a curious expression. "Did you see the rest of the team yet?"

"I ran into the guys when the meeting filed out. Corrine was on a call. I haven't seen Farrah yet."

Reagan nodded. "I'll let you two, uh, catch up." She glanced back toward Olivia before she added, "She's giving you a second chance, Savannah. Don't fuck it up."

They watched Reagan slip out the door without further comment. Olivia groaned. "Sorry about that."

Savannah held up her hand in acknowledgment. "So Reagan knows, huh?"

Olivia knew she was blushing. "Uh, yeah. She saw us kissing at the airport."

"Anyone else?"

"Just Farrah and Reagan. And Christine, but she's my sister, so she doesn't count."

Savannah stepped into the room and quietly closed the door behind her. "This is the room we first met in. This is where you told me about the Coleman Park view and the concrete jungle."

Olivia looked out at the glass to her left. "It's my favorite room here."

Savannah stepped closer, extending her hand to take Olivia's. "I missed you today."

Olivia gave Savannah a shy smile. "It's only midday."

"Feels like an eternity." Savannah sighed. "I hate working without you. Especially knowing you are just a few blocks away."

Olivia shrugged, unsure of how to respond. "So is that why you're here? Because you missed me?"

"Is that weird?" Savannah looked a little nervous.

"No, I think it's sweet." Olivia tugged Savannah a little closer by their joined hands.

"Good." Savannah spared a quick glance toward the closed conference room door before she pressed a lingering kiss to Olivia's lips.

"It's probably better we aren't working together," Olivia said, her mouth close to Savannah's, "because you are still the best kisser ever and I am having all kind of thoughts pertaining to non-work-related activities in the work setting that are distracting."

Savannah's soft chuckle was muffled by the skin of Olivia's neck under her lips. "Like drafting tables?"

"Precisely." Olivia mustered all her control to distance herself from Savannah's lips. She wasn't concerned about people finding out they were together. But she wasn't quite sure they *were* together.

Savannah placed another kiss to Olivia's mouth. "I was hoping to borrow your keys so I could pop into your place a little early to prep some things for dinner."

"Oh." Olivia was surprised by the request. "Yeah, sure."

Savannah leaned back against the table and pulled Olivia into a loose hug. "If it's not okay, Liv, that's fine."

Olivia settled into Savannah's arms and rested her head on Savannah's shoulder. "No, it's fine. I guess I wasn't expecting you to say that."

Savannah raised her eyebrow. "What were you expecting?"

"I don't know," Olivia admitted. "I'm not sure."

Savannah's expression as unreadable. "What time will you be done tonight?"

"I suppose five-ish."

"Okay." Savannah rubbed her hands up and down Olivia's back. "Dinner will be at six."

Olivia stepped away from Savannah but kept close as she replied, "Let's go get those keys before my meeting with Corrine, and then we'll track down Farrah so you can say hello."

Chapter Thirty

"Cooper, how many cloves of garlic?" Savannah called over her shoulder as she began mincing.

"Three. Four if you really want to make sure Dracula doesn't interrupt your date, but it may decrease your chances of getting laid." His voice sounded over the speakers of her tablet.

"You are such a perv." Savannah shot him a look and reached for another clove.

"Well, your outfit implies you're looking to have sex. I was just giving you a friendly warning about bad breath." Cooper smiled at her over the webcam and sipped his beer.

"Shouldn't you be in class?" Savannah said in response, ignoring his jab.

"Who would read you Abuela Carmen's recipe if I was?"

Savannah had been grateful when Cooper picked up earlier. After she had proposed making dinner for Olivia, she realized all her recipes and her cookware were in Chicago. Abuela Carmen had been Cooper's nanny for a few years during his early teens before her father bailed on his third wife when the money ran thin. She made a mean sautéed eggplant pizza on flatbread. Savannah stirred the ingredients in the pot and checked the time.

"You know, I can't remember the last time we cooked together," Cooper said.

"Coop, we had dinner together before Olivia left Chicago," Savannah reminded him.

"Yeah, but I mean, like, just you and me. We used to do it all the time when we were younger."

"That's because Dad was never around and you had an insatiable appetite," Savannah teased. "I had to feed you to keep you out of trouble."

"You make the best mac and cheese." Cooper nodded solemnly as he took another sip.

"Thanks, bro."

"And you look nice, by the way. I think she's going to like that outfit."

Savannah stopped cleaning and sat down on the kitchen island stool in front of her brother's image on the screen. "Thanks, Coop. I'm a little nervous."

Cooper nodded. "I figured if you were busting out Carmenita's eggplant panty dropper recipe, you might be."

"I'm just not too sure how she's going to take the news." She thought back to the tension she felt at the office earlier. She'd hoped it was mostly sexual, and it did seem that way, but when she asked Olivia for her keys, she seemed guarded even though she had been receptive to Savannah's affections.

"Well, I'm sure she'll take the news better than I did." Cooper frowned.

Savannah felt that familiar pang in her chest at Cooper's admission. "I need to live my life for me now, Cooper."

"I know. It doesn't make it suck any less, though."

"I just want to make sure I did everything I possibly could, no what-ifs, you know?"

Cooper leaned back in his chair and clasped his hands behind his head. "What are you going to do if she doesn't react the way you're hoping?"

"I don't know, crawl into a hole and die?"

"That sounds like a good plan. Any alternative endings lined up?"

"Nope." She made an oval shape with her arms. "This is my basket and these are all my eggs."

"Sav, if you keep discussing your menstrual cycle, you are never gonna get laid. Go stir your eggplant."

❖

"I'm totally freaking out, Chris," Olivia said into the phone as the cabbie honked at a meandering pedestrian.

"Why are you freaking out? It's not like you haven't had sex with her before." Christine sounded bored.

"It's not about having sex with her." Olivia's eyes were drawn to the cabbie's in the rearview mirror. She lowered her voice. "It's about all the other stuff."

"What other stuff?"

"The *I love you* stuff."

"Wait—what?" Christine sounded markedly more attentive now.

"So, you know how we agreed to have coffee last night?"

"Yes, I remember coffee. Go on."

"Well, it went really…well and she spent the night."

"So, you already slept with her. Good. What's the big deal?"

Olivia groaned. "I didn't sleep with her, she slept over."

"In your bed?"

"Well, yes."

"But you didn't have sex?"

"No."

"Did you want to?"

"Yes." Olivia paused. "Wait, that's not what we're talking about."

"It's not?" Christine sounded perplexed.

"No. We're talking about the *I love you* thing."

"Oh, right. So you told her you loved her when you were so busy not having sex?"

"No."

"I'm lost."

"Christine, focus. We had a nice night, there was no sex, but I wanted there to be, sure, but there wasn't. It was just a lot of cuddling and getting reacquainted in a PG-13 kind of way."

"I don't believe that for a second," Christine said.

"Well it was mostly PG-13," Olivia admitted as her thoughts were pulled back to the unconscious groping that sort of escalated before it was extinguished.

"And where in that mess was an *I love you?*"

"At the park before we went back to my place."

"You went to the park? Which part?"

"By the duck section behind that pretzel vendor—not important, by the way."

"I just want to set the scene, you know, taste, smell, sounds," Christine replied.

"It was quiet, warm, after sunset, we were on a park bench, and some kids were playing soccer off to the side, I think." Olivia humored her sister with details. "And then she told me she loved me."

"Oh."

"Oh? That's it?"

"Well, what did you do?"

"I kissed her."

"And?"

"And invited her back to my place to watch a movie and snuggle."

"But not have sex."

"No, Christine. No sex."

"So, let me get this straight, you're freaking out because Savannah is back in town and told you she loves you and you invited her over but didn't have sex but you wanted to and she loves you and you love her. And that's a problem?"

"Yes." Olivia nodded as the cabbie pulled up to her curb. "Wait, no, not exactly."

"What did I get wrong?" Christine sounded skeptical.

Olivia handed the cabbie the fare and thanked him as she closed the door and walked toward her building. "I don't know if I'm ready for all of this."

Christine sighed. "Olivia. Don't do this. Don't freak out for no reason."

"I have every reason to freak out, Christine. There've been weeks of no talking and now there is *I love you*. Freak-outs are allowed."

"You love her."

Olivia paused as she reached the front door of her building. "I do."

"Then why not just tell her and make it not so complicated? She obviously feels the same way that you do. Except she's a little braver."

"I resent that comment." Olivia pouted.

"Resent it all you'd like—I don't care," Christine said. "It's time you accept the fact that you need to be a little vulnerable once in a while, too."

Olivia buzzed her apartment and waited for Savannah's voice.

"Hello?"

"Hey, it's me. Buzz me in?" Olivia spoke into the intercom. The lock buzzed open and she walked through.

"Where are you?" Christine waited for the noise to fade before resuming their conversation.

"I'm in my apartment building, in the elevator. Savannah came by the office earlier today to get my house keys. She's cooking dinner for us."

"That's adorable," Christine cooed.

"I know," Olivia agreed. "I'm so fucked, aren't I?"

"Sounds like you are very lucky and shouldn't let your past behavior in these situations dictate your future."

"You sound like Yoda." Olivia paused at her apartment door and took a deep breath.

"No, but I'm still right. Have a good night with your girl, Olivia."

"Good night, Christine."

❖

"Are we really doing this?" Olivia asked.

"It would appear as though yes, we are." Savannah refilled Olivia's wineglass.

Olivia raised one eyebrow in challenge before she started. "Fine. Third grade, behind the seesaw on the playground at Brown Elementary, with Max Rubick."

"Typical. First kiss with a boy? I'm unimpressed," Savannah teased as she leaned back on the arm of Olivia's sofa, cradling her wineglass.

"Oh, yeah? You got something better?" Olivia pulled her knees up to her chest as she reclined next to Savannah.

"Absolutely." Savannah leaned a little closer to whisper, "I always have something better."

Olivia didn't miss the playful taunt. Throughout dinner and into dessert the sexual tension between them had been mounting. She thought it had hit a peak when they tumbled onto the sofa in a passionate kiss but had been surprised when Savannah had excused herself to open another bottle of wine. When she had suggested they play an abbreviated Twenty Questions, Olivia had agreed with the hope that they could continue what they had started a few minutes before. If the look in Savannah's eyes was any indication, they were right on track.

"First kiss—fifth grade, sleepaway camp, top bunk, Molly Parker. Who, I might add, was two years older."

"An older woman, you scoundrel."

"You're up. Do your worst."

"You might regret that." Olivia smirked. "Okay, most embarrassing sexual encounter. Who, what, and where?"

"That feels like three questions."

Olivia merely shrugged in response.

"Back of a Greyhound bus on the bench seat during a six-hour ride, with my college girlfriend, while her face was in my lap. We were interrupted by a male passenger who went into the bathroom next to us and asked us if he could join when he came out." Savannah paused. "We said no. At the time I was beyond mortified. In retrospect, it was kind of flattering. He was handsome and very polite about it, and he took the rejection with a gentle smile and nod. It could have been way worse."

Olivia laughed and shook her head. "Here I was thinking we'd had a few interesting sexual encounters, and I got beat by the Greyhound bus? Damn."

Savannah set both of their glasses aside. She shifted on the couch and wrapped her arm around Olivia's shoulders where she placed a few chaste kisses on the exposed skin. "You asked me about the most embarrassing, not the best. Ask me again."

The intensity of Savannah's gaze on Olivia's mouth made her stutter. "What was the best?"

Savannah moved closer, placing a leg on either side of Olivia's knees, straddling her hips as she looped her arms behind Olivia's neck and gave Olivia an impish grin. "The best what? The best orgasm I've ever had? That night you came to my hotel room by accident. I remember wanting you so bad it almost hurt, and when I finally felt your skin against mine, I thought I'd come just from the sensation alone."

Olivia let out a soft moan and gripped Savannah's hips, pulling her closer. "Yeah?"

Savannah nodded. "Or maybe it was the third morning of our vacation together in Phoenix, after you woke me up by caressing my naked skin and when your lips wrapped around my nipple. You made me beg for it. Maybe that was the best one."

Olivia slid her right hand off Savannah's hip and under her shirt, palming at Savannah's stomach as she let the memory wash over her. She'd been pleasantly surprised at how loud Savannah had been that day. It was one of her favorite memories.

Savannah closed her eyes and dropped her head back. "No, maybe it was in Chicago at my apartment when I had you on your knees from behind and when you arched back into me and we came together. My body so close to yours it was inevitable."

"You were unbelievable that night." Olivia licked up Savannah's neck. "You touched every place I needed you to. I had no idea sex could be so pleasurable."

Savannah ground her hips down against Olivia's when Olivia's lips finally connected with hers. They kissed passionately, hands moving greedily over each other until Olivia shifted them so Savannah was on her back, underneath her on the couch.

"I missed you." Olivia's breath was hot and fast against Savannah's lips as her hand worked its way into the waistband of Savannah's jeans and past her panties. She stroked along the slick, heated flesh as Savannah bucked below her, moving in sloppy, teasing motions until Savannah gasped and pleaded. Her fingers scratched along Olivia's shoulders and hip. "Tell me."

"I missed you. I need you, please." Savannah pulled back to look up at Olivia, her breathing labored and inefficient. "Please, Liv."

Olivia slipped inside Savannah and increased her thrusts as she asked again, demanding what had gone unanswered as she felt Savannah start to tremble with release. "Tell me, Savannah. Tell me again. Tell me how you feel."

Savannah whispered in understanding, "I love you."

Olivia watched the flood of emotion cross Savannah's face as she gave Olivia the reply she was waiting for. She saw the fear, the lust, the pain, the ecstasy, but it was the adoration that drew Olivia's lips back to Savannah's. She knew Savannah meant every word of it. And it gave her a sense of peace to hold her as she came down, cradling her close and kissing along her face and jaw. She felt whole and loved and it was beautiful. "Thank you."

Savannah's body vibrated with energy as she recovered. She snuggled with Olivia. "Liv?"

Olivia propped herself up on her elbow while the fingers of her other hand continued to caress along the flushed skin of Savannah's neck. "What's up, sweetheart?"

"I want this to work. I want to be with you. Can we try this again?"

"The sex? Of course," Olivia teased but Savannah pouted. Olivia sighed as Savannah entwined their fingers and held their clasped hands against her chest. "How can we make this work, Savannah?"

"I think it's working just fine right now." Savannah slipped her leg between Olivia's and pressed against her. Olivia moaned in response. "We're good together, Liv."

Olivia nodded in agreement. They definitely had sexual chemistry, but Reagan had been right on the flight back from Chicago. Distance was going to be a real problem for them. Olivia sat up, pulling Savannah with her as she reached for her wineglass as a distraction. "My life is here. My home is here, Savannah. I don't think I can be with someone that I never see. I like—"

"Roots. You like having roots." Savannah's expression was serious when she asked, "Do you love me?"

Olivia's lips paused on her wineglass. She licked the last drop from the rim before setting it down and facing Savannah. Christine's advice was fresh in her mind. "I do."

Savannah nodded. "Then let's find a way to make this work. I don't want to spend another moment wondering where we stand. Let me show you that this relationship is possible." Savannah cradled Olivia's face in her hands as she implored, "Let me love you."

"All right, show me." Olivia's throat felt tight as she let herself be guided off the couch toward her bedroom.

CHAPTER THIRTY-ONE

It had been three weeks. Three weeks of waking up next to Savannah. Three weeks of long, passion-filled nights and soft, nuzzling kisses in the morning. It had been three weeks of dates introducing Savannah to NYC and meeting up after work to unwind before falling into bed with each other, sometimes just to cuddle, sometimes just to taste one another. It had been three weeks of distractedly staring out the window while she was at work, wondering what Savannah was up to just a few blocks away. It had been three weeks of Savannah telling her she loved her every night and Olivia still not being able to say it out loud. It had been three blissfully perfect weeks, and Savannah's project in NY was finishing tomorrow and Olivia was terrified.

Multiple times over the past few weeks, Savannah had tried to broach the topic of what their lives would be like after the project completed, and multiple times Olivia deflected it. The other night a frustrated frown settled on Savannah's face and she went back to her hotel room to finish up some work. Olivia had been convinced she would get a call telling her that Savannah had been too tired to come back afterward. Which although it would have been devastating, she realized would have been completely understandable. She had been more surprised when Savannah called to let her know she was downstairs and asked to be buzzed in.

When Olivia opened the door, Savannah had the same weary look on her face that she'd had when she left, but there was something else there, too. Before Olivia could ask or back out of asking, Savannah's lips were on hers and she was kicking closed the apartment door with a "Let's go to bed, baby, it's late." Olivia didn't argue.

Savannah licked every inch of her body that night until she almost fainted from exhaustion. When she woke up the next morning there was a note on Savannah's side of the bed informing her that she had an early meeting and would call her later. It was signed with a heart.

That was yesterday morning. Olivia had not seen Savannah since, and the change in morning routine was devastating. Olivia missed her smell. She missed the way Savannah would let the shower water run until it was the perfect temperature and then coax her into it with promises of coffee and breakfast or even join her, if they had enough time. She missed the joyful feeling of seeing the clock at the end of the day and knowing that Savannah would be meeting her soon.

Things were so unknown now. She realized what she missed most was her infallible ability to ignore the obvious: she was in love with a woman who was about to leave and she still couldn't say the words out loud. But she couldn't ignore it anymore; Savannah's project was ending at the end of the day today and she was going to lose her out of fear.

Olivia had texted and called Savannah earlier today without any response. She figured Savannah must be busy finishing her project and prepping for the launch party, so she settled back into her chair at work with a frown.

"What's that face about?" Reagan asked as she leaned against Olivia's desk and sipped her coffee.

Since Reagan had been so supportive of her and Savannah's relationship, she decided to be honest. "Savannah's project wraps today. And she hasn't returned my texts."

Reagan paused, setting down her coffee with calculated precision before glancing up at Olivia. "When is she leaving?"

"I don't know." Olivia felt the tears well in her eyes. She had not asked Savannah that bit of information. It made the ending feel too real. All she knew was that tonight was the end of the project, and Savannah hadn't tried to initiate a discussion about their future again. It was like she had resigned herself to not knowing. "I fucked this up, Rea."

"What do you mean? I thought things were going well?"

"They were, are, I mean." Olivia tried to contain the sob that bubbled into her throat. "What if she already left? What if she just didn't tell me? She tried to talk about us but I just couldn't. What if the radio silence is because she's gone?"

Reagan's eyes widened in surprise. "Uh, I think you're freaking out, Liv. I'm sure she's just busy. When was the last time you saw her?"

"Yesterday." Olivia sniffled.

"So relax." Reagan gave Olivia a half-hearted smile. "Or be a total creeper and just call the hotel to see when she checks out and go be all Nicholas Sparks-y and show up at her hotel room with flowers, love sonnets, and naked apologies."

"I wonder if it's too late for that." Olivia reached for the phone as she typed on the keyboard in front of her.

"What are you doing now?" Reagan attempted to see the monitor, but Olivia shooed her away. "Wait, are you really calling the hotel? I was kidding."

Olivia ignored her and responded to the pleasant male voice on the other end of the phone. "Hi, yes, I was hoping you could tell me whether or not the person in room 457 had checked out yet?" She nodded to no one as she waited, intentionally avoiding Reagan's glare. She had laughed when Savannah had told her the room number she was staying in during their first conversation. When she commented on the coincidence of it, Savannah had admitted to it being intentional. Olivia remembered the warm feeling in her chest when she had heard it. "Yes, I'm still here...Oh...When was that? Okay, thanks."

Reagan tapped her foot impatiently. "Well?"

"She's gone." Olivia made no attempt to wipe away the tears as they began to fall. "She checked out yesterday."

"Shut up." Reagan shook her head in disbelief. "You're screwing with me, right?"

The panic started to set in.

Reagan sighed and pushed Olivia and her chair off to the side of the desk. "Liv, pull yourself together and move over."

Olivia just cried a little harder, gaining the attention of their coworkers. Her head dropped to her hands as Reagan nudged her away from the desk and bent over the keyboard. After a moment or two Reagan picked up the phone and mumbled into the receiver. Olivia didn't bother trying to listen. She was too upset. All Olivia could think about was the last thing she and Savannah had talked about before she woke up to the note on her pillow. Savannah had told her that she loved her. She had told her that she was elated they'd reconnected, and she'd kissed her cheek and whispered that she was ready to be happy. At the time, Olivia had felt like Savannah was telling her that she was happy to be with her. But now it just seemed like maybe Savannah was trying to warn her that she was leaving—like she was ready to be happy somewhere else. The thought made her insides ache, like her soul had fractured. Her sobs were interrupted by Reagan's warm hand on her shoulder.

"Liv, we have to go."

"Go where, Reagan?" Olivia fought the urge to shrug off Reagan's hand as a new wave of nausea swept over her. She shook her head and replied bitterly, "I'm going home, alone."

"No, you're going with me to the launch party for New Horizons' newest project. If we hurry, we can get there before it ends and you can catch her before she flies out."

"Reagan, didn't you hear me? She checked out yesterday. Not today. Yesterday. She's already gone."

"You don't know that."

"If she's still in the city, then where did she stay last night? Because it wasn't with me," Olivia challenged and crossed her arms as she tried to stop the painful hiccups lingering from her crying. "How do you even know where the launch party is?"

Reagan ran her hand through her hair with a sigh. "When Savannah told you she was in town, I called around to some of my engineer buddies to see if they had heard anything. I wanted to follow through, you know? See what they had done with our vision…" She shrugged. "Anyway, I just remembered that a friend of mine told me her catering company was recruited for the event, so I called in a favor and asked her to sneak us in through the kitchen. We can be there in twenty minutes, Liv. It's worth a shot."

Olivia gave Reagan a curious expression.

"What?" Reagan looked left and right before looking back at Olivia.

"You were checking up on the project?"

"That's your focus, Liv?"

"No." Olivia stood and reached for her jacket. "My focus is getting in front of Savannah and telling her I'm a jerk and that I love her. But I think it's cute that you're keeping tabs on the project."

"Hey, I may be a world-class slacker, but I take pride in the work I do when I do it, especially when it's as kick-ass as that New Horizons gig we had. I'm not about to let someone butcher it without at least knowing about it." Reagan blushed. "Stop looking at me like that."

"Let's go before I lose my nerve." Olivia grabbed her purse and headed for the elevator, hoping it wasn't too late.

❖

"Hey, Olivia." The woman in the white dress shirt and bow tie gave her a raised eyebrow as she opened the side door of the party for them.

"Oh, hey, Hannah. How are you?" Olivia made a mental note to throttle Reagan for neglecting to mention that her catering contact was their shared bedfellow.

"Fine. Hey, babe," Hannah addressed Reagan with a peck to her lips. "I put aside some leftovers for later."

Reagan beamed. "Awesome."

"You guys almost missed it. We're already boxing up the favors for people—you better get in there."

Reagan went to follow Olivia but stopped when Olivia turned to look at her. "I need to do this alone, Rea. Stay and help Hannah. Tell her I really appreciate this, okay?"

"Are you sure, Liv?"

Olivia looked over Reagan's shoulder at the poorly concealed death stare Hannah was sending her way. "Yeah, I'm sure. Go be a super girlfriend."

Reagan gave her a hesitant nod. "Good luck."

Olivia pushed through the kitchen doors toward the sound of the launch party and grabbed the first glass of champagne that sailed by her.

The room was bustling with activity. The New Horizons logo was etched into an ice sculpture on display in front of a digital frame that rotated pictures of what she assumed was the New York site space. She recognized a few of the people lining the far wall, giving them a polite wave as they glanced back at her in surprise. She hurriedly finished her glass and handed it off to a passing waiter while she scanned the crowd for Savannah.

"Olivia, this is a pleasant surprise." A booming voice interrupted her search.

She recognized the man from the Chicago launch. Savannah had been icy toward him and at the time Olivia couldn't understand why. "Hello, Mr. Dodd."

"Please, call me Ken—we're all friends here." His jolly red face shook with his empty smile. "Did you see the montage? The site came out great."

"I bet. You had excellent leadership…"

Ken's smile faded and he cleared his throat. "Ah, yes, that we did. Well, enjoy yourself, Ms. Dawson, and say hi to the team for me."

Olivia nodded because she was afraid that if she opened her mouth bad things would spill out. Over the past three weeks, Savannah had told her all about the behind-the-scenes meddling that Ken Dodd had been involved in; now that she was aware of his true nature, pleasantries seemed like a large feat to undertake.

The MC for the night took the microphone and addressed the audience, thanking them for coming to the launch party and telling them to be safe on their ride home. As the lights came on in the room and people began to disperse, Olivia finally got a glimpse of the dark red hair that had been so elusive.

"Savannah!" Olivia weaved through the crowd after the fast disappearing silhouette.

Two tall men in suits stopped immediately in front of her, and she crashed into one of them as she tried to follow Savannah's receding shape through the side doors of the conference room.

"Fuck, sorry," Olivia mumbled as she pushed his well-intentioned hands away from her and started to jog toward the far door. "Savannah!"

She pushed through the double doors and found herself alone in the coat room, standing in front of a large mirror. The face that looked back at her was flushed and panicked.

"Do you have your ticket, miss?" A small woman with dark-rimmed glasses emerged from behind a rack of coats, carrying a trench coat toward the other end of the room.

"Oh, uh, no." Olivia realized she had come in through the back entrance. "Sorry, I was just looking for someone."

"No one here but me, miss," she said as she handed the coat off to the man waiting by the other entrance. She looked beyond the man and asked, "Do you have your ticket, miss?"

"Yes, sorry, I thought I heard someone I knew here." Savannah's voice was music to Olivia's ears.

Olivia held her finger to her lips and took the jacket from the coat-check clerk, then carried it to the doorway. Savannah had her back turned toward the door. She was rummaging in her purse. She reached out for the coat, her attention elsewhere. "Thank you."

"You're very welcome," Olivia supplied quietly as she let her hand skim along Savannah's.

Savannah whipped her head toward her and a small smile graced her full lips as she sighed. "Olivia."

"In the flesh," Olivia said as she took the money from Savannah's hand and handed it to the waiting attendant with a broad smile. "Thanks, I found what I was looking for."

Olivia helped Savannah shrug on her jacket. She smoothed the lapels and looked at the curious expression on Savannah's face, feeling suddenly shy. "Hey."

"Hey," Savannah parroted as she adjusted the purse on her shoulder.

"Savannah, I—"

"Ms. Quinn, your car has arrived." A young man interrupted them and motioned for the door.

Savannah nodded and took a step in his direction before she paused. "I wasn't expecting to see you, I have to be somewhere…"

"Oh, I, well—"

"Would you like to ride with me? Wait—how did you get here?"

"It's a long story, and yes, I would love to."

"Okay, let's go." Savannah reached out and took Olivia's hand, leading her toward the door and into the night.

CHAPTER THIRTY-TWO

You didn't call or text me today." It had been quiet since they had climbed into the back of the town car. Savannah sat by her and held her hand, but she had been looking out the window for the past fifteen minutes, in complete silence.

"Today was a very busy day," Savannah replied as she watched the bustling city around them. When Olivia didn't acknowledge her, she glanced over. "How was work?"

"Long." Olivia pulled Savannah's hand into her lap. "Savannah?"

"Olivia," Savannah replied as the car broke through foot traffic and sped up.

"I'm sorry."

Savannah blinked. "About what?"

"Everything."

"Well, that's unfortunate." Savannah frowned, and her hand relaxed its grip on Olivia's.

"No, not about this." Olivia grabbed Savannah's hand more firmly. "I'm not sorry about this."

"You lost me." Savannah gave her a perplexed look.

Olivia let out a slow breath. "I love you."

Savannah didn't say anything at first. She remained still, her hand motionless in Olivia's grasp. "I know." Her response was quiet.

Olivia tried to quell the disappointment that bubbled inside her—she'd expected a different reaction. She tried again. "I love you and I should have told you all along, but I have a bad history of leaving the people that love me, mainly because I don't think I have ever really let myself be loved because it scares me, and I was wrong and I'm sorry. I love you."

Savannah leaned forward and cupped Olivia's jaw. Her fingers danced along the skin of Olivia's neck as she pressed a kiss to Olivia's lips. "Thank you. I love you, too."

Olivia warmed at the returned sentiment but before she knew it, the moment had ended, and Savannah's lips were off hers. She decided it was now or never. "I'm not ready for you to go."

"Is that why you decided today was the day to tell me you love me? Because the New York project is over?" Savannah's expression was serious, her voice soft.

"No. Yes, well, no." Olivia cringed as Savannah shook her head and sighed. "Wait."

"I have waited, Liv. I've waited and been patient and took what I could get from you. I told you I wanted to be happy, Liv. Is this your idea of happy? Waiting until the last possible moment to be honest and truthful with yourself?"

"That's not, I mean, no—" Olivia reached out and took Savannah's hand.

Savannah's gray-blue eyes looked at her intently. "What made you come by the launch party tonight?"

The directness of the question caught Olivia off guard. "I needed to see you. I wanted you to know that you were important to me, that I fucked up. I wanted you to know that I love you."

"And all those times in the past three weeks when I asked you about us and our future together and you didn't answer, what about those times? Why was tonight different?"

Olivia felt like she should be on the defensive, but Savannah's tone wasn't attacking. It was quiet, subdued almost. She looked directly at Olivia with great attention but not with malice. Olivia replied honestly, "Because your work here is done. And you're leaving. And I want you to stay."

Savannah nodded. "Olivia, I'm going to ask you a question. I want you to answer me with your immediate, gut reaction. Can you do that?"

"Yes."

"Do you love me?"

"Yes, I—"

Savannah held up her hand to stop Olivia. "Do you want to try to make this relationship work?"

"Yes."

Savannah smiled. "Okay."

Olivia frowned. "I'm lost."

The car pulled up to the curb and stopped. The driver popped the trunk and opened Savannah's door. "We're here, miss."

"Thank you."

"Shall I get your bags?"

"Yes, please."

Savannah exited the car and reached back in to take Olivia's hand. "I want to show you something."

Olivia let herself be guided out of the car by Savannah and looked around for the first time. They were parked in front of an apartment building and there was a doorman holding two small bags she assumed were Savannah's. "Where are we?"

Savannah thanked the driver and tipped him before she pulled Olivia toward the doorman without saying a word.

"Ms. Quinn! It's nice to meet you. They told me you would be coming tonight. Would you like me to bring these up for you?" He held up Savannah's bags with a friendly smile.

"We'll take them, thanks." Savannah released Olivia's hand and passed her the smaller of the two bags as she motioned for the elevator.

Savannah reached into her purse as the elevator doors closed and looked up only to hit the button to the fifth floor.

Olivia tried again. "Savannah? Where are we?"

The elevator doors slid open and Savannah exited without a response, walking toward the other end of the hall with a determined stride. She paused outside the last door and slid a key into the lock, opening the door and holding it open for Olivia.

The apartment was small but beautifully furnished with a welcoming, open floor plan. The wall colors were warm and tasteful and the granite of the kitchen island shone with a polished newness. Olivia watched as Savannah kicked off her heels and padded across the newly buffed hardwood floors into the kitchen area. She retrieved two wineglasses from the cabinet by the sink and held one up to Olivia in question.

"Uh, sure." Olivia had no idea what was going on.

Savannah reached into the fridge and pulled out a bottle of champagne. She popped the top easily and poured it into both glasses until they were full. "These are the closest things I have to champagne flutes at the moment, sorry."

Olivia took the glass Savannah had filled and waited for some sort of explanation.

"To one chapter closing and another one beginning." Savannah raised her glass and waited for Olivia to do the same before she sipped it and set it down.

Olivia reluctantly sipped her glass and placed it next to Savannah's on the counter as she watched Savannah shrug off her suit jacket and roll her neck in fatigue. "Savannah, where are we?"

Savannah answered her with a kiss. The kiss started out slow and deep before quickly veering into X-rated territory. As Savannah's tongue danced against hers, she had to remind herself to breathe. This kiss, this was a kiss that she didn't think she could ever forget. Savannah's hands slid into her hair, holding her close as whispered across Olivia's lips, "My apartment. Welcome."

Olivia's attempt to process that information was halted when Savannah's arms looped around her waist and her hands slid up Olivia's sides, teasing along her ribs. She could swear there was electricity in Savannah's touch because every part of her hummed in response to Savannah's closeness. She wanted to give in to it, to relish the sensation of Savannah's lips on hers after such an emotionally draining and stressful day, but she needed answers. Olivia pulled back and dipped her head to catch Savannah's gaze. "Your what? Weren't you staying at the hotel? I called, and they said you had checked out only yesterday."

"You called and checked up on me?" Savannah's smile was flirtatious.

"Yes. You didn't come by last night and I got worried. Where did you stay?" Olivia felt like she was two steps behind here.

"Here." Savannah took Olivia's hand and walked out of the kitchen toward the living room. She sat on the couch and pulled Olivia down next to her. "I needed a night to think and prepare for what I knew would be a big day." She shrugged. "So I came here."

"I don't understand, Savannah."

Savannah reached out and cupped Olivia's jaw. Her touch was tender and soft. "I resigned from New Horizons. Today was my last day. This is my new apartment." She paused. "I want to make this relationship work, Olivia. So I'm not going anywhere."

Olivia blinked in recognition. She couldn't believe her ears. "You're staying?"

Savannah's eyes shone brightly. "I'm staying."

The flood of emotions that hit Olivia in that moment overwhelmed her, and before she realized it, she was crying all the tears.

Savannah wrapped her arms around her and smoothed her hands up and down Olivia's arms. "Tell me these are happy tears, Liv, because I signed an extended lease."

Olivia laughed and stood from the couch, pulling Savannah with her and into her embrace. She kissed Savannah's smiling lips over and over, relishing the feeling of Savannah's warm hands sliding up her back, under her shirt, and gently scratching the skin. When those same hands gripped her ass roughly, she moaned. "*Savannah.*"

"Yeah?" Savannah kissed along the column of Olivia's neck.

Olivia struggled to resist the warm mouth staking claim to her skin. "I need—"

"What do you need, baby?"

"I need..." Olivia blinked and shook her head. She pressed her hands to Savannah's shoulders and gently pushed her back. "I need to know more."

Savannah leaned back and licked her lips. "Well, that went in a very different direction than I was expecting."

Olivia laughed and shoved Savannah playfully before she pulled her in for a quick kiss. "I'm serious."

"Okay, what do you need to know?"

Olivia settled back onto the couch, tugging Savannah down next to her. She was close enough that their thighs were touching. "Let's start with everything."

Savannah's warm chuckle greeted Olivia's imploring pout. She brushed one of Olivia's rogue curls behind her ear and traced her finger along Olivia's jaw. "Having you in Chicago with me, having you meet Cooper, waking up with you every day...I realized I didn't want to live without that. When you left Chicago, and everything fell apart"—she let out a soft sigh—"I panicked because in no time at all I had gotten used to something that didn't belong to me—an unexpected stability, even if it was temporary. And when you wouldn't take my calls, when I couldn't reach you...it was only then that I remembered something you said to me on the last night of my first visit to New York. Do you remember what you said?"

"I don't," Olivia replied.

"You told me that everyone needs roots somewhere, and that sometimes it just takes longer to find a good spot to set those roots." Savannah smiled and cupped Olivia's face. "You know what I realized?"

"What's that, baby?"

"I realized that I wasn't waiting for the perfect place to put down roots. I was waiting for the perfect person. Home isn't a zip code for me anymore, Liv." She placed her palm flat against Olivia's chest, over her heart. "It's a heartbeat. It's a feeling. It's you."

Olivia closed her hand over Savannah's and kissed her, quickly getting lost in warm, soft lips. When Savannah broke the kiss to rest her forehead against Olivia's, Olivia encouraged her to continue. "So you—?"

Savannah smiled and leaned back. "So when you finally answered my call, I decided to take a chance at being happy. Work had me coming back to New York, but to be honest, it hadn't been working out. We worked out a deal that would make the New York site my last."

Olivia nodded in understanding. "I ran into Ken at the launch tonight. He was pretty cryptic when I brought you up. Now I can see why."

"Yeah, well, you know how I feel about that asshole," Savannah said wryly before getting serious again. "When we reconnected here, I felt that same completeness I had with you in Chicago. I knew I'd made the right decision. But after weeks of telling you I loved you without you reciprocating, I started to second-guess my choice. It was a choice I'd made without consulting you, and maybe that was wrong. I was worried that maybe I was more invested in this than you were, and that terrified me."

Olivia cringed at the momentary lost look in Savannah's eyes, her vulnerability on full display. "I'm so sorry, Savannah."

Savannah shrugged and took Olivia's hand in hers. "You love me?"

"With my whole heart."

"Then it all worked out. How we got here is less important than the fact we're actually here." Savannah squeezed Olivia's hand once more. "So I called an old friend who worked as a Realtor and told her to find me a place to stay in the city while I figured everything out. It took a little last-minute juggling, but she was able to find me a place." Savannah's smiled broadened. "I knew I wanted to work on this, and I knew I needed to put in the time here, not jetting back and forth to a job that lost its shine once it no longer included you." She gestured to the room around them. "So here we are, on my couch, in my new fancy New York City apartment, drinking champagne out of wineglasses."

"What about your place in Chicago?"

"It was never really a space that brought me comfort. I never settled there. I packed up the essentials and moved some things to storage before I came out here. Cooper and Amber graduate at the end of the semester, so they're subletting for a while until the lease is up in a few months. That gives me a chance to figure out what I need, what I want. It gives me a chance to be happy."

"You're staying." Olivia had to say it aloud once more to make sure she wasn't dreaming.

Savannah pulled Olivia onto her lap and nodded. Her smile was blinding. "I'm staying."

Olivia felt like her heart was going to burst out of her chest. The woman she loved was here, in the flesh, looking absolutely gorgeous underneath her, and she wasn't going *anywhere*. That realization did all kinds of things to her, but in this moment, she could only think of one thing.

She looked down at Savannah, spreading her knees to settle into her lap. This was a favorite position of hers and Savannah knew it. She loved straddling Savannah's hips. She liked being on top and feeling like she was in control, when they both knew damn well that Savannah ran the show from beneath her in this position. When Savannah's hand massaged her hips and pulled Olivia's center closer to her own, Olivia understood they were on the same page.

She dipped her head and connected their lips as Savannah's hands moved up from her hips to caress her stomach through her shirt. When her hands cupped Olivia's breasts over her bra, Olivia let out a throaty moan.

"I hated not sleeping next to you last night." She sucked Savannah's bottom lip between hers and bit down lightly.

Savannah licked across her lips and dragged her thumb across Olivia's nipple, squeezing it when it pebbled beneath her touch. "Good, because I don't want to wake up another day without you."

Savannah's words plucked at her heartstrings while her hands brought Olivia to new heights of arousal. The pressure forming between her hips increased as Savannah's lips moved to her neck, her hot breath burning a path to Olivia's ear. Savannah sucked on her earlobe and panted softly. "You feel so good, Liv."

Olivia didn't stand a chance against that sex voice, not coupled with Savannah's hands and tongue all over her. She rocked forward, grinding her hips against Savannah's as she unbuttoned Savannah's dress shirt, a button or two falling victim to her impatience. She needed to feel Savannah's skin, she needed to touch all of her. "Mm, Savannah."

Savannah whimpered when Olivia's hand grazed across her chest and she bucked up against Olivia's slow downward grind.

Olivia saw stars and realized she wouldn't last long at this rate. "Savannah…"

Savannah nodded, and her hands dropped from Olivia's chest to massage the seam of Olivia's pants against her crotch.

"Fuck. Yes." Olivia rocked forward again, her rhythm getting more frantic the harder Savannah pressed against her.

Savannah slipped her hand into Olivia's pants and under the band of her panties, stroking her hot, wet flesh in that practiced way they both knew would bring Olivia to climax quickly.

Olivia's insides tightened, and her clit throbbed when Savannah wrapped an arm around her back and pulled her down hard on the next roll of her hips. Her gasp was silenced by Savannah's mouth against hers as Savannah breathed out, "I love you."

Ecstasy enveloped her, and she cried out, melting into Savannah's arms as her orgasm ripped through her entire existence. She felt a lightness and warmth radiate through her whole body as Savannah's words echoed over and over in her head.

She took a few gasping breaths and rested her forehead against Savannah's as she recovered. Savannah held her close and traced looping circles over her back. She pressed her lips to Savannah's and kissed her with everything she had left. "I love you, too."

She tucked her head against Savannah's neck and stayed like that for a few moments—Olivia wanted to savor this feeling forever.

Savannah's thumb brushed her cheek. "You're crying again."

"They're happy tears. You make me *so* happy." Olivia brushed the tears from her cheeks and leaned forward to kiss Savannah. "Now, this living room is lovely and all, but I assume this place has a bedroom?"

"Mm-hmm, the bedroom is great, but the bathtub in the en suite is what really sold me on this apartment." Savannah's lips chased Olivia's perma-smile.

Olivia laughed and stood as she slowly began to undress. "Well, in that case, why don't you start the tour there and we'll get a fresh start in your new digs."

Savannah caught the shirt Olivia tossed in her direction and dropped it unceremoniously to the floor as Olivia's hands slipped around

Savannah's waist and tugged at the button of her slacks. "Sounds like a plan to me, Liv."

"Good." Olivia pushed the offending slacks off Savannah's slim hips and hooked her thumbs into the black lace panties before her. "Now let's get you out of these clothes before things get a little too wet."

Savannah moaned, and Olivia pulled her close. She wrapped her arms around her and whispered, "Welcome home, Savannah."

About the Author

Fiona Riley was born and raised in New England, where she is a medical professional and part-time professor when she isn't bonding with her laptop over words. She went to college in Boston and never left, starting a small business that takes up all of her free time, much to the dismay of her ever patient and lovely wife. When she pulls herself away from her work, she likes to catch up on the contents of her ever-growing DVR or spend time by the ocean with her favorite people.

Fiona's love for writing started at a young age and blossomed after she was published in a poetry competition at the ripe old age of twelve. She wrote lots of short stories and poetry for many years until it was time for college and a "real job." Fiona found herself with a bachelor's, a doctorate, and a day job but felt like she had stopped nurturing the one relationship that had always made her feel the most complete: artist, dreamer, writer.

A series of bizarre events afforded her with some unexpected extra time and she found herself reaching for her favorite blue notebook to write, never looking back.

Contact Fiona and check for updates on all her new adventures at:
Twitter: @fionarileyfic
Facebook: "Fiona Riley Fiction"
Website: http://www.fionarileyfiction.com/
Email: fionarileyfiction@gmail.com

Books Available From Bold Strokes Books

Alias by Cari Hunter. A car crash leaves a woman with no memory and no identity. Together with Detective Bronwen Pryce, she fights to uncover a truth that might just kill them both. (978-1-63555-221-8)

Death in Time by Robyn Nyx. Working in the past is hell on your future. (978-1-63555-053-5)

Hers to Protect by Nicole Disney. Ex–high school sweethearts Kaia and Adrienne will have to see past their differences and survive the vengeance of a brutal gang if they want to be together. (978-1-63555-229-4)

Perfect Little Worlds by Clifford Mae Henderson. Lucy can't hold the secret any longer. Twenty-six years ago, her sister did the unthinkable. (978-1-63555-164-8)

Room Service by Fiona Riley. Interior designer Olivia likes stability, but when work brings footloose Savannah into her world and into a new city every month, Olivia must decide if what makes her comfortable is what makes her happy. (978-1-63555-120-4)

Sparks Like Ours by Melissa Brayden. Professional surfers Gia Malone and Elle Britton can't deny their chemistry on and off the beach. But only one can win… (978-1-63555-016-0)

Take My Hand by Missouri Vaun. River Hemsworth arrives in Georgia intent on escaping quickly, but when she crashes her Mercedes into the Clip 'n Curl, sexy Clay Cahill ends up rescuing more than her car. (978-1-63555-104-4)

The Last Time I Saw Her by Kathleen Knowles. Lane Hudson only has twelve days to win back Alison's heart. That is, if she can gather the courage to try. (978-1-63555-067-2)

Wayworn Lovers by Gun Brooke. Will agoraphobic composer Giselle Bonnaire and Tierney Edwards, a wandering soul who can't remain in one place for long, trust in the passionate love destiny hands them? (978-1-62639-995-2)

Breakthrough by Kris Bryant. Falling for a sexy ranger is one thing, but is the possibility of love worth giving up the career Kennedy Wells has always dreamed of? (978-1-63555-179-2)

Certain Requirements by Elinor Zimmerman. Phoenix has always kept her love of kinky submission strictly behind the bedroom door and inside the bounds of romantic relationships, until she meets Kris Andersen. (978-1-63555-195-2)

Dark Euphoria by Ronica Black. When a high-profile case drops in Detective Maria Diaz's lap, she forges ahead only to discover this case, and her main suspect, aren't like any other. (978-1-63555-141-9)

Fore Play by Julie Cannon. Executive Leigh Marshall falls hard for Peyton Broader, her golf pro...and an ex-con. Will she risk sabotaging her career for love? (978-1-63555-102-0)

Love Came Calling by C. A. Popovich. Can a romantic looking for a long-term, committed relationship and a jaded cynic too busy for love conquer life's struggles and find their way to what matters most? (978-1-63555-205-8)

Outside the Law by Carsen Taite. Former sweethearts Tanner Cohen and Sydney Braswell must work together on a federal task force to see justice served, but will they choose to embrace their second chance at love? (978-1-63555-039-9)

The Princess Deception by Nell Stark. When journalist Missy Duke realizes Prince Sebastian is really his twin sister Viola in disguise, she plays along, but when sparks flare between them, will the double deception doom their fairy-tale romance? (978-1-62639-979-2)

The Smell of Rain by Cameron MacElvee. Reyha Arslan, a wise and elegant woman with a tragic past, shows Chrys that there's still beauty to embrace and reason to hope despite the world's cruelty. (978-1-63555-166-2)

The Talebearer by Sheri Lewis Wohl. Liz's visions show her the faces of the lost and the killers who took their lives. As one by one, the murdered are found, a stranger works to stop Liz before the serial killer is brought to justice. (978-1-63555-126-6)